Max's brother was staring straight at Darian, blanched as he noticed the human's attention.

Darian got the eerie feeling he had seen something he was not supposed to see - as if he had caught a child stealing candy. Peering at the condition of the bound Mantarian, he noticed a hand. A free hand, working quickly and deftly in the wraps of twine at the prisoner's side.

The Drago beside Adam was furiously wriggling against the ropes. Some of his knifelike scales had already poked through the lines holding the two prisoners. They both stared at Darian, gritting their jaws in frustration as they wrestled against their tight bindings.

The shock of imperative drive thrust itself up to the human's mind, making him gasp for breath.

"HEY! THEY- THEY'RE LOOSE!"

He took a step towards the brigands before his head snapped around to make sure the rest of the crew had heard him.

They had – most of them were starting to move in the same direction Darian was moving. Captain Vrue had also turned, and with an angry sneer on his face bellowed a command to his charges.

"BUST THEM DOWN!!"

Darian was overtaken by crewmembers rushing to respond to the bark of their commander. He had already learned that the Captain hated pirates - hated them more than anything else on the planet. The human jerked his head to look back to the front mast, suddenly worried about the ferocity that would be unleashed on the escaping men. But as he looked his eyes were distracted by movement in the air off to the side of the galleon beyond where the prisoners were tied. The emergence of a solid shape rapidly moving towards the *Archer* through the clouds.

Darian's eyes bulged and his chin dropped as he saw what was coming straight at them.

BLOOD and BROTHERS

a story of Zefphyr

Kurt Kennett

Illustrations by
Mary Minch **and** *Skech*

www.zefphyr.com

ISBN 978-1-4357-0510-4

Manufactured in the United States of America.

First International LuLu.com edition: December 2007

For Jennifer

pReface

Humanity frowned on the scientists, branding them incompatible with a just society. But the researchers wanted to continue their work, for it was all they had.

They saw the cloudy, wind-swept planet as a haven. A hideout. A sanctuary from prying eyes.

It was different – strange and powerful. Wrapped in cloaks of harmonic energy that the scientists plundered with their machines and raped for their tests and their experiments. For their version of nature.

And they brought their flora, their fauna. Workers and helpers, partners and children. But they found the planet inhabited by a precursor race. Felids - learning and growing, evolving on their own path with their own spirits and destiny.

The scientists took the rustic cats. Ripped them from their homes, molded them and put them with the other life forms the humans had brought and created.

From all their animals and from themselves the masters took whatever they needed to follow their destiny. They made the seeds.

They were, to a one, driven. Cold.

But their servants and builders were not. The helpers saw the sentience in the seeds of life. Saw themselves in the genetic creations. Some broke away – ran away with the seeds they could save or steal. They could not let their brothers languish in servitude and slavery as toys.

And so began the struggle for control - A battle for life and death. For what was... humane. Heroes and villains rose and fell, until the eve of the greatest conflict. The greatest destruction.

The meltdown.

All that the scientists had brought and built was destroyed – at once and finally, with the greatest of sacrifices. Only scattered remnants of technology and tools remained. All that were left struggled - some stumbled together, some apart. Across the planet the varieties spread and grew, changed and evolved.

For a thousand years.

one

Darian Carver burst through the side doors of the Navy barracks. Momentarily blinded by bright sunlight, he crashed headlong into two young Impalans and stumbled over their falling bodies. Entangled with the creatures' long limbs, the human tried desperately to keep from ending up in a sprawl on the ground. He recovered his equilibrium and twisted his head to look back at who he had run into. Fellow cadets, but lower classmen – he took the appropriate action of cursing at them for getting in his way. Then he ran flat out towards the stairs to the activity field.

Darian knew that Max Ford would only be fooled for a moment by the simple trick he had pulled. They had been sitting in Darian's barracks room when the human had politely excused himself, abruptly leaving without explanation. While his Mantarian friend was gullible, he was certainly not stupid. Darian knew from many interactions with Max's race that he could not compete physically on a level playing field, and he had long stopped trying.

As the human slid on his buttocks down the metal banister at the side of the stairs, he grinned widely at the thrill of being pursued. "Got him again!", he huffed out aloud to himself as he reached the bottom of the stairs. Starting across the grass field, he ran between creatures of various size and race that were exercising and socializing in the mid-morning sun. Halfway across the track field he risked a quick look back – fully expecting to see the Mantarian's powerful bulk charging out of the barracks doors.

Unfortunately for Darian, the seven foot tall creature was already at the bottom of the stairs – scarcely a hundred meters behind. His friend's head was bent forwards on his thick horse-like neck, showing eyes set in a determined glare and short pointed ears folded tightly back.

Darian laughed a curse as his head whipped back around. He put all the energy he had left into his legs as he weaved around and through the throngs of people talking and lounging in the middle of the field. He knew right away that Max would catch him – even running upright using only his hind legs. Evolved from equine genetics, the Mantarian's lower body powered him like no other type of creature on Zefphyr.

Oh well, at least I'm as good a rider!

By the time Darian reached the hovercycle lot on the far side of the track field, Max was literally on his heels. Swiping his ID card, the human sucked in a breath and turned to face his friend, looking completely cordial. "Ah, Mister Ford. So glad you could make it today." Darian radiated satisfaction and turned smoothly and slowly to pick a hovercycle. Though he tried as hard as he could to stifle the effects of his own exertion, as soon as he was facing away he had to gulp for breath.

Max said nothing. With a glare of frustration the large male gritted his teeth and shook out his short mane of hair. His ears stayed folded back, and he gruffly swiped his own ID before stomping over to choose his cycle.

The snub-nosed hovercycles they chose were powered the same way as every other vehicle. Simple convectional thrust engines gave the craft measured freedom from gravity, stabilization, and forward thrust. Gull wings made of sail fabric pulled taut over thin metal wireframe came up out if their midsection, extending towards the front. Folded up very tightly for storage, bringing the wings out took a few moments. When deployed they used embedded crystals to garner, channel and store raw power from the abundant energy fields that wrapped the planet.

Both the cadets chose cycles that had already been used to excess. As he prepared his craft Darian made a point of stifling a grin as if he was irritated from having to wait for Max to catch up.

"You are one annoying human," Max growled a deep grating sound. "Left alone for three days, and the first thing you do when you see me is take off. I thought at least you'd be lonely."

"Oh of course," Darian chuckled, thickly laying on sarcasm. "Doing without you for more than a few minutes is indescribably painful. And besides, I ran out of interesting things to do. I sorted my books, cleaned my clothes. Hell, I even read a book. You took your own sweet time dealing with your mommy and your daddy and your sis-"

"Look, I can't help it if my family visits at cycle break and yours- well... doesn't." Max finished clumsily. It was clear that halfway through the sentence he didn't know how to find an end to it - one that wasn't barbed. The Mantarian's throat tightened and his sleek short facial hair ruffled in embarrassment. He squatted down on one knee and looked intensely at his cycle, obviously glad his eyes were given a reason to avoid Darian's face.

Darian didn't move. "My father would come if he could," he explained. He knew Max could tell he was lying, but he didn't know what else to say about his only living relative. "He's... away. Two years now. Busy."

"Yeah, right. Too busy to spend a single day at cycle break with his only son. Everyone else's parents are around - Navy or not. Pssh. What would get him here?"

Darian sighed and squatted down by his own machine to hide his reddened cheeks. He wanted argue for his father, but he knew Max was right – he'd been alone for all the time that cadet's families were allowed to visit.

Cycle break at the Queen's Naval Academy was the one time that Darian had to put mental effort into planning what he was going to do. All the other time he was kept busy with training, or was engaged with other cadets in social and physical activities. But break was when the families came – when the parents and siblings were permitted to visit the island that served as the Academy grounds. Twice a year, for three days at a time. Darian had been in the academy for five years, and was about to start his last cycle before graduation. He'd been alone during almost every break he'd ever had.

"What do you talk about with your family while they're here?" he asked quietly over the sounds of their mechanical tinkering. He looked over the top of his cycle and from the expression of difficulty he saw on the Mantarian's face, he could tell that the his friend was caught off guard by the question.

Max appeared thoughtful for a long moment, but did not look away from his adjustments. "Guilt," he said suddenly.

Darian raised his brows and widened his eyes.

Max didn't look at Darian – he just smiled at the silence that conveyed the human's astonishment. "My parents guilt-trip me constantly."

"About what?"

"That I'm 'the one'. You know - the 'family jewel'." Max drew up and tested his craft for stability, rocking it slightly back and forth. Then he turned to Darian and formed a box with his thick, flat-ended forefingers and thumbs, looking down through them. "Just picture it - seven Mantarians in a penniless family putting blood, sweat, tears and all their hope for their good name in the future of one... sacred... son!"

Darian blinked incredulously. "Crap! I mean… wow. That's-"

"Nice, eh?" Max laughed a deep rolling sound, dropping his hands. "I'm not there with them, stitching up endless racks of power sails. I don't cut my fingers to shreds on Atillian crystals. I don't starve. So they save all that up for me. All they feel – come here at cycle break and give it to me." He slumped backwards in the chair – smile gone. "Sometimes I wonder if I'm just their... insurance policy."

"Huh?" Darian balked, taking a moment to think. "You mean your salary when you graduate?"

"Yeah," Max answered evenly. "And the twenty years worth of it that's a lump sum for them if I die."

"Come on, that can't be what it's all about. They can't treat you that way all the time they're here." Darian had stopped fiddling and also stood.

Max took Darian's movement as a sign they were ready to get started. He mounted his cycle and started his engine. "No, you're right," the Mantarian answered. "It's not all bad. After they tell me about all the hard lessons they have been learning about self-sacrifice, they make damn sure I'm healthy." He grinned in embarrassment. "It's nice to know people care about you, but I think your mother giving you a full physical exam is kind of weird, don't you?" With a roar of his engine, Max surged forwards.

Darian was surprised that Max had taken the lead – but pleasantly so. So many times Darian had to push Max to do things. Even from their first days at the academy, it had been Darian pulling the shy and reticent Max to try the cycles for the first time. The human always had a hard time believing someone who was around power sails all his life had never actually gotten to use one for recreation.

Neither one of the young males could remember precisely how they'd met five years ago, or what had cemented their friendship. Max had always been there, ever since Darian's father had not. The human smiled as he also rocketed forward, forming up swiftly and easily beside his friend.

As they approached the exit, the lot lieutenant suddenly emerged from the checkbooth. He waved at them to indicate they should stop before leaving.

Darian was instantly miffed, glancing to Max at a loss. Being upper-classmen, their ID cards should have given them rights to take out the cycles any time they wanted, without further validation.

They stopped in front of the short and fat bearlike humanoid and put their engines on idle, but kept the humming v-shaped wings fully deployed. The much older male was obviously unimpressed by the two younger ones in front of him.

"ID check not working to your booth today, sir?" Darian asked in a light, quizzical air.

"Oh, it's working fine, cadet corporal Carver," the Lieutenant returned, his thick accent layered with boredom. "Travel's restricted 'cause of the hullybaloo going on over in the valley. Graduation day today for the seniors. Rules say I can't let anybody but them near there. Got that big boat coming in to be taking them away." As he spoke he walked around them, old eyes scrutinizing their craft.

Darian didn't watch him but heard his slow, sauntering steps. He tried his best to sound nonchalant. "Why would we go there, sir?"

The lieutenant stopped right behind Darian's cycle and let the human's question hang in the air for a moment. "Oh, you're going there all-righty," he sighed. "Every cycle a couple of uppers – full'a piss – sneak off to watch that big ship, dreaming about what's coming for 'em."

He started walking slowly again, around to stop directly at Max's side. Slowly he leaned in close to peer at the Mantarian's face.

Darian looked down to the front of his cycle, and then calmly over at Max. Max mirrored the same slow movements, looking back away from the Lieutenant. Darian could see in Max's eyes the strain to remain confidently relaxed, and knew somehow that he was being wordlessly asked to take the lead.

It had become a natural and comfortable process of deferral. Over time in the academy, Darian's style and social air, not to mention his academic scores, had all pointed in the same direction as his father's – operations and command. At first subtly, then formally in cadet ranking, he had taken a lead-ership role in the barracks 'house' group they were in. While dependable and hard working, Max had chosen to follow the pathway of an enlisted man.

Darian saw both other males gazing at him, and he tried to keep his voice as level and confident as possible.

"When the 'uppers full'a piss' go, sir, how do they get there?" Darian saw Max's eyes widen at the candor, and struggled to keep a straight face himself. He forced his stare past Max to the lieutenant.

"They go the same way you're trying to go," the old male stated flatly, unimpressed. "Usually I knew or be knowing their pap – or their marm. I can judge their character, so to speak. Know if they're gonna get caught."

Darian's brow furrowed, and he saw Max's face fall and his throat force down a soft swallow.

"Know your pap," the lieutenant continued after a moment of considering Darian. Then he gazed at Max, and the Mantarian turned his elongated muzzle forwards in silence.

"Don't know you."

Darian could see the deflation in his friend – the Mantarian's shoulders went down and the short fine hair on his cheeks instinctively ruffled. Frustrated, Darian braced himself and prepared to take on his most commanding tone. He had practiced – though he would never admit it to anyone, even Max. "Lieutenant, sir. This is upper-class cadet ensign Maximillian Ford. Engineering specialty, Delta-Seti classification. As his cadet corporal I take full responsibility for the extra-curricular training exercise we are embarking on today."

The lieutenant chuckled openly at the bravado, but continued to stare into Max's face.

"Oh, this one needs looking after, does he?"

Though he tried to stop it, Darian could feel his own cheeks redden in embarrassment. Max's eyes closed his chin came down in resignation.

Defiance welled in Darian and he blurted an answer, no longer caring about being disciplined for insubordination. "He's fine on his own sir, thank you sir, very much." His own protective reaction surprised him – but in his chest Darian felt a swell of righteousness. Max didn't deserve to be looked down on.

The lieutenant's eyes were cold and steady for a moment, and his jaw clenched. "Yup, I know *your* pap for sure. You're just like him. Exactly." He paused, then looked down and emitted a chuckle. "Full'a piss I say. Same thing every cycle."

Max's eyes open in bewilderment.

Darian found a smile forming on his face, but he saw the lieutenant's eyes come quickly up again. When he spoke his voice was stern.

"Same warning I give every cycle too. You get caught and ain't nobody never does this again". He paused for effect. "And I'll be telling whoever tries why – and who – cadet corporal Darian Carver."

Max started his engine. Still looking past him at the lieutenant, Darian did the same. The lieutenant turned and sauntered back inside the checkpoint as both young males blasted out of the lot.

two

Not ten feet from the lot exit, Max opened up his engine to its maximum setting. Maneuvering towards the trees and hedges leading away from the common grounds, he poured out frustration on his hovercycle. Clenched feet and hands wrought out staccato motions on the wing trim controls, and his left foot jammed hard against the accelerator.

How is it that the world forces everyone else to stick their necks out for me? he thought angrily. Just for once, he wanted to do something on his own and have it work out for everyone

In contrast, things always seemed to 'click' for Darian. Whether it was luck, skill, or something in the stars, Max wasn't quite sure. He just knew that he always felt at least one step behind.

Darian was always the one out ahead, the one teaching Max how to fly, and the one getting the most out of the experience. The human made the decisions about where they would go, what they would try, and how far they would push themselves.

Now, with his frustration and anger to feed him Max flew at a breakneck pace. He scarcely weaved around large obstacles and bobbed only slightly to clear hills or to duck under bridges. Far from the large settlements of Zefphyr, the island that served as the academy's home was sparsely occupied. As he blasted along through the misty highlands with only the scenery in front of him, he realized how different the world looked without Darian ahead of him.

Is this what it's like for him? he thought. *Nobody to follow.*

It became hard for the Mantarian to hold onto the feeling that drove him. At first he resisted the urge to look back and find Darian, a comfortable point of reference. But the loneliness continued to rush in, and he realized his left foot was beginning to hurt from being shoved up against the accelerator. The feet of his race were tough – but their hearts and minds were softer.

As he moved to cut back on his speed the sound of his engine died down and he finally felt completely alone. He shifted his weight to weave by a set of trees and onto a narrow plain, then finally gave in and looked over his shoulder. Darian was staring at him in open concern. Realizing most of his anger was burnt off, Max threw the human a quick smile.

Darian's face relaxed and he grinned, deftly working his board to gradu-ally close the gap between them. They flew low over an open mesa, and the human had to yell above the howling wind. "HEY. YOU ALL RIGHT?"

Max stared back at Darian for a moment, trying to think of a witty re-sponse to explain his angry behavior. "THOUGHT I WOULD SLOW DOWN FOR YOU," he hollered.

Darian's brows furrowed, but his smile turned into a competitive grin.

Max was elated that the simple jibe had found purchase, and did not break his stare. "KNOW YOU DON'T LIKE GOING THAT FAST," he teased.

Darian did not break the stare either. Curiously, the grin he had turned confident. Too confident. "THREE WORDS FOR YOU!"

"WHAT?" Max yelled, not being able to help but lift a questioning brow. Something suddenly felt strange. He waited for more words as they streaked across the plain. At the back of his mind grew a familiar tingling sense.

"WATCH THE DROP!"

Max shot over the cliff edge. His shock at doing so was only matched by the shock that his best friend had been able to trick him – twice – in less than an hour.

The wind current coming up the cliff immediately caught his extended wings. As the shear flipped over his hovercycle, Max's firmly bound feet pulled him around with it. Buffeted by uncontrolled spiraling gusts, he quickly began to spin. His foot slid away from the accelerator, but the engine kept running, pushing the winged craft out through the air away from the cliff face. Max just held on, trying as hard as he could to maintain his sense of up and down as he tumbled. It felt like a minute, but in mere seconds he cleared the cliff updraft.

Feeling the loss of pull from the wind shear, Max worked to pull in his cycle's wings. It took him two tries to do it. With the wings out of the way, he used his powerful legs to grip onto his machine. Allowing his weight to stop the spin he became properly oriented, and was able to take a look at how far he was from the ground.

Bad idea. His heart jumped in his chest as he realized that there were less than a hundred feet left in the fall to the rocky outcrop near the ocean shore.

Cutting the engine was the usual next step, but Max felt like it was the wrong one. He was going to need the craft's thrust to brake his speed, since he gone right through the cliff updraft that would have otherwise slowed him down. Again using the strength in his legs and bringing in his arms to grab the cycle, he pointed the rear of it as best he could at the ground. At the same time he used his back foot to increase the engine's output.

Less than ten meters to the ground, Max knew he was going to make it. Nail it. He felt the downward speed decreasing, and knew the hovercycle could handle taking over the descent. Even though the forward speed was much faster than he'd ever gone before, his pride overwhelmed his fear.

Watching the rocks come up at him, he let go of tight control. The cycle's wings folded out smoothly, giving the engine's power a boost. He looked back towards the cliff as the craft took over, trying to see where Darian was.

His friend would have been expecting the cliff drop and, having performed the action hundreds of times before, would have almost instantly put his engine to idle and yanked in his wings. The point was to use the relatively flat underbelly of the cycle and ride the fantastic rush of wind from the cliff updraft.

Max saw Darian had evened out his vehicle at the bottom of the cliff, and was just starting to redeploy his wings. The Mantarian preened, feeling the rush of air in his face as he blasted on in triumph, knowing that with the extra speed he was still outpacing his friend. But instead of slowing, he flew on.

It's going to be interesting to see how he saves face while he asks me to show him how I did that.

three

The large valley plain next to the ocean was surrounded by a thick layer of underbrush. Darian approached the edge of it, turning over in his mind many clever things he could say. He even rehearsed some of them in a whisper. Pulling back the large brush branches, he saw his friend sitting quietly on a short ledge, peering out towards the valley.

"Ah, Mister Carver. So glad you could make it today."

Max's voice was such a clear mimicking of Darian's comment from earlier that the human completely forgot the jibe he had decided on. He saw Max smile at Darian's obvious loss of focus. Caught, the human couldn't help but smile back. Even though he hated to lose, he knew the feelings he'd had back at the lot gate had been correct.

"Well, like I said - you don't need me to take care of you." The human came over to sit down next to Max, and himself looked out at the curved plain that led to the bottom of the valley. The clouds had parted and sunlight was streaming through them, leaving a patchwork of shadows on the gold and green grasses that filled the bowl in front of them. Thin trees swayed in the winds, while the sound of a calm rustle of their leaves descended on the pair.

"So, what are we doing?"

"You're the corporal, -sir." Max often sarcastically accented the last word. Most often he did this in public where he could see Darian squirm in front of others. "It's your 'training exercise'."

Darian sighed, refusing to respond to the challenge. Besides, he didn't want to talk about their differences. "Well, this is terrible!" he snorted indignantly. "We can't see anything."

"What are we supposed to see?"

"Well, the big grad is over there-" Darian pointed with a stiff finger out across to the top of the valley, where a patch of pristine white buildings sat surrounded by tall thin trees.

"And the airship?"

"Supposed to come from the over the ocean, fly up the valley over the plain. Maybe we missed it."

They sat in silence for a moment. Max's ears stood up straight and twitched, opening wide.

"I don't think so."

"Why not?"

"Listen."

"To what?"

"Sssh." Max put up an open three-fingered hand and looked at the sky to his right.

Darian heard a rustle of branches in the soft wind, and what he thought was the buzzing of an insect. However, the sound did not seem to waver and very, very slowly was getting louder. He was puzzled. "What is that?"

"Those are class-one power sails," Max grinned.

Darian's eyes widened as both young men eagerly looked around and up through the brush, trying to spot the origin of the buzzing. As the volume of the noise increased, a low rolling vibration also began filling the air.

Max turned to Darian, looking slightly worried from the awesome low-ness of the sound. Darian realized that he had the same slack expression on his face, his eyes pushed open wider than normal. He smiled at his friend – fully excited by his own deep-seated fear response. Max chuckled.

The power of the vibration still increased, becoming a throbbing bass that they could feel even in the ground through their feet. All Naval Academy cadets had heard and seen quantum repulsor engines, and Max had even worked with a few in his training as an engineer. Overwhelmingly the main basis of transport on Zefphyr, they pulled or pushed as necessary against the planet's peculiar omnipresent energy fields. For at least three hundred years they had been common technology, enabling gradual expansion and interaction of the various races that had survived the meltdown.

At once both young men became aware of the direction of the modulating sound – from the end of the valley away from the buildings. Not being able to see well through the brush, they both pushed forward out into the open. Breaking through, Darian stopped dead in his tracks and grabbed hold of Max's arm. They saw the first bit of the ship appear off the far side of the valley's bottom – cracking around the sheer rocks that met the ocean.

The bowsprit at the front of the sky boat poked into view beyond the sea -washed rocks, christening the view of the wide bow and forecastle. Immedi- ately following it was what seemed like an enormous shimmering mask of blankets – billowing sails extending in all directions, bursting and humming with energy. Starkly defying gravity, the ship floated gracefully through the air, its engines holding it strong and steady on course.

As the vessel turned around the island's edge and headed for the valley, Darian stole a quick glance at Max. His mouth was still slightly open and his eyes were glazed, glued to the radiant and intricate masterpiece in front of them. Darian's heart leapt as his eyes snapped back to the ship.

A heavily angled mast sprang into view, flying a bright blue flag that flapped in the golden rays of the sun. The galleon's attitude adjusted, tilting it backwards slightly as it ascended above the plain. At the same time the roar of the engines was finally heard at full volume, rolling across the field and overpowering the vibration and buzzing from the sails.

"Wow!" Max blurted – almost having to yell to be heard. His breath came in starts as he blinked, still half-chuckling at his own reaction. "That's a big ship."

"Uh, yeah," Darian stammered. His face hurt from his grin. They both watched in awe as the gigantic boat turned to cruise up the valley toward the small buildings. Darian's arm came up to rest on Max's shoulder. "One more year," he sighed. "One more year and we're on it."

Out of the corner of his eye, Darian saw Max's slack-jawed expression slowly spread into an easy smile. Max pulled his gaze away from the specta- cle to study the ground at his feet for a moment, then looked up at Darian.

"You think it'll be... like we talked about?"

"Exactly." Darian responded with natural confidence. "We're meant for that. Both of us." He felt the Mantarian's gaze steady on him. "One more year," Darian emphasized, "and we're out there. For real."

Max looked back to the ship and they shared the regal view once more. The huge craft had finally reached the buildings, and its small army of riggers and ropers began to secure the huge triangular sails. At the same time, a raised receiving dock that was dwarfed by the ship extended its largest access gangways. Flocks of dock hands began to secure the many sturdy rope lines required to affix the ship to its berth.

Darian sighed at the controlled commotion. Looking down to make sure of his footing, he started to hop and walk down the slight hill towards the valley plain.

It didn't take Max long to object. "Uh, Carver? Let's not, ok? We're going to get caught."

Darian didn't even turn around, much less skip a beat in the timing of his controlled descent. He walked quickly around a set of overhanging branches and separated the line of sight from his friend. Continuing to move forward, he looked for the simplest route through to the plain. After a moment he heard Max starting to follow. Darian felt a flash of pride, but was also aware of his gratitude. He knew true trust was earned and he felt a familiar glow of appreciation that he had earned Max's.

Then Darian had to stop, stymied by a wall of brush.

A jovial voice came clearly from behind him. "You're going the wrong way."

The human rolled his eyes as he turned around and stepped back through the tangled vegetation. He glimpsed the sheen of the light brown hair of the mane at the back of Max's head. The Mantarian was moving easily towards the edge of the plain, out into the open.

Darian paused, standing up straight and blinking. He had purposefully taken the lead, to push them both where he knew they wanted to go. But now he was the follower. It was if Max had suddenly broken new ground. Darian raised a brow for a moment, but then tried to recover equilibrium. He grasped at a mocking tone to get Max's attention. "We're going to get caught."

Oddly, Max did not stop or even slow. He kept walking, the outstretched fingertips of his hands touching the tops of the long grass as it was swept by random drafts of wind. The Mantarian's eyes were fixed on the vision of the ship in the distance, and on the movements of its crew as they rushed about.

Darian's competitiveness welled up – and also some bravado. He started to run. With a 'whoop' he shoved past Max harder than he needed to, laughing and jogging through the thick thatches of grass out into the open. Doing so gave him what he needed – a connection of some sort with what they both wanted to be. What they wanted to do. He slowed and looked up to the ship in front of them, beautifully hovering off in the distance.   As   Max stopped beside him, Darian realized his heart was caught in his throat.

The Mantarian's voice was edged with exasperation - Darian always pushed things just slightly too far. "You're crazy. We really are going to get caught." They both turned to look back at how far out they had come. More than a quarter of a mile – really out in the open now.

"No we're not!" Darian responded in irritation. "Besides, if we do it's your fault – you started it."

"Your responsibility," Max countered, smugly. "You're in charge."

"Yes," Darian shot back. "Yes, I am, Ensign." He stood up straight, trying unsuccessfully to match his friend's height. He stifled a blush as he saw Max was trying very hard not to laugh at him. Many engineered races had been placed on Zefphyr - the seeds of all that was. For the peoples that coexisted happily in the Queen's dominion, there was a common expectation of tolerance, and a celebration in the differences in physiology. However, sometimes those differences were hard to ignore.

"And when we are on –that-," Darian said sternly as he pointed across to the ship in the distance, "I will make sure to remind you of it."

The colossal ship was still perched at the dock near the buildings, but Darian and Max could see many shapes moving to and fro on the access gangways. They both stood still, watching and waiting.

"How long will it be there?" Max queried.

"Only a few minutes. They're just loading the grads and their gear. Then they're off to Station."

"And you know this how?" Max said as he folded his arms over his massive chest.

Darian turned his head and looked at his friend, his face suddenly a picture of resignation. Not hearing an immediate answer, Max turned as well to return the gaze. "My father told me," Darian responded, eyes cold and glassy "The day he signed me up. The day he left." He looked down at the grass for a moment, then started to walk slowly forward. Max followed him.

"I haven't really seen him since then, you know that. I hear about him from time to time, and I know he hears about me. But that's it." Darian measured his speech – slowly and methodically plodding through the past as his feet plodded the ground. Their steps were shared, and he knew Max was listening.

"If I'm so much like my father, why do I miss him?   It doesn't seem like he misses me. Everybody I've met likes him, or at least has heard of him. I appreciate how well known he is. Just wish I knew more of why."

"Your family has been in the Navy for a hundred years," Max said. "Leaving its mark on people. You and your father are a familiar continuation of that part of the... family. Something they know they can rely on, and trust to act a certain way."

"What, and you don't think they trust you yet?" Darian asked. "I mean, sure you're the first one of your family to join up. But you do everything right. People like you."

"To trust me they'll have to see what I do when things get rough. If I screw up, they'll expect anyone in my family that comes after me to screw up. To fit whatever pattern I set. I still have to show people what I'm like."

"I know what you're like," Darian said in frustration. He blew out his breath, and stopped to turn and look up at his friend. "I just wish I knew more what my father was like, so I could be as successful as he is. I mean, you get to see your parents and your brothers and sisters way more often than I get to see my father."

"Oh yeah, what I have is fantastic," Max snuffed in sarcasm as he cut Darian off. "Endless lessons in self sacrifice."

"Why do you think your parents are giving you these lessons?"

"I told you back at the lot – guilt."

"You think they're really that mean-spirited?".

Max opened his mouth and nothing came out. After a moment of staring blankly at Darian, he shut it again.

"Come on, Ford, they think you're the best of them. The very best of who they are as a family." Darian's tone made it seem like the situation was obvious. "Everything they ever have been in history, leading up to now. You know - from... the first seeds. The first ones like you." He looked squarely at his huge friend, tone strongly compassionate even through his words were superlative.

"Oh yeah," Max chuckled at the audacity. "Some half-baked genetic slush and a thousand years stumbling around in the dark to produce... me! Hah! I'm not exactly the best example of my race, you know."

Darian snorted, but continued his opinion. "If they didn't think that, you wouldn't be the only one in a have-not family to be here. Really - I mean it. Do you think your parents are doing less than what they think is the absolute best for your family?"

"Of course not," the Mantarian sighed, his eyes searching the distance for a moment in the direction of the massive ship. "My mother said... right before she left. She said that after five years away from home, they're just making sure that there is something of them... left in me. You know, when we graduate." Max smiled weakly, and took a deep breath.

His face lightened a shade. Then two. His eyes opened wide and his mouth slowly began to gape.

Darian's smile dissolved equally as slowly into a puzzling look as he watched the large Mantarian. Fear seemed to creep impossibly across the short space of air between them as his friend's visage changed without explanation.

"What? What is it?"

Max did not break his gaze, fixed beyond Darian into the distance towards the buildings and the ship. He stuttered his response. "I- I think we just got caught."

Darian spun around, and both of their faces became almost identically slack-jawed. The galleon's sails were deploying again – and an overwhelming number of crew, on the ship and on the docks, were pointing at them and beginning to move in their direction.

Darian grabbed Max's uniform's far shoulder at the nape of his neck, taking an unconscious step backwards. His shocked face was still fixated on the ship as alarm klaxon sounded in the distance.

"Wha... wha... what did we do?" Max continued to stammer as he took a step backwards with Darian. The scale of the response that was coming at them just didn't make sense.

Max jerked around, away from the spectacle to look at Darian for direction. His expression changed again - from one of shock and surprise to one of pure terror. Instantly he reached up and grabbed Darian's hand that rested on his shoulder. Yanking backward with his strong legs, Max almost jolted the human out of his shoes.

Darian was catapulted forward off his feet. His face hit the back of Max's neck, and his left arm flopped around his friend's other shoulder. The human's legs banged against the Mantarian's buttocks and rear thighs. Darian grabbed desperately for purchase as Max shot forward beneath him.

The wind knocked out of him, Darian heaved for breath as he tried to hang on and find out what was happening. A thunderous roar suddenly filled his ears, accompanied by a shattering, splitting sound of an enormous impact. Huge vibrating waves of force washed over them from behind. In utter panic Darian crammed his eyes shut and sunk his nails into skin and fabric as he clutched Max's back and neck.

He was aware of constant increase in velocity as he felt Max's muscles underneath his whole body contract and work in frantic powerful harmony. Only then did Darian realize what was happening – Max was carrying him on his back, running flat out on four legs towards the buildings and docked ship. Or away from something else.

Flipping his eyes open, Darian first saw how fast they were moving – the ground a painted smear. He then looked back over his shoulder to where they had come from, into unfolding devastation.

Another ship. A cargo boat – relatively small, but still large enough to ply high in the winds of Zefphyr. Powerless and therefore soundless on its own but for the noise of its crashing into the ground. Directly at them from behind.

Thousands of splintered shards of metal and wood flew past Max and Darian as they raced away. Mixed in were huge clumps of ripped up grass and dirt from the valley plain. Max tore across the ground, dodging wildly through the raining carnage. The bull rush of sound coming from behind them was overwhelming. Darian's consciousness filled with sinking defeat as the surge of impending death came at them.

Just as Max's labored breathing began to weaken, the wracking sound from behind them started to subside and the vibration lowered in tone to a stuttered, scraping sound. Max still ran steadily, but Darian could tell that his friend was almost spent. He looked back again to see the mangled, fiery hulk of the small ship gradually slowing behind them, shuddering and grinding through the dirt and grass towards an inevitable halt.

"MAX – Max! It's OK! It's stopping now!"

Max came up off four legs, still running but upright. Darian marveled in the moment at his friend's body, but at the same time wanted to relieve the Mantarian of the burden he carried. He abruptly let go of Max's shoulders - awkwardly jumping down to run on his own. They didn't have to move much further before they finally stopped. Darian looked to see how far they had traveled – they were more than halfway to the academy buildings from where they had started. It didn't seem possible to the human that they could have moved that fast. The crew on the galleon were still mustering, pointing and running towards them.

Max gulped loudly for air. Doubled over, he fell onto his knees in exhaustion. Darian came beside him, out of breath himself from the sheer trauma of the experience. He tried to cautiously put a hand softly onto the Mantarian's back. But Max bit out harsh words, one per breath as he soaked in necessary oxygen. "Don't... you... EVER... tell... ANYBODY... I... just... did.... THAT!" Gobs of saliva dripped from his mouth and droplets of sweat ran freely down his face.

Darian snatched back his hand, deeply confused by the words. His face hardened for a moment as he pushed through with his concern over his rescuer's exertion. He leaned over to firmly palm Max's back. "Are you going to be-"

"I'll be FINE!" Max yelled more harshly than Darian had ever heard him speak. The human was embarrassed to his core, at a total loss for words as a cold steel rod rolled through him. Max had just unquestionably saved his life – taken an action in an instant without thinking. The shame that his friend emitted was baffling.

A creaking, shaking vibration came through the air from behind them as a piece of the crashed ship's shattered hull broke away and fell to the side. Both young men turned at the sound. The vessel had stopped completely, its smoking wreckage strewn over a half-mile of the torn-up valley. Not a large craft, but bulky.

Max got up, and both he and Darian stood and stared at the mess that lay in front of them. Flame and smoke poured from the top and back of the collective rubble as it continued to settle in place.

"We... we've got to get... out of here." Max stammered through his still-wheezing respiration. "They... they're gonna find us. We're not supposed to be here! If we get caught - you heard the lieutenant."

Muffled yelling started to come from behind them in the distance. They both swung around, to see many people running towards them across the plain. The enormous galleon was starting to move as well – its ropers and riggers having worked swiftly to let out some sails, allowing the ship enough power to move and offer assistance.

"Carver, come on – we've got to go!" Max called, moving to Darian and stretching his arm out towards him. The human was frozen as the crowd approached.

We've been caught, he wanted to say. There was no point leaving now – they needed to help, to stay and be part of whatever rescue and recovery could be mounted. Darian knew that there could be survivors. "We need to stay and help!"

"They're coming! They'll be here to help in a second and they'll do more than we ever could! If they catch us..."

Darian was lost in the shock of their ordeal, and could not think clearly through the logic of what Max was saying. But in his heart he knew he was responsible for both of them being there. If they were caught, it was going to come down on both of them.

On Max.

Gaping into the Mantarian's worried, face, he realized he had put everything his friend's whole family had devoted their lives to in jeopardy.

Darian knew he could not let his friend fall on disgrace.

fOUR

For Max, the trip back to the barracks took forever, and had been nothing but awkward. Barely a word was spoken between the two young males. They had skittered and slunk back along the length of the torn-up valley plain, through the long grass to where their hovercycles were hidden. Max watched Darian sink further and further into despair. He felt as if he had to mentally pull the human every mile of the flight back to the academy grounds.

Once clear of the carnage of the crash, Max knew Darian would dwell on the same haunting images that he himself fought off. Those of people hurt and unconscious, needing help inside a smoking and burning wreck.

It was clear to the Mantarian that he was the sole reason Darian had allowed himself to be taken away. Never afraid for himself, Darian had acted based on what *might* happen to Max. To his career, his life and to his family. They were running away from what might become rather than standing up to face what was.

They returned to Darian's quarters in silence. Max followed his friend inside and watched as he collapsed down into the desk chair. The sudden change in light level was like commitment to a dark prison cell. The Mantarian's heart sunk as he watched Darian cover his face with his hands. *He can't even look at me,* he thought with a shameful ruffling of his face fur. *He knows that if he does he's going to wish he made a different choice.*

Max blew out his breath as he sat down into a splayed-out pose on the bed. His face took on a sullen mask as he listened to their murmuring breathing echo off the walls of the room. Inside, he knew he was waiting for Darian to speak. To take the lead, and readjust their roles back to normal.

Darian finally cracked his hands away from his face, and looked over at Max quizzically. "Ford, what did you mean back there?"

Max was caught off guard, confused as he struggled to replay events and understand the question. After a few moments he realized his face was screwed up into a puzzled mess. He widened his eyes slightly, pleading for enlightenment.

"When you..." Darian faltered, delicately catching himself. "After you saved me you said..."

Max bent his neck and put his face down into his hands. What he had done was something that he didn't want to see broadcast to the world.

"Oh, man," he started with a sigh. Then he spoke quickly, but kept his hands to his face. "Look, I'm just nobody's... *horse* - ok?" He hated the word the humans used for his less evolved ancestors. He'd seen the pictures - the historical documents of the first settlers on the planet, and the 'animals' they had brought with them. Before the meltdown and the genetic tantrum that led to so many types of mixed sentient life forms.

"I can... my people can... *do* that... but... we're-"

Max stopped as Darian's questioning expression vanished. In its place grew obvious empathy, and the relaxation of enlightenment. Max suddenly felt connection – the friend he knew so well had flashed back into the room.

"Ford..." Darian started, then stopped and looked thoughtful. "...Max."

The Mantarian's eyes widened slightly at the deliberate use of his first name.

"I can't think of you in any other way but as my friend. And as my equal. That's it - OK?" He looked serious for only a moment more, to cement the words. Then he looked down, suddenly conspicuous.

Max smiled slowly as he saw the tension recede from both of them. But in the short silence the weight of Max's shame and regret returned. He tried to cling to the old and familiar roles that they knew so well. "Just don't tell anyone I did that, ok? I'll end up being your... valiant... steed, or... something."

A wry, mischievous grin came across Darian's face. But before Max could respond a hard knock came at the door. Both young men sat bolt upright and lost all color in their faces. Max's eyes glazed over and he stared at Darian with a parched mask of worry, gulping down a lump in his throat.

Darian got up and the took two slow, heavy steps towards the entrance. His hand rested on the doorknob for a moment as he struggled an inhalation. Then he flung open the door.

A tall and wide pig-like being – quartermaster by uniform – was flanked by two absolutely enormous Ursid military policemen. All three of them glared at the human, backs stiff and shoulders starkly parallel to the floor. The male in the center spoke right away, a harsh grating sound that seemed to reverberate off the walls.

"Cadet Corporal Darian Carver."

Max saw Darian freeze as the address was hammered into his face. The Mantarian's neck muscles became taut and he could feel the blood rush into his cheeks. He imagined that Darian was experiencing the same thing.

"Y- Yes sir?"

The quartermaster's eyes stabbed past Darian directly at Max. The Mantarian glumly stood up and stared, waiting for his own name and rank to be called.

"You are to be immediately detained," the male continued, rotating his eyes back to the human. "You will accompany me to audience with Proctor Rempel."

"Sir, yes Sir." Darian weakly acknowledged.

Max still expected to be directed to join them, but no more words came. Darian took a tentative step forward, and glanced back to Max with a starkly worried face.

The door to the room rolled slowly shut on its hinges.

ƒıⱴε

"Your father is dead."

There was no hesitation in the words. No subtlety or empathy.

Darian's eyes lost focus, and he slowly rotated his vision down to the stone floor. The sentence ran over again in his mind.

Your father is dead.

He felt nothing. Reaching down inside, he turned the words over and tried to feel... something. Anything. Blankness came back at him. After a moment, it was all he could do to realize that, in fact, he had no immediate feeling. A moment more, and he also realized that the way he was acting was completely wrong in an Admiral's presence. He snapped his eyes up to stare at the man.

On the other side of the broad black desk stood the rigid, tall and pale human that any cadet knew instantly by sight – Admiral Rempel. He stared, motionlessly waiting for a response.

Darian blinked, dazed by his own confusion.

"Not the best of news," Rempel continued. The man did not flinch a muscle of his face beyond what was absolutely necessary to utter the words.

Darian heard them, but still seemed at a complete loss as to how to act. His heart drove him – he knew it did. Why wasn't it doing so now? He'd just been told his father was dead.

Rempel's face changed. Barely – but Darian noticed it. An air of confusion surfaced in his eyes. Then something that chilled. Suspicion. "When was the last time you spoke to him?" The words were not stated rudely, but still the question was obviously not a query - it was a command to proffer information.

"S..sir... not for... cycles... Sir. Two." Darian stammered his answer – confused by the tone suddenly taken by the Academy Proctor.

Rempel continued to stare at him for a moment. Then his eyes left Darian and wandered, as if he was trying to put together a puzzle in his mind. Using pieces that wouldn't fit.

Darian gulped again. His own inner turmoil was compounded by Rempel's posture and tone.

As Proctor, Rempel was known throughout the Academy. Not just as its chief executive and director, but also as its brick-and-mortar unflinching foundation. The man was regarded as simply having no empathy whatsoever. He believed in numbers and in hard real facts, driving the academy like one would drive a ship crewed by robots. The only real thing you got from the Rempel was a level of irritation, as if he had a dial controlling it which did not go to zero.

Finally, Darian felt he had to say something. "An accident, sir?"

Rempel paused – looking as if he was trying to understand and analyze the nature and motivation of Darian's question.

"No," he spoke quietly. But nothing more.

Darian was very uncomfortable now, quirking a brow while scrunching up one cheek and the edge of his mouth in perplexity. "Were others killed, sir?"

Rempel tilted his head almost imperceptibly forward, to regard the younger human through the top of his eyes. "Yes." His voice lost none of the hard edge - he seemed to be straining to hold himself back.

Darian's face flushed in of frustration. *A battle then?* he thought. *What am I supposed to do? Play twenty questions?* "Sir, am I to guess, sir?"

Once again, Rempel did not answer right away. He simply closed his eyes for a moment – as if he was trying to solve a riddle. He took a quick frustrated breath and his eyes flitted open. "No. You are... not." The last word was said very slowly, in a darker tone. Rempel watched intently for a reaction from Darian.

The only reaction Darian could give was one of perplexity. He just stood at attention and blinked, waiting for more information.

The Admiral looked even more frustrated by this lack of reaction. His voice grasped back onto an edge of anger, and he started to speak very, very quickly. "Your father, it seems, was directly responsible for decisions which resulted in the loss of his ship." He turned and started to pace in front of his desk, biting out the words. "The destruction of which caused the death of almost all crewmembers."

He stopped and looked at the only window, a small square high on the wall. His voice was weaker for a moment, something that surprised Darian. The Admiral had never spoken with anything but absolute strength and conviction. "Including my daughter."

Darian's face flushed with shame. He found it hard to breathe - hard to do anything but gawk at the Admiral. He hadn't known the man was a father. He had never heard the daughter's name. The only Rempel anyone ever talked about was the cold machine in front of him.

With a labored sigh Rempel swiveled and took two steps towards Darian, his face stretching as he restrained his anger. His eyes blazed red and his words came slowly in stabbing sentences. "The... *few*... survivors barely managed to return to Federated territory on a heavily damaged support ship. One that crashed on its return. Right here. This morning. Into our graduation field at the valley, right in front of the cadet revue." He quickly moved his hand up in front of Darian's face between them. A single finger stabbed out of his hand.

"One." He paused, letting the lone word sink in. "One member of the crew from your father's ship survived." His hand came down. "And nine from the support ship. That's all."

Darian gulped, but he had no choice in action. He just stared back at the Admiral, his mind buzzing. Rempel had to know already - must know. *He must be playing games with me*, Darian thought. *How could he NOT know that Max and I were there? I- I have to...*

"Sir... I... this... this morning... I was..."

The door behind Darian opened with a subtle hiss, causing him to smartly clamp off his confession. Rempel's eyes widened ,face going to an angry frown at the intrusion. All Darian could see was the Admiral's attention snap to the door.

Rempel bent his head forward, looking past Darian through the top of his eyes again as he bit out loud words to the person entering the room.

"Lieutenant, you are EARLY!"

The voice that answered was distinctively strong and even. Hard-soled taps of feet complemented its echo off the glassy marble floor. "My apologies, Admiral. I... have not slept since our return, and... seem to have lost my sense of time."

Darian's eyebrows went up and his eyes widened at the timbre of the voice. Obviously a female felid - and by the sound of the proper and prim accent, one from the well-developed north. But the human could also tell a level of fatigue and twinge of pain at the edges of the distinctive accent she had.

Through his time at the Academy, Darian had always been impressed with felids, both the muscular men and the equally powerful but lithe women. The human had seen young felid men fight, and their speed and agility made them daunting adversaries. But nobody – no one – messed with the females. The women had an extra evolutionary edge of a large primary talon embedded in each hand. These long, lethal "razor claws" gave them a distinctive ugly bulge in the knuckles. Even when the claw was not deployed there was the subtle reminder of hidden danger.

Darian's only experience of the feline humanoids had been with the polite, aristocratic ones that formed the lion's share of the Queen's government. Humans, Ursids and the hard-headed and horned Impalans still formed a large portion of the populace in the federated territories, especially in the Navy. But the felids' sense of morality, greater purpose, and community made them perfect for the higher social station. Darian had only ever seen pictures of the southern variety, the mystical reclusive aboriginal types that had somehow retained their tails.

Rempel stood stock upright in front of Darian and turned away, pacing back to his desk. His shoulders were hunched up high and his head was tilted forwards. The woman who had entered the room came up behind Darian and took up a position off to the right. He could hear her coming to attention.

Rempel reached his desk and spoke towards it, still looking away from them. "Mister Carver, this is Lieutenant Linsey. She is the sole survivor from your father's ship."

Darian's heart fell into his stomach, and he couldn't stop himself from glancing over at her. When he saw her he had to blink. Her left arm was in a tight sling clamped close to her body across her chest. Her face was badly scratched, but the rest of her was covered by a brand new uniform, and she stood stock-straight in the standard Navy attention pose. The tan tone of her short fur and her green eyes could be considered normal, but her fiery red hair was striking. Her small waist and thin forearms belied what strength and speed Darian knew all felids had.

Linsey did not look back at the human - she just kept her eyes straight at Rempel. When Darian looked back at the Admiral, the man was staring pointedly at him. His stomach flip-flopped and he cursed himself for being caught off-guard.

"The information regarding your father's... failure... has already gotten out." Rempel stated flatly. "Many other cadets have lost parents in this tragedy. Good people who were prime examples of those we need." The man did not falter in his gaze or in his tone. It was clear the Admiral's categorization was made to exclude Darian's father. His mouth continued in a set frown, as if he was daring the young man he held in his view to speak. "We build trust here. We build family. The life of one person is equally important as another. When a choice is made in contradiction of this, all of us suffer. All of us bear the brunt of the broken trust. Your father broke this trust."

"This boy is not his father," Linsey cut in, strong and loud enough to tell that she knew what command was. Darian had never heard a single person in his life cut off Admiral Rempel. His breath caught in his throat and he could feel a bead of sweat instantly appear on his temple, as every muscle in his body tensed for what he expected would be the closest thing to a nuclear explosion from the man. The room hummed in electric silence for a moment as the Admiral's eyes widened.

"...sir." Linsey finished much more quietly.

Rempel focused back on Darian, steamrolling through Linsey's comment to complete his thought.

"Your father's actions were selfishly reprehensible. They tell me... everyone tells me.. you are precisely like him." He scrutinized Darian, nodding to himself in apparent agreement with the assessment. "The Navy... our family... has been crippled. If you stay here, I dare say that you will face scrutiny and recriminations that cannot be predicted. People will not trust you. They will see your father when they see you. Hear your father when you speak. And when their lives are to be put into your hands they will remember what he did."

Darian looked down at the floor, turning over the words in his head. But in the moment, he could not fathom a response. Where else did he have to go?

"I do not think it wise for you to stay here. And there is nothing else I can do with you. You are a casualty - much like the others who died." The man trailed off, and Darian's blood started to scream in his ears at what was being implied.

"Sir, he has done nothing to deserve expulsion, and he must be given a chance. He has no other family but the Navy, now." Linsey answered directly for the human. Darian's head perked up and he risked another glance at the woman.

"He is but one cycle from graduation," she continued. "You must let him continue as a ward of the ac-"

"Do NOT tell me what I must and must not DO!" Rempel yelled, cutting Linsey off and quickly striding straight towards her, eyes fixed at her face. He passed Darian and went to stand a bare centimeter from her nose. Speaking very loudly in a rush he rammed out words into her face. "I have given you deference here due to present circumstances but my patience is wearing quite thin, LIEUTENANT. The miracle of your being able to pilot that burning scrap-heap of a supply ship back here notwithstanding, you are the *best* example of the *worst* type of priggart pussycat peacock I have ever met. You *will* shut your mouth until spoken to. Do I make myself CLEAR?"

Linsey just looked at him for a moment, then responded in a slow, normal and even tone. "Yes, sir."

Rempel glared at her, then backed up and turned sideways to look at Darian. Darian went eyes-front so quickly his neck hurt for a moment. He heard the Admiral breathe out in a huff.

"Mister Carver, I do not envy you in the slightest. I doubt anyone will trust your family again." He paused, and rotated to face his desk again."You shall be escorted to your quarters. You will be given compassionate leave for sixteen hours, and then you will resume your standard training schedule."

With his final words, the door on Rempel's office sprang open. Darian blinked once, and saluted Rempel as he had been repetitively trained to do. The Admiral just frowned and gestured in annoyance at the door.

SIX

As the door shut behind Darian, Linsey breathed a barely perceptible sigh of relief. Rempel was blaming Darian for the actions of his father, which to her was already unacceptable. But to have the boy spend the rest of his life paying the price for decisions that he didn't make – that was something that riled her anger. She'd seen enough lives lost or torn apart, and knew that even now other young cadets were getting the bad news about their parents.

The felid fixed her jaw and tried to stand stiffly. She had lost her left razor claw in a fierce close-quarters fight – an injury that would scar her for the rest of her life. The searing pain in her left hand was only partly dulled by the drugs she had been prescribed. She thought she could still feel the phantom of the missing piece of her anatomy, as a dull ache that she had been told would never go away.

Linsey still didn't really know why she had been called to an audience with the Admiral. After the crash and the emergency medical treatment on her arm, she had intended to immediately depart to her reserve quarters in the felid capital. However, as she was leaving she had received Rempel's urgent request. Desperately wanting sleep, she had decided to arrive at her appointment early.

The old man watched the door close behind Darian, then turned and strode quickly up beside her. Too close for comfort by far – she knew right away he was trying hard to put her off balance. To gain back the footing of his dominance.

"Lieutenant, in case you have not noticed I do not like your attitude. You have an unhealthy disrespect of protocol. It is an insult to our traditions, and does not serve you well."

Linsey remained silent - the last thing she wanted was a fight. But she also knew that she was beyond the point where she could deal with a boring conversation. *Cut through it*, she thought. *Get it over with...*

"Admiral, your daughter. She-"

"You are here for a reason." He spoke with intensity, forcing his words over her own as he avoided her eyes. It was as if her desire to connect on some kind of emotional level had caught him with the incredulity and repulsion of a bad stench. He had to take a full breath before he continued.

"Your recent experience is invaluable. As the only Admiral within range considering time and distance, I have been… directed... to take action." He frowned even more staunchly and looked at the arm she cradled.

"I need to know one thing, and quickly."

Linsey was slightly puzzled by the sudden change in attitude and direction with his words. She had wanted to explain what had happened - especially the details of his daughter's final moments. Why else would he have called the only living witness to him, before she even had a chance to recover? She looked sideways at him and cocked a brow.

"Is your injury manageable?" he asked.

Linsey paused a moment, quite confused. "Sir?"

"The Galleon *Archer* is departing as part of a flotilla. They will attempt to re-establish a new frontier line for the Federation near Cestica. Captain Qorl Vrue has put in a direct request - specifically for you." He paused for a moment as his voice changed to a regretful tone. "To be his second officer".

Linsey's eyes widened but the rest of her face remained stoic, covering a torrent of emotion as her mind whirled with questions. *Second officer? But... already? I just made full Lieutenant! Have other ships been destroyed? Is it really that bad?*

"Can you ship out?" Rempel continued, apparently frustrated at not receiving an immediate answer. "If it is too much for you then I can gladly-"

"Sir, I will serve in any way required." Linsey answered without really thinking. The words came up from her heart – from a wellspring deep inside underneath the surprise and confusion.

Rempel paused, and seemed for a moment depressed at her acceptance. Linsey had known his daughter - she had outranked the felid by a single bar. If it was the Admiral's progeny that had survived, then no doubt she would be getting the offer of promotion instead of Linsey.

"Good." His response was short, and his face did not change in any way. With barely a motion he removed a small handful of gold metal bars from his pocket.

"I would not normally be the one to promote you, but as I said we are constrained by time and place. We will have to accept the roles we are required to play."

"Sir - Dellia. She did the ri-"

"LIEUTENANT!" Rempel gripped his robes at the waist and bent his head down as he struggled to maintain his composure. "If I... ever... wish to speak on that subject with you... at any point, I shall ask you directly." His face came up, eyes closed. When he opened them they were glassy from his strain.

She did it right, Linsey tried to will him to understand with her eyes. She struggled to keep her mouth shut. *Dellia knew she was going to die. And she still did the right thing.*

Linsey's throat tightened but she held steady. She knew he needed to get by it. Needed to hear now what she had to say, or he never would. But he continued on, abandoning the path that would at least start to bring him closure.

"Lieutenant Katherine Linsey, in light of your recent accomplishments and selfless service to the Queen's Royal Navy, you are hereby promoted to Lieutenant Commander."

Far beyond exhaustion and almost in a dream-state of emotional wear, Linsey could barely reach out her hand. But she did, and he dropped the bars into it. Rempel then turned and walked slowly away from her.

"You may or may not be aware of this. Only one other member of the Navy has ever achieved this rank in their career as quickly as you."

She knew he was speaking of his daughter. But there was no pride in his voice, no hint of satisfaction or belying of emotion of any kind. His anger had made him say the words purely to make her feel out of place.

By the time he turned around at his desk and sat down, his customary frown was back on his face.

seven

Darian's room felt large and alien, as empty as his mind was of any kind of feeling. He slumped against the wall inside the door.

Your father is dead.

Staring at the floor, he went over and over the same four words in his head. Each time he let the sentence dangle. Waited to feel it. The loss, the hurt - something. Something like when his mother had died – a long time ago. Loneliness.

He felt nothing.

Minor guilt panged him – he couldn't believe he wasn't reacting. Even reacting inappropriately. Everything was the same as before. Didn't he miss his father? Hadn't he wanted to see him, at cycle break? At any time in the past few years?

And what had his father done? How could he have violated the trust of so many? Rempel had said that no one life was more important than another. All Navy members trusted each other to be considered equal. On the surface Darian agreed - it seemed simple. Would he act as his father did?

He suddenly chuckled at the absurdity of it all - the sound echoing for a moment in his room. He smiled, forced a frown, then chuckled again. Blinking, he tried to imagine what might have happened. He tried to see the pain, the struggle, or the choice that must have been made. He dug for a crisis to hold - to uncover and expose so that he could focus on hurt. Hurt that had substance.

I guess I would feel like this about anyone...

The door chime sounded.

Max.

The cold shock of Darian's feelings flooded through his mind and body, and he shook with wide eyes for a moment. On autopilot, he drew in breath and his hand shot to the door handle. But then he looked at that hand, and he let out the breath. It was there – feeling. What he'd been looking for. It just wasn't directed where he thought it would be. *This isn't the same,* he thought. *Max wouldn't be the same as someone else.* He gulped hard. *And people can see that.*

"It's me. I know you're there," Max's voice came. "Quick – open up."

Darian jerked the door open, looking at his friend with his face white as a sheet.

"You took it all on yourself, didn't you?" Max queried, his face suspicious. He paused, then nodded almost imperceptibly as he acknowledged his own assumption. "You took the heat for me again."

Darian blinked, mind disconnected from the morning's events.

Max shook his head in disbelief. Then his teeth gritted in anger. "Look! I don't need you to take care o-"

"My father's dead."

Max stopped suddenly, and the dry silence between them hung in the air. Then the Mantarian swallowed and licked his lips. He blinked, his mind apparently derailed from its path of thought. "Wow."

"Yeah." They stood there, looking at each other, for a moment more – Darian feeling Max study him. There was no change in the expressions of either young male. Darian stepped back and rested against the open door. "You coming in?"

Max glanced left and right, then entered quickly – rotating so that he looked at Darian the whole time as he slid in. "What... what happened?"

Darian closed the door, and then continued to face it. His heart was still pounding from the feeling that had rushed through him when Max had rung the door chime. "He..." Darian started breathlessly. "He messed up. Big time."

"How big time?"

Darian turned, and slumped against the wall again for a moment, before looking tiredly at Max.

"Whole ship. Two- actually." Darian's brows went up, still fascinated at his own detachment. "Almost everybody died."

"Everybody? How-" Max appeared as if he was having tremendous difficulty trying to conceive of a situation that could have had the results Darian was describing.

"The... crews, yeah. All but one, on his ship, anyway." Darian gulped and stared at the wall so that he wouldn't have to face the scrutiny that anyone – even Max – would give him.

"Wow. That means..."

"Yeah. Going to be lots of unhappy people."

Max still stared at his friend. "What... does that mean for you? People keep saying how you're just like your fath-"

"Exactly like him." Darian corrected, still staring off into space.

"I mean- uh-" Max grimaced. "Never mind. Are you O- uh... of course you're not OK, but-"

"How are you?"

Max balked, flinching as if a heavy raindrop had come out of a clear sunny day and thunked down onto the end of his nose.

"H... how am I?" Max stuttered. "Dare - you just lost your dad. What do you mean how am I?"

Darian smiled very slightly at hearing the shortened, familiar version of his first name. "I... I didn't feel anything, Max. When Rempel told me."

A pause came as Max took in the words. "And now?"

Darian shook his head slowly, staring a thousand miles into the distance that wasn't there. He still smiled, coming close to chuckling again from the audacity.

Max shifted his weight, eyes compassionate and large as he moved a step towards his friend. He appeared as if he didn't know what to say, but still wanted to offer something. Whatever was needed.

Darian looked straight at him as he moved. "I'm not feeling any kind of -"

The door chime going off jarred them both – Max's eyes widening as he flinched. Then his face turned quizzical. Who would come calling right now?

Darian's heart fell. He guessed that it was probably another cadet – one who's parent or parents had been killed by his father's apparent selfishness. "Great. Here we go. You might need to help me fight somebody off..." he muttered.

Darian turned and opened the door, revealing the calmly standing Katherine Linsey. Darian blinked and again went white, heart pounding up into his throat. "L-Lieutenant... I-"

Linsey smiled slowly, but said nothing. Darian felt Max immediately on his shoulder, peeking around - his eyes staying wide as he gazed at the beautiful female.

"I... I wasn't expecting you."

"You are busy," Linsey responded, her eyes alighting on Max. "I apologize for the intrusion."

"No! No- it's... it's fine. This is... Ford. Max Ford. He's... uh... my..."

Max jutted out his hand around Darian and reflexively offered the standard line he gave to women he met when he was with the human. "I'm his comic relief."

Darian frowned – hard. Not the time for jokes – or for fraternizing. Especially with a superior.

"He's my.. friend." Darian finished with a slight roll of his eyes.

"You will be needing your friends," Linsey answered, looking down at Max's hand. The hand he was reaching for was at the end of the broken arm bound to her chest. She smiled in response to the gesture, and gently dipped her chin in acknowledgement.

"Uh- sir! Yes, Sir. What.. why-" Darian realized the lapse in protocol and tried to recover.

"It's fine, corporal. You've had a bad day. As have I." Her mouth set in a line. "I came here to speak with you for a moment. I have to leave shortly."

Darian blinked again, glancing to Max and then back to Linsey. "Uh... okay. Do you want to..."

"Come in, yes. That would be suitable." Linsey finished for him, looking at Max again. The Mantarian stepped backwards into Darian's room away from the doorway and grabbed a chair for her.

Darian coughed and stepped to side up with the door – allowing space for her to pass. She repeated a small nod to acknowledge the courtesy, and stepped into the room. As he shut the door behind her, Darian noticed the shiny new commander's bars on her lapel. "Uh... sir – ma'am. What would you like to speak with me about?"

Linsey stared at Max for a moment, as if querying if he was supposed to be present. The young male looked back at her with a mirror of the questioning face – not for a moment perceiving her unannounced query.

"I wished to check. On you. The Admiral is... not the warmest person I have ever met. And," she paused for a moment. Then she took her eyes from Max and turned to look into Darian's face. "I am leaving on another mission in only a few minutes." She seemed to search for her next sentence. "I knew your father."

Of course you did, Darian's mind bluntly pulsed. *He killed all your friends.* He opened his mouth, then closed it - trying to find a footing for his words.

"You were on his ship," is all he could manage.

"Yes," she continued, using a soothing tone starkly unlike the Admiral's hard-edged manner. "I was there. Was part of... what happened." She looked into his face for the briefest of moments, as if trying to recognize him from the father's face. A face Darian knew she must have seen every day. "It's not going to be easy for you." Her voice turned to a strain. "To be here."

"Why? I mean, people will be angry. But it wasn't me that-"

"As the Admiral pointed out, your father made a decision that was... and... will forever be... unpopular. An action in character - a character everyone here seems to think you have. He made a choice that some others would not have made."

"What choice?"

Linsey looked into his eyes – searching. As if she was looking for something that would give her a way out of the conversation.

"He chose to try to save... some... people. People he cared for. Instead of... a greater number of others." She eased it out very softly, feeling the words for truth. The people she spoke of were not cold equations to her, as they were for the Admiral. "The choice he made, and when he made it, took away the choices of the others. And unfortunately... his solution did not work. For anyone."

Darian blinked. Still no feeling for his father. He tried to envision the situation she described – using any number of situations he knew could occur on a solar galleon plying the winds of Zefphyr. Why wasn't she being more specific?

He realized that the details of the situation didn't matter – that it was done. He also realized that he did feel something – he felt for the people that she was describing. Anger for the Navy officers that had been lost, and for Linsey as the only survivor. He felt for the Admiral. His face was hot and his eyes were watery as his throat suddenly got tight. The two things the academy hammered into all its cadets stuck in his mind.

Responsibility. Family.

Looking at the felid, he suddenly was aware of Max, who's concerned, empathetic eyes were looking around, back at him.

"It doesn't matter. It's over. And there's nothing you can do about it," Linsey said with finality, making a definite effort to close the conversation. "Nothing anyone can do now."

Darian tried to latch onto the anger, to somehow show her how sorry he was. Even the deep remorse he had from fleeing the crash site that morning. But he was lost. "What- then what do I do?"

Linsey just looked at him for a moment, as did Max. The Mantarian's throat and face taut with stress.

"You don't give up," she said. "You continue to be who you are. Who you were yesterday. Not something others will try to make you out as."

Darian thought of Max – about how people treated him because his family was not of a proud stature. The human wondered what was going to change for him, now that his father had been disgraced.

"I'm not my father," he intoned softly.

Linsey nodded at him as if she'd known he was going to say that. "You never were. And you never will be. No matter how much people tell you they know you, or know exactly what you will do." She glanced to the floor as and took a breath. "I don't blame you for what happened."

Darian just looked back at her, his chest shaking. He had no clue what to do or what to respond with, even how to feel.

"Promise me you will not give up." Linsey stated flatly, and rotated her green eyes up to look at his. Her face was compassionate, but the undercurrent of command came through in her voice. She was trying to give him an order.

Darian nodded curtly, finding himself reacting more to the order than to the compassion. Trained to respond to the voice that Linsey was using, he felt the welling of his resolve.

Linsey spent only a moment more looking at him – then without another word she turned and exited the quarters.

Darian gazed in the silence at his closed door.

"I won't give up," he murmured.

two

years

later

eight

Linsey resumed consciousness slowly. She smelled smoke, and tasted ash. Light-headedness was compounded by a constant pain in her chest and on her legs - a weight. Something... or... someone.

A big... hairy... male. Her mind was jarred awake, but the shock subsided almost immediately due to what she sniffed through the dank smoke.

An Ursid. Vrue.

"Captain?" her voice came out, but faltered into a squeak at the pressure against her from his enormous bulk. He was covering her body, which was shoved up against a very solid bulkhead. She struggled to get enough clean breath to talk, but sputtered and coughed at the acrid air. She suddenly felt frightened. Was he dead?

Vrue moved slightly, stirring.

"Captain! Are... are you all right?"

His huge frame shifted and leaned on her more. Bearing the crushing force, Linsey just waited, trying to breathe through the stench of burning flesh and hair that wafted into her nose.

Vrue moved back slowly, shaking his head and blinking. Then he looked at her – his face appearing confused as he puzzled back the pieces of what had happened. Linsey looked beyond him, and Captain Vrue caught her glance, to swivel and turn on his knees to look.

The entire left side of the cabin was gone – open to the dark clouds of Zefphyr. The edges of the hole were burning, and parts of cannons and the crews that had operated them were strewn about the room. Linsey coughed again and covered her mouth with a hand while her eyes widened in shock. Then she looked at Vrue as he surveyed the damage.

"Ow," he grunted. "My head." He held it for a moment, then looked at her. "Miss Linsey – you all right?"

Linsey looked down at herself, realizing that apart from becoming rumpled by having Vrue lying on top of her, she was undamaged. She then realized that Vrue must have protected her – covering her with his body as the...

"I will be fine, Captain. What... what happened?"

Vrue nodded to acknowledge her status, then looked around again. "They fired their cannons. I... uh.."

"You jumped in front of me. When..."

Vrue paused, then looked at her and chuckled. "Sorry about that." He started to get up.

Linsey gave him a wry look for an instant – irritated at the apology. She was extremely relieved that her mentor had survived, but the Captain seemed to apologize for everything, no matter what was happening. It never stopped him from doing what was right, but he seemed to have a touch of regret in everything he did. It was a trait Linsey knew was too often associated with his people – and after two years she was getting used to it.

Vrue appeared flustered, his huge well-muscled bulk shifting as he continued to get up to standing. He had to duck a bit so as not to hit his head on the cracked bulkhead beam above them.

"Well... You were in my blasted way! I'll write you up for it later, shall I?" he jested. "Besides – we're both still here." He turned his head and gestured stiffly to the rest of the destroyed room. "Can't say as much for the others."

"How long were we out?" Linsey wondered aloud as she rose.

They could hear feet thumping on the deck above, and the first officer calling their names and ordering for fire control teams.

"Minute or two I reckon. Nobody woke us up. And the ship's still up in the air." He was quiet for a moment, as if testing the motion of the ship. "Liable to stay up by the feel of it."

"Are.. you sure you are all right?"

Vrue shrugged, but then turned around, looking over his shoulder as he did so to try to see his back.

"I've a bit of a scorch, I think..."

Linsey covered her mouth with her hand in shock again - the entire back of his uniform was in tatters. His lightly haired back stuck out, burnt crisscrosses showing where debris had hit his thick skin as he had covered Linsey with his body. His trousers were scorched as well, showing holes where his flesh was charred and the hair gone. "Oooch," he mused aloud. "I might need a new uniform."

"Sir! I..." Linsey blurted through her hand, her eyes wide. She looked away from his partially-bare burnt bottom, feeling heat in her cheeks.

"I've had worse, Lass." He chuckled and turned around again – offering her his hand to stand her up. At that moment the calls came from above again.

"Captain! Commander Linsey!"

Vrue's huge baritone came out rumbling in response, seeming to shake what was left of the cabin. "We're down here, Mister Craig!" He paused and looked at Linsey. "And we're still breathing!"

More shouts and angry voices could be heard above them. Vrue frowned in response and lowered his voice so as not to hurt Linsey's sensitive felid ears.

"We best get topside, Miss." He started to move.

Linsey followed and they quickly climbed the cracked short staircase to the main deck – trying to see through the smoke to avoid the broken splinters of wood that seemed to be everywhere.

First officer Craig was standing at the top of the stairs, looking at them with the blanched pallor of someone who had seen a ghost. He also appeared confused to see that Vrue's uniform was burnt and tarnished, and that Linsey's was paradoxically in completely the opposite condition.

"How's the ship, Mister Craig?" Vrue rumbled to break his first officer's stare.

"Uh – Sir. Strong back. Like her Captain- sir. She'll hold. We are now rounding up survivors from the ships that we put down." He glanced off to the side of the ship where the shouting was coming from, and frowned in disgust. "Humans, Dargs, a few Kestens and Mantarians. Even one stinking Venerian. I'd just as soon leave them out here on some atoll to starve." He wrinkled his nose and paused, looking at his Captain again. "Are you..." he trailed off, glancing at Linsey then down into the smoke coming out of the compartment they had been in.

"Fine. List me a damage report please." He turned to Linsey. She was still looking away – intently upwards to prevent herself from staring at his

exposed rear end. He smiled and turned to face her. She gulped and thankfully lowered her hot face to look at him.

"Miss Linsey. If you could fetch me a new nick of trousers and jacket..."

Linsey snapped her eyes up, moving immediately towards a storage
locker at the side of the vessel. "Sir, yes Sir."

Craig started immediately. "Sir, the gunnery crews...?"

"They're gone, Mister Craig." Vrue answered, and looked at his first officer for a long moment. "Looks like we traded souls for souls." He looked
out over the edge of the ship – towards the smoldering fiery debris field on
the ocean far below. Disabled lifeboats that were all that remained of their
foes. "Not a fair trade."

A skiff from the Navy ship was running around and picking up prisoners
– each stop denoted by voracious yelling and insults from the Navy crews that
were tasked with the chore. Vrue noted the enemy survivors with a sneer.
"Roughs. Bastard roughs."

Except for small settlements that were able to defend themselves as a
unit, anarchy reigned outside the Queen's frontier. There was no safety, no
medicine, and no rules. The 'rough', it was called, as were the beings that
chose to live in it. Gangs of brigands, pirates and thieves - those on the run
from society.

"If it weren't for the Queen's command of mercy, I'd jack us up a mile
high and toss all of 'em over the side. Let them think about what they done,
all the way down. Still wouldn't put us equal. One of my people's worth
fifty scum roughs. A hundred. They all deserve to be gutted."

Craig looked out as well, then back at the Ursid. "Sir... I don't know
what to say, sir."

"Carry on, Mister Craig. We lost some good people. We need our first
officer to step up now."

Craig nodded eagerly, his face turning quickly to fierce resolve. Vrue
smiled at this reaction – obviously pleased that Craig was able to be commanded so easily and so effectively. He wasn't the best officer Vrue had ever
seen, or the most creative, but he was the most loyal.

"Get to it, now. Get us cleaned up."

"Yes sir." he said as Vrue turned to the side of the ship to gaze down at
their defeated foe.

Linsey silently sided up to him, a new uniform for him slung over her shoulder. "Captain?"

"Ah, Miss Linsey, thank you." He motioned for her to hand him the uniform, then gestured over the edge of the ship, in the direction of the remains of the ship from the rough that had been attacking them. "Take a look down at that, now. Keep your eyes over there."

Linsey did, turning and peeking over the edge. However, she was almost immediately distracted from her gaze by the fact that the Captain started to change clothing. He shucked off his dirty half-melted boots, then his burned-up jacket and trousers. With no regard for modesty he dressed quickly beside her.

To distract herself, Linsey thought of the two ships that had been traveling with them. She looked around them at the blue and white clouds for a moment, as if trying to see something they both knew was no longer there.

"We took a beating this time," Vrue murmured as he pulled on his new pants. "The *Kristoff* and the *Raven* are nowhere in sight." Vrue referred to their two light escort ships. Small and fast but with limited capacity, the two had more weapons than armor. "They haven't been destroyed. Probably captured – since we aren't seeing more debris down there." He sniffed.

"Captain Culley..." she murmured. The Captain of the *Kristoff*. Linsey had really liked her – one of the very few female Captains in the Navy. "And Captain-"

"Trey. Yes." Vrue answered quickly to cut her off, not wanting to dwell on the thoughts. But then he paused, just watching her as she considered their comrades who had disappeared. He came up beside her to lean on the railing. "No gun crews left and we're listing. Our engines took a few. And we got to house these stinking prisoners now."

Both officers looked down over the side and studied the smoke from the fires burning below them on the ocean waters. "The remains you're looking at was the strongest, for sure," Vrue said. "But... we'd have had a longer fight if their buddies had stuck about." He finished with another scowl. "Cowards. I'd like to rip their arms off. Watch them squirm."

Linsey blanched, and looked down at the deck. The Captain's constant violent musings on what should be done with pirates were not something she typically disagreed with, but she still didn't like the colorful images he described.

"Sorry Miss Linsey. I got me reasons for hating them, and they're good ones - you know that."

She did - the Ursid settlements were near the rough. Less than ten years past over a hundred of their women and children had been kidnapped by a large group of desperate brigands. A rescue attempt was badly botched, and resulted in the death of many hostages. Linsey knew Vrue originally had six sisters, but he only ever talked about one of them in the present tense. She never asked about the rest.

The Captain looked out and down at their defeated foe. "We'll need some medical supplies to patch up our wounded. Can you fix us up on the comm net for a delivery?"

"Yes sir, right away sir." Linsey responded, and started to move away.

"What is it you're always saying to the crew?"

"Uh..." Linsey stammered, not quite knowing what he meant.

"Don't give up." He smiled. "That's it." He repeated it softly to himself as he gazed off into the distance. "Don't give up, Aye."

nine

"I give up!"

The Impalan sergeant threw his clipboard onto his messy desk, stomping around to fall into the chair behind it. The seat creaked loudly from the sudden strain of dealing with his furred bulk.

"I am *convinced* you don't know what you are doing – even after *six* months of doing it!" He continued to yell without really looking at Darian, and he put his face into his hands, rubbing the palms into his eyes. "How long does it take you to get it into your head that there's a *reason* you look at what you're moving around?!!"

Darian sighed. He had followed his sergeant into the doorway of the office, and stood loosely posed against the frame. His dejected eyes were half closed, and he barely raised his head enough to look at his superior. "Oh, would you calm down, man," he said in barely a whisper. "Why does it matter how I stack a bunch of boxes?"

"Boxes of what?!" the older horned male burst out at him. "Do you even know what that stuff is? Huh?!" He leaned forward and his eyes dazzled with frustration. "You don't know! But *I* do! The ones you so gallantly stacked six feet high are high explosive. T-4!" He paused for effect and Darian watched tiredly, his bored look unchanging as he strode slowly into the room.

"You are the laziest, sloppiest, most... ANNOYING ... *kid* in the Navy." He nastily spat out the words, fur on his head ruffling. "Where did they grow you, huh? Scraped you off the bottom of some... reject bin? Dammit! They send me the idiots, I swear!"

Darian sighed and looked sheepish, but he'd heard worse. *Hopefully I won't pick up any extra work*, he mused as he tried to look repentant.

"You want to report to work one day and see we had a fire? There wouldn't be anything left. Just a big glowing hole in the ground where a bunch of *our* guys *died* because you were stupid and stacked a bunch of T-4 in the same place. You want that?"

"No." Darian quickly managed the simple, correct response. He stuck his hands in his trousers, fumbling them around his dirty, pulled-out shirt. His messy hair effectively obscured his eyes as he stood waiting to see if it the sergeant was finished yelling.

"Do it *right*, dammit!" the sergeant squawked.

At that moment Darian's dirty and disheveled work partner Brad entered from behind them and chucked another clipboard at the sergeant's desk. It landed loudly and slid down the small pile. Without a word the young man turned began to leave.

"And - YOU!"

"What?" Brad intoned, continuing to move towards the door. He then turned back, putting his hands on his hips in an annoyed pose. "What'd I do?"

"Nothing! That's the problem! You and your senior goof-off partner here."

Brad sighed, and looked at Darian in obvious disappointment. He strode back across the room to the sergeant's desk. At its edge was a large distinctively shaped electric blue bottle. Still looking irritated, Brad grabbed the dirty glass that sat next to the bottle and began to pour.

The sergeant looked incredulously at him as the glass was filled. But then Brad handed it to the older male, changing his face to a look of compassionate understanding. He said nothing.

Their boss looked at the drink for a moment, before he put it to his lips and drained it in one swig. Brad smiled. Darian cocked a brow and looked at the bottle.

The red and black banner around its neck had one word - *Killeagh*. Besides being able to effectively strip grease from engines, the Ursid brew was one of the more potent and popular inebriants available. It also had certain other qualities that Darian knew Brad found particularly useful. There were many stories his work partner had told him about wild nights with young women and a couple of the special blue bottles.

"We do things right when things are properly labeled," Brad said soothingly. "It's not our fault if the dock boys deliver things without a label. That's like they're lying to us. You don't like it when someone lies to you."

Brad quickly took the glass from the angry sergeant and filled it again, then handed it back with a flourish. The Impalan emptied the glass down his gullet. He belched loudly, and Brad continued.

"I think some times they're trying to make fools of us. Make a fool of you. They do it on purpose - to make our jobs harder. I'm sure they laugh at us."

Brad looked over at Darian for support, something to add to the soothing spiel he was giving. Darian sighed and shook his head slowly.

This time the sergeant took the bottle himself, pouring another glass as he ruminated on the words he heard. Apparently the liquid had started to show its effects, as incredibly he nodded his head in approval.

"Bastards. You're right."

"Of course I'm right," Brad said in soft encouragement. "You taught me everything important. You're a great teacher. Now..." He glanced to Darian with a sly grin as they waited for the sergeant to drink his third full glass,

"Now... I think you should go tell the dock boys to do their job right. That they're making it impossible for the rest of us. Making us– you. Making *you* look bad."

Now their superior was bleary eyed - only a minute after starting to drink. Darian was surprised at how fast the change was. He watched Brad connect his eyes with the older male. "Go tell them. Tell them how you feel."

The sergeant stared at Brad for only a second before he got up and brushed roughly past Darian and out the door.

"Magic!" Brad mused. "Ah, Killeagh. I say it, they think it." The young man sat on the desk, which pushed some of the clipboards onto the floor. He shook his head and rolled his eyes, looking at Darian with angrily bent brows. "You need to learn to use that stuff if you want to get by here."

"Not sure I want to learn what you're teaching." Darian folded his arms across his chest, tired and unimpressed.

"S'up to you, wonder boy," Brad intoned dismissively as he started for the door himself. "Clean up the orders all over the floor. The Killeagh will have worn off by the time he gets back."

"What? Why is that my job?"

Brad looked back at Darian for a moment as he sauntered out of the room. "Cuz I say it is. You want me to go tell the sarge how he should feel about you?"

Darian's face burned.

"I didn't think so. Get to work."

As Brad left, Darian turned to regard the messy room. Six months in the supplies depot and before that six months work with the salvage crews. He felt like he'd done all that drudgery in the same day. Flopping down in the chair next to the desk and staring at the mass of work, he blew his long bangs up and closed his eyes. *Too much. Too long. And I don't care.*

"Rough day?"

The deep but soft voice rumbled, but its tone lit off a spark in Darian's brain. His head whipped up and his eyes snapped open.

"Max!" he blurted out at the sight of the Mantarian. "I mean... uh... Ford!" He stood up quickly, knocking some clipboards onto the floor as he smiled a huge smile. "How can you be here? I thought you were on the Ranger!"

Max Ford smiled and approached his friend. Dressed in a very proper, clean and starched Navy uniform, he stepped inside and looked about for a moment. "I'm back. Visiting. Came here to... uh... see where you'd gotten to."

Darian followed Max's gaze about the disheveled room. Then he looked back down at himself, and started shoving his shirt in. "Oh! Uh.. well. Just... working hard. You know. Heh." He didn't know what else to say. "Wow. It's so great you're here."

"Well, only until tomorrow. Then it's off to Station again."

Darian twisted his face into a staunch look. "You're not going back on the Ranger? What happened?"

"Nothing bad." Max smiled. "They're... uh... moving me up."

"To what?"

Max looked pensive – but just for a moment. Then he just dismissively shook his head. "I don't know. Something... different, they said." He looked at the clipboards on the desk and on the floor near Darian's feet. "Glad you're still here. Wouldn't know where else to find you."

Darian gulped, and was still just staring at the regal Mantarian. "Uh.. yeah. Yeah. But I'm... moving up too. Getting out of supplies soon."

"Oh yeah? When?" Max voiced his interest, and looked keenly at his old friend. "Where to? On a ship?"

"Uh, I don't know. Something... different."

Both men stood and stared at each other for a moment. Darian's could feel his cheeks slowly flush at the lie. But there was no smugness at all in Max's posture or tone – he simply was waiting for the next move. As he always had with Darian.

"Are you too busy to hang out..." Max stated uncomfortably.

"What? Uh- no! Heh. No." Darian shook his head and started to pick up the clipboards and put them back onto the desk. "Let's get out of here. Let me just... put this stuff away I-"

"Can I help?" Max asked, and took a step forward.

Darian's frustration at himself seeped out. "Nothing I need an engineer for, thanks." He quieted his voice, but the tone in it remained. "You leave this to me and I'll leave gallivanting around the frontier to you."

Max silently looked at the floor.

Darian immediately felt pained in his chest - an unfamiliar feeling. *That was mean,* he reproached himself. He picked up the clipboards and put them onto the desk, trying to glance at each one of them so they at least went into the right piles. He sighed. *Whatever. Like he cares.*

He fumbled with the last clipboard, then stopped and stood stock still, reading it. He blinked, then flipped over the single page to see if there was any more to the order he was holding. His mouth hung open, and then he cocked his head.

Max waited for a moment, then cleared his throat while he watched. "Look, Carver, I'm... I don't want you to be stuck here. I'm sorr-

"It's her." Darian just started nodding to himself. Then a twinge of excitement came into his voice, as one side of his mouth curved up goofily into a half grin. "This is amazing! It's her, Ford!"

"Who?"

"It's... It's Linsey!" He put a hand on his head and chuckled. Then his voice went soft. "Lieutenant Commander Linsey. The requisition is for her." He looked back down, scrutinizing the board. Then he yelled. "Brad! Get in here!"

Max blinked, seeming interested – at least at Darian's reaction. "What is it for?"

"Brad! Get your lazy ass in here or I'll swear I'll report you!" All of Darian's attention was on the clipboard.

From the other room came a bored yawn, then muffled laughter. "Oooo. Darian's gonna report me."

Darian winced in frustration. "Just get in here, ok?" he pleaded. "I'll buy you a new bottle of that... blue stuff."

When Max spoke he sounded incredulous. "What... you keep track of her or something?"

"Brad! C'mon! I'll even give you the next run... ok?" Then he finally looked at Max to answer him. "I haven't seen her since... well... you know."

Max blinked and nodded, looking slightly puzzled, but still quite curious.

Brad came into the room. "Ok, I get the next run. So can I go now?"

"When does Flipper get back?"

"How the heck should I know?"

Darian sighed and slowed down. His tone adjusted to have the same in-dolence as Brad's. "When is he *supposed* to get back?"

"I dunno. Uh... four. Something like that."

"Ok. Well, get Stan and start filling this pronto." He handed Brad the clipboard.

Brad clearly did not like Darian ordering him around. "Why? Is this my run?" he countered, skeptical of the urgency.

"No, it's mine."

Brad mumbled his annoyance. "Next one better be good. This is a lot of stuff." He stomped out of the room.

Max interjected, bobbing just slightly on his forefeet and putting his hands behind his back. "I... uh... had eating and... drinking and doing point-less things like that in mind. Not... delivery boy stuff."

Darian fixed his mouth, turned and stared in irritation. *Delivery Boy, eh?* his mind bit out.

Max reacted to the anger from Darian, and put out the palms of his hands in a calming gesture. "Okay, okay. Where is she?"

"It says the delivery is for the high docking yard on Careenus – pretty close but above the clouds here. To get that high up with a load we have to take the jump skiff that Flipper's got right now."

Max brightened. "Oooh. Cool. I can do a jump skiff."

Darian smiled back, enjoying the feel of the familiar camaraderie. "My turn to drive."

Max made a stern face and folded his arms across his chest. "Again?"

ten

The packed jump skiff shot up along the steep side of Careenus mountain riding a curtain of fire. A bizarre anomaly from the other smaller landforms nearby, Careenus was a towering pillar of rock. Max held on beside Darian and enjoyed every moment of the constant acceleration. The closest thing to it was when he ran down on all four legs – taking off in the open fields near his family home to chase his brothers and sisters. The main difference in this case was that Darian seemed to like to do crazy rolls, and change direction frequently.

"You do this often?" Max shouted over the din of the engine.

"Not often enough." Darian yelled back grinning, obviously enjoying the rush of riding a rocket. "And I only drive nice when I've got a passenger!" They slowed slightly and leveled out as the ground shrunk beneath them. "Sorry, didn't mean to be rough on you."

"Oh, I've been on rougher rides than this." Max rumbled, letting up a bit on his clutching of the skiff's side. He wanted to counter the bravado. Get back into the comfortable play between them. Find something that wasn't the sullen attitude he'd gotten from Darian in the supply house.

"Oh yeah?" Darian quipped quickly, sounding very interested. "Where?"

Max could not mistake the excitement and envy in Darian's voice. He didn't want to rub it in. His adventures around Zefphyr were... different... from the adventures in a storage and supply house. They were everything Max had always dreamed they could be. "Uh... all over. Lots of missions near the frontier and past it." He realized he might not be going down the right path, and tried to sound bored.

Darian stiffened with envy for a moment, then he looked away, off towards the direction they were flying. "You're really first-rate now."

Max took in the words, and sat in contemplation. Not knowing how to respond, he tried to swing the conversation around again to something positive. "Uh, thanks. But... you..."

"I'm in a crappy dead-end job with no future, no fun, no risk and no reward." The words flowed from him in what seemed to be a practiced statement. Like he had said it to himself a hundred times. "Keeping the Navy safe from another generation of Carvers."

Max gulped, trying to find something to offer to make up for the obviousness of the difference between them. "What I'm doing is not all it's cracked up to be, you know."

Darian gulped, hard. His throat muscles stretched. "Yes," he responded slowly, his eyes suddenly wet. "Yes, it is."

Max hurt. He knew he couldn't lie any more, and that they had to find a way to get through the trip together. He watched Darian surreptitiously. His friend's face shifted through a bewildering array of emotions, finally settling on a thin attempt at indifference. Max tried to relax, but it was so alien for him to want to detach himself from Darian.

As they reached the top of the enormous rocky pillar, Darian maneuvered them through the clouds towards the small supply vessel that waited there.

Fundamentally different from a Navy corvette or galleon, the hauler they drew up on was bulky and wide. It seemed to have too many masts, and large humming sails of various drab colors cascaded in huge arcs from one side of the boat to the other. Almost all of the deck space seemed to be covered in crates and boxes, stacked far too high for any realistic margin of safety. Three small cannons adorned its stern.

For running away, Max thought. *Shoot at who's following you, but run away.* Simple logic for those without elaborate means to defend themselves.

They were waved down by one of the crew and guided to land carefully on the main deck, squeezed up beside the main mast. A flurry of activity ensued as other deckhands moved to secure their skiff.

"Yer late," the crewmember who had guided them in mumbled as he came up to Darian.

"We're early. Got your things." He craned his neck around, searching for any sign of the distinctive Felid Navy commander.

Max looked around too. Neither one of them touched the supplies. They just scanned from one position to the next on the ship, expecting to see Linsey stride out to meet them.

"You... uh... looking for something?" the crew member questioned, watching their bizarre behavior.

"Uh... yeah. Lieutenant Commander Linsey."

The man looked at one of his deckhand cohorts, then back at Darian and Max.

"These supplies are for the lieutenant," Darian explained with confidence.

"Don't know a Linsey." The man gruffly leaned forward and lifted a bag from the pile of supplies.

"Well, the requisition has the name right here."

The man just shrugged. "We're a federated hauler, but this ain't a Navy ship. We're headin' to the Arcadian shoals. Guy you're talkin' about is probably there, waiting."

Darian's face fell, and he blew out his breath in exasperation. Max just sighed and shrugged, standing there. Darian appeared upset that he'd let Max down - their trip now seemed to be a stupid waste of time and energy that could have been spent on much more pleasurable things.

Darian's voice took on a frustrated tone. "Girl. Not a guy." He started to unload a bag himself. "Arcadia? You mean... near the rough?" Even federated carriers that were permitted to carry cargo for the imperial Navy avoided the rough unless the fee was high enough.

The man nodded, and then stopped unloading to glare at Max. The Mantarian had not moved at all, and was watching the others work with a bored expression.

"Hey - you management or something?"

"Huh?" Max responded, not quite understanding that he was expected to help unload the supplies.

Darian explained. "He's my friend. An engineer. He's not in supplies."

The crewman just looked at Max for a moment. "Engineer? You mean, like... fixing engines and stuff, right?"

Max replied on his own behalf. "Uh... yeah."

The man abruptly turned. "Captain!" he bellowed towards the front of the ship. Both Darian and Max looked over in the direction of the call.

"Aye, Mister Kidell? Have they got what we're supposed to deliver?" The female voice was strong and sure, but had an edge of a dark accent to it. Max had to peer around a large crewmember to see her.

Short and slightly plump, the creature that approached them was completely blue from head to toe, had four orange-yellow eyes stacked two-on-two, and seemed to be missing a nose. She also wore an outlandish pompadour hat – much too large for any real purpose but being outlandish. Out of the brim of the hat stuck a bold purple and blue feather. Max tried not to smile too widely as she sized him up during her approach.

Kidell didn't answer the question – he just indicated Max. "Engineer. Him."

Max blinked, but did not shy away. He was proud of what he was. Darian stopped to watch.

"Ah." She put her hand on her chest. "Captain D'ara. And you are?"

"Ford." Max intoned shortly, but glanced at Darian for support. None came.

"Neat. Mister.. Ford." She tipped her hat comically, reaching way out to grab the edge of it. As her face changed to a smile the color of her feather shifted, within seconds becoming a deep orange.

"Come here lad. We're in a hurry and I need to borrow you."

Max blinked twice at the sudden obvious change in her appearance. He looked reflexively at Darian again. But this time he was more aware of himself doing it, and more aware that Darian still was doing nothing to lead. *He's learned very well to do nothing in the past two years.*

"Uh... what seems to be the trouble?" The Mantarian stepped down and away from the skiff towards her. Her short stature made her face awkwardly level with his waist. He didn't know if he should stoop, or simply stand there.

Chuckling, D'ara craned her neck upwards to look at his face. "Engine's been acting up, and we gotta take that load you brought out to Arcadia - highest priority. I wanna know if we're gonna make it." Her blue face resembled a smile, and she blinked the lower pair of eyes at him. "Can you help us?"

"Okay. Uh... where's your... engineer?"

D'ara smiled. "You're looking at her."

"I thought you were the Captain."

Dara's feather subtly changed color again - this time flashing to a deep pink. She nodded her head curtly and explained.

"That I am. It's not a Navy ship, lad. We do what we can, and what we can afford." She paused, looking over his prim and neat uniform. "Can't afford no fancy Navy engineer like yourself. So... I take what I can get when I can get it."

D'ara pointed to a short staircase, at the end of which stood a yellow ladder. "Straight down there."

Max moved, and D'ara followed him all the way down into the hot engine room chamber. In the new, tighter environment Max immediately felt more at home. Still - he was used to Navy protocol, Navy Captains, and other engineers being around. D'ara sounded like a hack.

"Wow." He remarked at the sizes and shapes of the equipment in the room.

"What?" D'ara responded with a chuckle. "You've never seen a girl's engine's before?" She smiled, seeming very proud of her vessel. "Hauling engines for a hauling ship."

Max sniffed the acrid fumes. "Avedyne coils, right?" He waded forwards a bit and looked over a piece of equipment down into the bowels of the machines. "You're burning metal down there. Carb inducer's gone."

D'ara smiled even more widely. "You see, you get what you pay for. I pay nothing, so I got nothing. You Navy boys... heh. You just know."

"They train us well." Max smiled back. "I'm not sure what I can do. You need a new inducer. Without one there's no way you'll get all the way to Arcadia."

D'ara sighed in open frustration. "I guess we're going nowhere fast then." She contemplated for a moment, then turned and started back up the ladder. Max thought for a moment – wanting to help or give options. Even though this wasn't a Navy ship, he had been taught to always explore the options in any situation. "You... just need a new inducer. Or one that will work well for... your trip."

D'ara laughed and looked back at him as she ascended. "Yeah. Try getting one of those on short notice. Navy may have supply houses in this corner of the empire, mister, but we don't. When I say I can't go when the priority is this high, they ain't gonna wait. They're gonna give the job to somebody else. Just lost me some money and both of us some time." Her feather abruptly changed to a rich dark blue as she continued upwards on the ladder. Max shrugged, and followed her.

Back on deck, Darian, Kidell and the other crew had almost finished unloading the drop skiff. Darian looked up and brightened at seeing Max re-emerge from the ship's bowels. "You guys all done?"

Max dusted off his hands on his pants. "Uh... no. Not really. They need a new inducer. They're not going anywhere until they get one."

Darian looked at all the unloaded supplies, and he had made a mental track of their type – almost all medical. Someone was in trouble. "But... these supplies need to go out to... to her." His pleading voice stuck out. He swallowed and continued. "Can we get you an inducer?"

Max responded for D'ara, looking at Darian. "If you've got a spare in your supply house you're ready to give up, or another skiff like this one you're not using." He folded his arms over his chest again.

Darian was silent. They didn't have another jump skiff, and he had no idea if they had the required part. They probably didn't. He looked sadly at D'ara, shaking his head.

She was not looking back at him. She was looking at Max - keenly. "Why another skiff?" she queried. "Skiff's not going to get us to Arcadia."

"Well," Max responded, and pointed to the rear of the engine on the skiff. "That inducer on the skiff engine looks almost new. Even though it's not rated for your ship here... it would hold to get to Arcadia and back. For sure." He looked up at Darian.

Darian looked at D'ara and his eyes brightened.

D'ara's gaze was still fixed on Max. Except now she was smiling. Widely. Her feather was bright yellow.

"Ohhh... No." Max protested. "Full stop. Wait a second now, this isn't a Navy shi-"

"Boys!" D'ara shouted loudly with great cheer. "Yer hereby comman-deered!"

Max's eyes widened as he redoubled his objection. "But! I've got to get back down there. My transport to Station goes-"

"Max, it's *her*," Darian implored, seeming surprised that Max could protest. "These are medical supplies, almost all of them. She could be hurt. We have to get these things to her."

"We can't decide based on who it is! Darian - another crew is depending on me. What about all of them? They need me to get where they're going."

"They're not injured! They're safe on their ship. How could they be as impor-"

"Haven't you learned *anything*? You can't take choices away from people. That's what your father did. What happened to *you* because of that?"

Darian's face flashed fiery red and his breath caught. He looked ready to explode as he seethed words through clenched teeth.

"You filthy bastard."

D'ara stepped her diminutive body between them, a hand reached up to each of their stomachs. The feather in her pompadour hat changed again to a jarring green. Both young men looked at it, surprised. She called sternly up at Max to draw his attention. "You'll get a different transport when we get back, or we can drop you on the way."

Max turned his head down and blurted an objection at D'ara. "It's in completely the other direction! And- you're not Navy! Neither one of you has the authority to do thi-"

D'ara steamrollered over Max's protestations, cutting him off with a surprisingly loud commanding voice. "What are you, green?! On a ship riding the winds, boy, there's only two things. What a lady *can* do and what a lady *can't* do. And boyo, you're on my ship. So's I *can*."

Feather shifting again to the bright yellow she smiled, enjoying the finality of her decision. She tipped the brim of her outrageous hat again.

"Gentlemen! Take that there part down to my engines. You're both coming for a ride!"

eleven

Linsey and Craig were given the tiresome job of sorting through the prisoners and lining them up on the deck, a process that took much longer than Linsey had anticipated. All the roughs were male, and many of them made leering comments or jokes at being handled or ordered around by the pretty felid. She gritted her teeth through it but was a little rougher on some of them than she otherwise would have been.

When she got to the end of the line, a reasonably well-dressed older Drago and a young male Mantarian were the final pair. "I've seen you before." Linsey squinted at the latter, frowning at him while she drew her hands behind her back in a relaxed pose. He appeared dirty, smelled as if he hadn't bathed in a month, and one of his ears was torn. Her mind raced to try to place him, but came up empty. She decided to try something roughs respected - intimidation.

"Where was it?" She growled and stuck her nose in his face, gritting her teeth. Linsey got the reaction she had wanted. The young male stared at her surprised – apparently baffled that he was supposed to remember a prior meeting.

"I.. I don't know. I.. I haven't been caught be-"

"Shut up!" the Drago beside him cut in curtly. He rocked on his heels, grinding she sharp claws on his lizard-like toes into the boards of the deck as he scowled at her. In response to the command, the Mantarian boy stopped and looked down at the deck, snapping his mouth shut.

Linsey's eyebrow perked, but she did not leave the young one - sure she had seen him before. She continued, using a harsher tone to ensure his attention.

"What is your name, rough?"

The boy did not respond, by movement or by words. His face muscles tightened as he braced himself against the question.

"He doesn't have to talk to you, honey cakes. None of us do. You've got rules – you've got to take care of us. Feed us and wipe our bottoms." Low guffawing from the other prisoners erupted, and the Drago grinned a toothy grin.

Linsey turned to coolly watch them all for a moment. Unfortunately, she caught sight of Craig – smiling and looking at the deck. Her face reddened, and her eyes stabbed invisible daggers at him. *He's undermining me now? What is this – a boys-only club?*

As the roughs quieted down, she feigned sniffing the scaly aggressor. "Pirates don't wipe their bottoms, apparently." This elicited another guffaw from the line – and a hard look from the Drago. He was a daunting specimen, but she decided to use that to go even further. "And as for feeding you – I'll give you a mouth full of loose teeth if you like."

He struggled against his bonds. "Hah. Right. You want to try it – untie me, you prissy pussycat. I'll show you your place."

Craig broke in before Linsey could respond further. "That's enough Commander."

"Yeah. That's enough... Commander." The Drago parroted at her in a high voice. "Shut your yap. Can't speak unless spoken to. Gotta ask permission to take a piss."

Irritation flickered across Linsey's face – but she pushed her feelings down, turning to walk in front of him. The bored face she put on showing no signs of intimidation. Then she abruptly slammed a balled fist into the soft center of his midsection.

The male's eyes bulged and he doubled over, fighting for breath. He slid to his knees and coughed loudly as he tried to recover from the wind-stealing punch. Drago bodies were covered in hard and small flexible scales that naturally protected them from almost any type of injury. But they still felt impact or pressure - especially when they weren't expecting it.

"Now," she continued, but in a sweeter voice than before. Turning to the Mantarian, she proffered the same question again. "Your name, boy."

"Adam!" the Mantarian answered immediately. "My name's Adam, all right? Leave him alone. He's right. Aren't you... Navy people supposed to have rules or something on how you treat your.. prisoners?" His tone was plaintive, and he looked at the Drago with concern.

"Hah! A pirate that's talking about rules. That's a new one." From behind Linsey, Vrue's baritone rumbled a laugh as he approached. His eyes blazed, but his massive frame stood relaxed. It was hard to imagine the Ursid disapproving of the conduct of his second officer.

"How about she shows you some more of the rules about pirates on my ship? Hmm?" He growled and stared at the young one. "Every breath you take is a theft."

Linsey glanced back at her Captain, then once again looked at Adam with a frown. She didn't want the boy to give Vrue a reason to let out his anger. "There are no rules out here. Pirates are fond of reminding us of that whenever they can. I suggest you stop your whining and answer our questions." She lingered for a moment more, then turned away and strode back to where Commander Craig, Captain Vrue and a few of the deckhands were standing. Internally, she puzzled over the boy's name – not one she had heard before, at least for a Mantarian. But the eerie feeling of recognition of his face stuck with her.

Craig stood with his arms crossed on his chest. He looked as if he wanted to stoke the embers of the fire he knew was in the huge male. "What shall we do with these bastards, Captain?"

Vrue was silent for a moment, considering. Then a wicked grin flickered through his face. He looked sideways at the angry deckhands and officers – all of them with murder in their faces for the loss of their comrades.

"Hm. Maybe we keep them below decks and away from my eyes. Close to our wounded. That way when some of our loyal and brave are being tended to the same people can make sure our guests here are good and... comfortable."

Linsey coughed, and turned her head to look at her Captain. She knew he wasn't serious – none of the captives would survive even ten minutes. He glanced back at her, and her eyes implored his to do what was right. Even though she knew inside he strained for vengeance.

Vrue took a breath, and scratched his chin. "Miss Linsey – our medical supplies. Where and when?"

"The Arcadian Shoals, Sir. Priority dispatch."

Craig looked a bit confused. "Why so far out? We should head back deeper within the frontier." He turned to the Captain, but looked at Linsey with a disapproving face.

The Drago Linsey had punched struggled back to his feet, but did not pipe up with any more comments. Instead, he appeared to be listening intently to the conversations of the Navy officers.

Vrue noticed this, and deepened his sneer. "These buggers are dangerous. Need to be taken back to a prison compound, or be better confined than what we can offer. Especially in our state."

Craig piped up again, sounding happy to be agreed with. "Yes, sir. That's what I was thinking."

Linsey flushed at the discussion happening in front of the prisoners. She didn't mind being wrong, but the fact being pointed out publicly where they needed to keep absolute control and authority...

"But Miss Linsey was thinking of our wounded, Mister Craig. Them first. Any medical supplies we get will do for triage, but not much better than that. The shoals are on the way to the resupply post at Karst." He paused, and looked at the Drago in the line of prisoners. "Doesn't matter how I feel – it's what we should do. Get the invalid off the boat - gotta think of our own people before these dirty sods."

Craig nodded curtly. "Yes Captain. I'll set a course."

Vrue then looked at Linsey. "Lash 'em to the foremast, Miss." He winked at her. "Tight as you like."

twelve

With all its sails extended, the supply ship broke through the thick clouds of the atmosphere and streaked away from the far side of Careenus tower. The latent power fields that wrapped Zefphyr were channeled and purified to energy that thrusted its way through to the boat's engines.

The carb inducer replacement had been quick, and for Max, easy. Captain D'ara was impressed, and very happy with her temporary charge.

Max enjoyed the work for the most part – finding the equipment a tougher challenge than the well-kept machines of the Navy galleons. Not only were the mechanicals unfamiliar - the work environment of the supply ship was distinctively different from the one Max understood and respected.

He found himself looking around for a commander - someone to report to or check in with. A few times he tried to engage with the other crew members, before recognizing that their mental capacity was pretty much equal to their station. He quickly saw why Captain D'ara had taken advantage of the opportunity while it had presented itself. People who knew what they were doing and how to do it were hard to come by. Rank meant nothing – knowledge was the real power.

In the first day out, the young Mantarian tried to spend as much time as possible with Darian in the hope of bridging the gap that they had both become painfully aware of. To Max, it was more important than ever - Darian seemed to languish once aboard the ship. He was given menial duties and dragged his feet with each task. And Max saw no anxiety in the human about his performance, certainly not like he himself had. No overt feeling that he was shirking his duties elsewhere or that he was coming up short of expectations. Max started wondering if it Darian would have felt any differently no matter what was happening – whether the apathy was even for this particular circumstance.

Emerging from the engine rooms, Max went looking for his friend and found him at the side of the ship, staring off into Zefphyr's thick windswept clouds. Coming so he could see the human's face, Max was pleasantly surprised to see a smile.

"They don't let you out much, do they?" He queried, walking up and wiping off his hands.

Darian turned – his eyes wide and visibly moist, and his face flushed with excitement. He sighed as he looked at Max, then turned back to look out at the fantastic view.

"Never. Just to Careenus, or the archipelago near the supply house. That's it." He paused, his voice creaking on the words. "I've hardly done anything. Certainly never been out this far."

This far? Max thought. *We've barely left.*

He blinked, and watched the back of Darian's head. He thought for a moment, and his heart told him that they had to work through the difference in their station. Not avoid it.

"Do... do you think that's going to change?"

Darian closed his eyes and his head tilted down. A long silence came before he answered with a grumble.

"What do you think?"

"I think anything's possible. I've seen a lot go on already."

"Yeah, you've seen it all." Darian sniffed, and raised his head again – face reddened and wet. "Been out here... all the time - doing what we always dreamed of. Talked about for so many nights over and over again. I remember we talked so much everyone else in the cadet house got sick of us."

Max remembered, but he didn't back down. His words came out slowly and carefully. "Are you mad at me? For... what I'm doing. Where I've been and what I've seen?"

Darian turned and stared right into his eyes.

"How can I?" He took a shaking breath of the cool air to try to calm himself. "Yes. No. I don't know. I'm feeling what I'm feeling."

"You can't blame yourself for where you are, at least not entirely," Max answered evenly. "You can only take responsibility for the choices you make." Max felt his previous Captains talking through his mouth. His training and his experience. It felt rock solid inside him – but the fullness reminded him that it was something Darian didn't have.

"What choice did I make that put me where I am. And you where you are?" Darian protested, still looking into Max's face. "My father made my choice! I'm paying for it. I've paid for it for two damn years, with no end in sight." His gaze turned angry. "Nobody's every told me exactly what happened, or what choice he had to make. Why would he choose what he did? I mean, he died! If he was gonna die, why screw up *my* life? What - was he trying to teach me a lesson? Or was he hoping that the world..." he glanced his eyes around upwards at it, "the world would educate me on the error of his choice?" He stared at Max for one more moment, then abruptly turned, yelling out over the edge of the ship. "I'VE LEARNED THE LESSON!"

Max clenched his jaw, and just stood there. He didn't feel he had anything left to give.

"Problem here, gents?" Captain D'ara's voice came forth, and the diminutive blue lady walked towards them from the forecastle. "Something between you two that's gonna run my ship tighter than I like it to run?"

"No, Captain. We... we're old friends." Max responded immediately. "We just-"

"What the hell do you care?" Darian growled in a low tone towards D'ara, wiping his eyes while still facing out from the edge of the ship.

Max steeled his teeth at the comment.

D'ara frowned, and there was a distinct rumbling from her throat.

"Mister Carver," she bit out. "You take that tone with me again, on my ship, and Navy or no Navy I will hang you from a yard-arm as ballast." She paused, all four of her eyes bearing down on Darian's back.

Darian turned slowly, leaning loose against the railing. But then he nodded, eyes cast down to the deck.

"Mister Ford." She continued after a moment. "Would you please attend to repairs on the mizzen sail? And please take your... old friend... with you." She huffed once, seemingly to calm herself. "He needs some time out of my sight."

"Captain, yes ma'am", Max said quickly, and took a step forward to grab Darian on the arm and haul him away. Darian didn't resist, and was easily pulled away from the diminutive woman.

"What are you, nuts?" Max's voice whispered to Darian, his eyes wide as the two men stumbled towards the mizzenmast. "Man, if this was a Navy boat you'd... well-"

"I'd be put into supplies," Darian finished for him. "Wow. Big punishment."

Max stopped pulling him at the sail, standing back and looking at him.

"Look – this isn't a joke out here. It's not just pushing supplies from place to place. These are *people* on this boat. You've lost supplies before, I'm sure. Try losing a person." He paused and his soft eyes bored into Darian's, brows bent down. "It's not fun."

Darian's shoulders slumped and he sighed.

"Yes... sir." The tone was so dismissive it was clear that all he wanted Max to do was stop talking and leave him alone. Max gritted his teeth in frustration. He'd seen Captains get annoyed with new recruits who didn't pay attention to what was important. Now he knew how they felt.

"Ok," he huffed. "I don't know what is up with you, but we've got a job. On these ships, when people give me a job I get it done. I don't know what you're used to, but right now you're with me. We're working." He turned without waiting for an answer, and grabbed the ropes at the side of the mast, starting to haul himself up. *You better be right behind me,* he growled to himself.

Darian did climb, although not very quickly.

"I don't know what the point is. I can't fix stuff the way you do," he complained. "I haven't learned anything interesting for two years. I've forgotten more than I can remember - especially all the technical crap."

"It's not crap," Max gritted. "It's important and a ship this big doesn't go anywhere without using its sails. You know that much! Just listen to me and I'll tell you what to do, ok?"

"Okay.." Darian sighed in defeat.

Max gruffly grabbed the sail edge and looked along the connecting lead to the mast, where energy from the crystals embedded in the fine fabric was being channeled. The wind blew fiercely about him, but he squinted, then listened. "It's twisted somewhere," he muttered, and looked out at the wide beam where the sail was tied.

"How do you know that?"

"Cuz I've fixed about a million of these when they're twisted. That's why."

Darian moved out along a bit, then gripped the sail at the bottom, looking at it.

"Hey! Careful! Don't touch the yellow parts."

"Hmmm. Ok. I can't remember why not."

"Cuz they're the channel fibers. They'll put about a billion kems of energy through your hands in less than a quarter of a second," Max moved out next to his friend. "Have you forgotten what a sail does?"

"Of course not. My family doesn't make these things like yours does, but I remember the basic stuff from the classes three years ago. It makes the... you know... power from the planet's ambient fields... go into the ship. It... works the engines."

Max rolled his eyes. "Geez, you HAVE forgotten a lot." He turned back to the sail and beckoned to it. "These sails aren't that bad - Class twos. A sail is like a big magnet for the free power all around us. Takes it in, the crystals amplify it and harmonize it." He explained. "Then they put it into a great big stream in the masts. Held together by the electromagnets there." He pointed to the mizzenmast. "If those magnets go, the mast would blow up because all the accumulated energy would collapse in on itself." He smiled, glad to be able to explain his knowledge and feel confident in his role.

"I remember now – yeah. So why's all this power in the sail, then?" Darian queried, looking at the bunched yellow fibers at the bottom of the big white drapes that were pushing the ship.

"Big amplifier. All the power goes into those coiled threads. They're not insulated 'cuz they'll conduct the power onto just about anything. Touch them and you'll release the energy, instead of it going into the mast. Get it?"

Darian nodded, and looked out along the yardarm at the complicated mass of yellow. "Wow."

"Yeah – wow," Ford chuckled and smiled. "Other colors are fine, but stay away from the yellow. I've seen people who've touched those things. It's not pretty."

"All I've seen are clipboards and boxes," Darian responded, continuing to look at the huge complicated weavings in the sail. The hum from all the power was awesome and deep. Max watched the human ponder.

"This is probably the closest I'm ever going to get to this. Like.. ever." Darian mused as he opened his hand to feel the soft glow of the energy next to him. "Out here doing this. The high point of my life, I guess." His voice was strained as his hand inched slightly closer to the yellow fibers.

"Carver, come on," Max uttered in exasperation. But he didn't want to pull Darian away from what was probably the most interesting thing he'd seen in a long time. *Keep him involved*, he thought. *Don't let him sink back down where he's only thinking about himself.*

"I need your help. Go out to the end – carefully. And let me know where you hear it get louder."

"Louder?"

"Yeah. It'll get louder near the twist, since some of the energy in the fibers is being released."

"Cool." Darian smiled. Max smiled too, then moved with Darian outwards. He stopped about halfway along the yardarm, but Darian kept going as he listened and looked intently at the yellow fibers.

"Watch the line on the bottom." Max called out, looking below Darian's feet to the hardened rope along the wood they were standing on. "Don't get your foot caught in it."

"Okay." Darian called back, stepping over and squatting. "I think I found it - here." He reached his hands towards the sail.

"Don't touch the yellow!" Max yelped.

Darian snatched back his hands, but looked at Max in irritation. "I'm not an idiot! You just said not to touch that part."

"Yeah, but don't even put your hands near the fibers when they're twisted. A power spike will jump the gap. I just needed to know where it was. Now come back here."

Darian squatted, looking intently at the bundle of threads at his feet. "What do we need to do? I'm remembering things. I can do it."

"No, you can't." Max answered right away, loudly with a frown. "I do most of it from here. Besides, it will take too long to explain it to you."

"Just tell me what to do."

"No! Get back here." Max's voice was imperative now. He hated people who didn't listen. On his Navy ship someone would already have berated Darian for his non-compliance. You learned quickly who to trust and who was going to listen the first time - and who wouldn't. Max was not used to being with Darian and feeling a distinct lack of confidence in him. He was disturbed by Darian's insistence on playing around.

"C'mon Ford! You get to do this all the time. This is the first time for me. When am I going to get another chance like this?" Darian reached out and touched the white part of the sails, above the point where he had indicated the twist was.

Max's eyes went wide as he saw the touch.

"It's warm," Darian smiled and called back. "But... prickly."

"Look," Max countered, licking his lips. "I told you not to touch it. Leave it alone. Let me handle it from here, please?" He knelt down near the mast, deftly working with the fibers that connected the sail. Knowing exactly how to move them and how to chain them together.

Darian smiled, still feeling the sails. "I can *do* it, Ford. I..."

Max wasn't listening – he just barked out a command. Speaking in a way he'd never spoken to Darian before in his life. "Carver, get your DAMN hands off the sail!"

Darian scowled and turned, angry at the words. He moved his hands back, and got up. A gaze with narrowed eyes and set brow was focused directly on Max's face.

Max frowned right back at him.

Darian took a stiff step along the thick beam back towards the mast – still glaring at Max and not noticing his foot caught in the rope. He tripped and fell.

"Darian!" Max saw him fall, and saw him reach out to stop himself. A shock of fright erupted through Max's mind as he saw Darian's hand come dangerously close to hitting the yellow bunch of fibers at the base. Then Darian fell sideways, so that he was hanging off the back of the yardarm. Max whipped around, and started nimbly tearing away at the fibers connecting the sail to the mast – knowing exactly which he could safely touch. The sail immediately started to shimmer as the energy running through it drained away. He continued to rip, a sweat quickly bursting out on his forehead.

"H- Help!" Darian yelled. He reached out to better his grip – and closed his hand directly around the yellow twisted strands.

Nothing happened.

Max stood at the mast, holding onto it and gaping at Darian. The inner light which seemed to come from the sail had completely disappeared - the energy flow cut off by Max at the mast. The power in the sail flowed around inside of it, instead of being directed to the propulsion of the ship.

Max was already halfway to Darian when the human let go of the fibers, and readjusted his grip.

"You idiot!" Max yelled. His deep voice had lost all of its natural soft-ness, and his face was stretched out, teeth bared in anger.

"Hoy! What's the problem up there!" Captain D'ara's voice came - a healthy amount of irritation in it. "When you're gonna cut half our power you gotta let me know first, you daft buggers!" She growled at them as Darian hung and Max tried to help him back up.

With the sail disconnected, the ship had almost instantly slowed, and the other sails flickered and strained as the power imbalance swept through them. A slight drop in altitude resulted, and the wood of the ship vibrated.

"What are you trying to do? Cripple us out in the middle of nowhere?!" D'ara stomped to the bottom of the mast and glared up at them.

Darian was back on the yardarm, heaving and looking rather scared. Max didn't care.

"I *told* you to watch your stupid feet! Dammit." Ford looked down at the Captain and answered her with deference. "Sorry, Captain, ma'am. Will have it fixed in a minute. Just... if you can equalize for a moment... uh... ma'am?" He tried to sound competent but not commanding. He knew exactly what the Captain would have to do to get the other sails to work properly now, with the mizzen sail temporarily disabled. It was very complicated work.

"You get yer horsed ass down here, Mister Ford the engineer!" D'ara seethed. "You and your charge there. I'll get somebody who's competent to handle it from here."

"Captain... uh... yes ma'am." Max grimaced as he tried to swallow his anger and embarrassment. He glanced once more at Darian before grabbing him roughly by the shoulder and rumbling the deepest he could muster.

"Why don't you just jump down, huh? Do me a favor - try to land on your head!"

thirteen

In Vrue's quarters, Linsey and Craig stood in front of their Captain, and Craig listed off a summary of the injured and the dying. Their battle with the roughs had been costly. Twelve hands lost, four more on the way due to lack of medical supplies. Another half dozen injured.

"These gangs of roughs won't last that long. The Queen's got a mind to finish them all off inside the year. Push our line out past the Soleste volcano, if you can believe that. With us half dead and stretched thinner than one of cook Kelley's broths." He snorted, then remembered that the cook had been one of those who had died. "Hmph. They'll keep sending me new bodies to throw at them. People who need training. You two have been around for a while. They'll move you off to places you are needed more than you are here." He blew out his breath.

"Once we get the medical stuffs we'll start the long trek back – but we can't be down long. Mister Craig, I want you to muster a repair crew – anybody who knows anything about fixing this tug up." He paused for a moment and changed his tone. "Miss Linsey – you seem to have an affinity for one of our roughs."

Linsey's eyes widened, but she responded with no pause. "Uh... sir, no sir. Just thought I recognized a face."

"No. The other one. The one you poked."

Linsey's eyebrow raised, and she visibly gulped.

Vrue smiled, and quietly looked at her for a moment, then turned his head to look at his first officer. "Mister Craig, that will be all. Off you go."

Craig was flustered, and turned sideways on his way out to look at Linsey, clearly wondering what the Captain had in store for her. Linsey wondered too – was he going to say that she had been too rough on the prisoner, or not rough enough?

Once the door was closed, the Captain got up, and started to pace in front of the stained glass window at the back of his cabin. It let in a little bit of light from outside – mostly just giving an indication of the harshness of the weather. Linsey looked down to watch his feet pace.

"Sir, I'm not sure I'm the right person to get information from these men. They're not liable to respect me or take my questions seriously. Also, you and Mister Craig have had more time out here with this type of scum, and... are male."

Vrue was silent for a few moments more, then nodded as he looked at his window. "Yes." He sighed in deflation.

Linsey relaxed, but still felt confidence - he would know what to do.

"Pretty soon now, whether I like it or not, you two are going to be leaving me to go out and deal with things on your own. When you do, you'll have to make decisions on what's important, what questions to ask and which direction to go, without having me around. The world will try to break you." He turned the upper half of his body to look at her, and smiled. "It'll be the test of my leadership – what happens when I'm not around."

"Sir, yes sir." Linsey responded again. "If I... get into a jam... I shall think of what you would do." Vrue had been her mentor for two years. She'd almost always agreed with what his choices were, and had invariably learned from them. She felt a bit worried – did the Captain feel like she couldn't handle the responsibility?

Vrue just stood waiting, offsetting his brows at an angle to at her to encourage a further response. When none came he turned and walked around his desk, then sat upon it. He quietly crossed his arms.

Linsey's expression changed – feeling like her answer had been the wrong one. Blinking, she just looked nervously at him.

"Out here, you do what *you* would do, Linsey." His words came slowly, and he stared into her eyes so that she would remember. "Mister Craig – he's my first officer. I picked him for a reason. It's his station and the limit of his desire for his life. If that's the same as yours then I've been misjudging you."

He paused as he let her think about his words, but kept his smile. "But I don't do that very often, I don't think."

Linsey brightened, her face showing mild surprise. "Sir... I am glad you think me capable. And I will use my best judgment."

Vrue looked at her for a moment more before continuing.

"Linsey - a man made me who I am. Built me, so to speak. Built me up so hard I'd never break. But I been tempered by what's happened to me, out here. You've been tempered too – and you've been lucky. You look at me sometimes, when I'm ranting on about them roughs, like you're afraid of me. Seeing you afraid has made me think. Made me want to tell you something the man who built me told me. A long time ago. For every time you've got to make a decision in rough air out here." He sighed. "And we're in rough air now. Queen needs all of us."

Linsey was intensely curious. She blinked, then nodded to encourage him to continue.

"If you're faced with choices you don't know how to make – you ask yourself one thing. One thing I ask myself all the time." He searched her eyes as he spoke, pupils penetrating to see if the words had purchase. "What would you do if you weren't afraid?"

Linsey's expression changed, and she looked down at the deck in contemplation.

"Afraid of me," he continued. "Afraid of roughs, or afraid of some Admiral who's going to judge your every thought. Or worse - your crew watching you break, right when they need you. What would you do - if all that wasn't hanging over you?"

Linsey thought of herself, alone without Vrue to guide her. She did feel frightened – unsure. But somewhere inside was the answer Vrue had just given her. To go beyond the fear to who she was and find the answer there. She knew instinctively she could find the place inside herself he was talking about, if she looked. Linsey relaxed, connecting to his words.

Vrue seemed to notice her realization. "You'll never be a first officer, Linsey."

Her head snapped up and she looked at him in shock, her heart dropping.

He just widened his smiled at her, enjoying the reaction. "You're for better than that."

fourteen

Darian and Max didn't speak to each other. They just sat at the table in the small galley – both with scowling frowns on their faces.

The dressing-down from D'ara had been particularly humiliating. She had made numerous references to the "high and mighty" Navy - explaining at length about how much everyone had been deceived by the stories. Then she had ordered a simple deckhand to fix the disabled sail.

Max had visibly steamed all the way down inside the ship, obviously unaccustomed to failure and being publicly dressed down.

Darian felt overwhelmed with indignation. How come he couldn't have fixed the sail? Didn't Max even trust him enough to follow simple steps? Do a few simple things? Sure – he had tripped on the yardarm over the stupid rope, but he had been distracted by Max's harsh words. He sniffed and mused, grumbling and picking at the gouges and slivers in the battered galley table.

"You had to mess around, didn't you?" Max finally said, not trying too hard to keep disappointment out of his voice. He huffed, "It's my fault. You work in a supply house. You had no business doing stuff up there."

"D'ara ordered us up there. You're the one that put me out on the yard." Darian snorted back at him. "Why'd you do that if you didn't want me to... touch stuff?"

"I thought maybe, just maybe, you'd be teachable a bit. Get a charge out of being up near a sail, on a real ship out here."

Darian's eyes widened. "Teachable? What – from you? Do I have a sign on me that says 'teach me o wise one' somewhere that I don't know about?!"

Max gritted his teeth, and let a pause hang in the air. His brows were knitted and to Darian it looked like he was physically holding himself back.

"You should."

Darian's hands gripped the table.

"Oh yeah? Well, you're a fantastic teacher then. Much better than I ever was with you." He snorted and his voice was thick with icy sarcasm. "Heh. I bet you needed all the help on your big Navy boat, too. Without me there, doing what I used to do. Somebody watching you and taking care you don't get in trouble and ruin your precious family."

Max's brows came up, but only for a moment. "Yeah. That's why I'm out here. Getting onto the flagship." The Mantarian's eyes glared.

Darian's mouth dropped open.

"That's right." Max continued. "Second engineer on the flagship. I didn't tell you before because I thought maybe you didn't need to hear it."

"Oh, and I need to hear it now?" Darian's voice cracked. Working on the most important ship in the Queen's fleet – Max was living Darian's dream. How had this happened? How could it have gone so wrong?

"Yeah." Max finished getting up, and turned around. "I came to visit because I wanted to see where you were. How you were making yourself... better. But you're not. You're a loser."

Darian couldn't speak. His reddened face blanched with shock and his chest shook with shame.

"You've given up. Did you come out here to find Linsey again just to show her that?" Max finished as he passed to the door of the small room. He turned back for a moment, and Darian felt himself being sized up, considered. Through the past and into their present. Then Max frowned and turned away, his words edged with sadness instead of anger.

"Stay away from me."

Darian stared at the table for a long while, feeling the tears on his face and the lump in his throat. Wanting it to go away, to recess back to the numbness he knew so well.

But it didn't.

fifteen

Coming up from below decks, Max's feet dragged as his mind slogged through his feelings. He pushed them away and shoved them down, reminding himself over and over that he was on a ship in the rough - a place he had to keep his wits about him. He couldn't deal with Darian right now - couldn't face any more than he had just faced. He had responsibilities, and he'd already let his crew down once.

His sensitive ears picked up the sounds of explosions that had rolled across sky. Snapped out of his feelings, he reacted on instinct and moved – fast – the rest of the way up to the main deck. The air around them was mostly clear, with only scattered grey cloud. Max stretched his neck to look about and around for the source of the noises he had heard.

"Ahoy, Cap'n. Mark at five forward!!" a crewmember near the stern yelled out, pointing almost straight out the front of the ship. Max looked in the indicated direction.

Too distant to see properly, a cloudy, ghostly background of a jetstorm cloud was perforated by flashes of light. Rolling across it and followed in time with fading thunderclaps, it was obvious that something was happening. Something big.

"That be a battle, there, Mister Deeg," Captain D'ara shouted from the bridge. "Big guns, big ships, for us to hear them from where we are." She then glanced at Max, before turning to her helmsman and giving some quick instructions that Max was too far away to hear.

Max began to walk to the control center of the ship. As he moved, he noticed the ship's speed increase and the glow from the sails brighten considerably. The bow swung quickly to be at right angles to the battle.

We're running, he thought to himself in surprise.

"Captain! We need to see if we should hel- "

"No we don't Mister Ford. We're a lightly armed supply ship, and in due consideration for the skins which cover our bodies, we need to remove ourselves from our current location."

"But Captain!" Max was incredulous. This was entirely counter to all situations he had ever been in. You simply did *not* ignore a battle. It didn't matter who was fighting – it was always better to know than not to know. He licked his lips and made his deep voice as stern as he could. "What if it's a Navy ship? They're fighting in a storm cloud. What if they need help? There are lives at stake!"

"Yes, there are lives at stake – ours." D'ara scowled at him and set her arms across her chest – dipping the brim of her pompadour hat as her head tilted forwards. Her feather glowed a strong crimson. She obviously did not like to be visibly questioned on the running of her ship, especially by a member of the Navy.

"We need to investigate. If we don't, then-"

"If we do, Linsey won't get her supplies." Darian's voice came from behind Max. His eyes were light, but his face was hard. "That's all that matters." He nodded in D'ara's direction. "I agree with the Captain."

Max turned to scowl at him. "She doesn't need your agreement, and you don't know what you're talking about – this is your first time out here." He turned back, and switched his face to an imploring one. "Captain – my... my comrades may be at risk."

"We are all at risk, Mister Ford. All the time we are out here. You know that." She lifted her four eyes upwards, in the direction of the receding flashes and sounds. "As do they. I don't meddle in things which are not my business."

Max's mouth closed, and he blew a frustrated breath out his nose.

"She's right – it's none of our business." Darian echoed at Max's back. "We've already got a job to do – an important one." His tone was even, full of conviction.

Max looked up at D'ara once more, then turned and stomped by Darian, to head back down below decks. His eyes fired a glare that could melt metal as he roughly passed the human. "You have a lot to learn about what's important."

sixteen

"Why do you Navy turds think you own everything out here?" The Drago bit out the question, sneering as he stood lashed to the foremast. He leaned on the ropes – legs weary from the amount of time he'd already been put there. "We should be able to do what we want. Not just what the Queen says we can do."

Linsey was in front of him, hands behind her back as she listened to his words. She smiled – trying to seem as relaxed as possible to contrast how she knew the older male prisoner must be feeling. "Queen's laws only say what you can't do. Included in that are raping, pillaging, and taking things that do not belong to you. Those laws are meant to last for generations, not only for a nasty, brutish and short reign."

Although she had not interrogated pirates from the rough before, she knew their lot and their philosophy: Take - because you're stronger than those that have whatever it is you want.

The familiar younger Mantarian lashed next to the Drago looked expectantly at him now, waiting for an answer – clearly wanting some simple logic to counter Linsey's statements. The felid woman noted Adam's continued deference, remembering that Mantarians were impressionable, strong minded, but almost never leaders.

"Huh. What about all your blessed taxes? Hmm? All the power and wealth for one person? Your imperious skank of a leader. That's just your 'legalizing' of takin' what don't belong to you. What about if we don't want to be part of her empire? What if we like it the way that it is? Choosing our own path. Survival of the fittest pushes the fittest forwards – while you weak minded idiots wallow in protecting those holding you back."

Adam calmed at the Drago's reasoning words. Linsey pitied him, and could see how much devotion there was. The power the older one had chilled her.

"Are you the fittest then?" Linsey strode forwards, even closer to the Drago. "You and your... band of miscreants here? Hunting, killing... and oh! Getting caught! By wallowing weak minded idiots like me." She gritted her teeth in a smile and leaned dangerously close to his ear. "How embarrassing."

The Drago's face crunched up into a hateful, seething mass, and the ropes holding him audibly strained. He breathed heavily and stared into Linsey's face, trying to murder her with his gaze. But he said nothing.

"Awww... what's the matter? Cat got your tongue?"

A low growling voice came back at her. "I am going to tear off your head and sh-"

"Commander Linsey?" Karthow the helmsman was beside her. The Drago's taunt stopped, and he listened carefully to what was coming from the crewmember. "Uh... sir. The Arcadian shoals are directly ahead. Shall we slow our velocity?"

Linsey looked directly ahead of the *Archer* – noticing the difference in the density of the clouds and the clusters of foliage-covered islands getting denser below them. "Yes, Miss Karthow. Please do. Start a locality sweep for signs of the supply ship we are meeting here. I will inform the Captain and Commander Craig."

"Aye, sir." A generic derivative of a scavenger race, the Tebryn blinked slowly through the thin black fur mask about her eyes, then moved away.

Linsey followed her the short distance to the bridge, then slid off to the side of the ship, where Craig and Vrue were speaking in low tones. Linsey could tell the Captain's usual lecturing tone from many steps away. *Hopefully he's teaching him some manners.*

"Captain, Commander. Miss Karthow has just informed me that we should arrive at the shoals in a few moments."

At her words all three of the officers scanned out from the bridge – squinting in an attempt to see the supply ship on their own. Linsey always loved it when her superior eyesight let her upstage the equipment on the ships. It gave her solace that biology was just as good sometimes, if not better than technology.

However, the technology did work faster this time. A steady beeping from the locator was followed almost immediately by a finger pointed by Karthow. Linsey visually followed the direction of the digit, and saw a small support craft anchored to a hill on one of the larger islands in the shoals. Captain Vrue immediately barked out orders. "That's them, Miss Karthow. Take us in."

In only a few minutes, they had dropped their altitude and lined up with the supply ship - the deckhands securing the two boats together just above the ground. A short makeshift gangplank was put between them as they hung in the air. Captain Vrue stayed at his own bridge – standard operating procedure when prisoners were aboard. That meant Commander Craig took the duties of meeting D'ara's crew and getting a manifest of the supplies that had been delivered.

Linsey immediately saw the disparity in appearance between the two ships. The supply ship was an order of magnitude smaller, but much cleaner – especially after the battle the *Archer* had experienced. And all of the crew she could see were in good shape – even for a supply ship. Looking beyond Craig and D'ara as they talked, she was surprised to see two Naval uniforms amongst the supply ship's crew. One of them a... Mantarian?

Linsey did a double take, and her head whipped about to look at the prisoner of the same species tied to the *Archer*'s foremast. She looked back again to the one in the Navy uniform. "Amazing," she said quietly to herself. She'd seen many varied Mantarians before - it was too great a coincidence to have them look so alike. Jumping onto the short rickety span between the ships, she slipped quickly around the deckhands as the supplies were transferred. *I know I've met ONE of these two before!*

"Hoy. You!" she called to them as she pushed her way onto the supply ship. Both of the young men in Naval uniforms turned at once at her voice. Linsey stopped suddenly, shock radiating from her face at the sight of the pair. The Mantarian was a spitting image of the prisoner – older, and stronger on first glance. But it was upon noting the human that the pieces clicked together and a rush of recognition came over her.

"Carver." Linsey said slowly to herself. She swallowed, but smiled. She was curious now. Standing there for a moment, she tried in vain to remember the Mantarian's name, but failed. She tried to run over their previous meeting in her mind. *Well, I wonder what brings them all the way out here?*

At meeting her eyes, Darian's face glowed with excitement. His Mantarian companion's didn't seem to be as open, but certainly became more relaxed at seeing her.

"Uh... Something wrong Lieutenant?" Craig had turned as he'd heard Linsey's shout – and he looked at her with mild annoyance. He swiveled his gaze from her over to the two young men, then back again.

"Sorry Commander - nothing. I simply recognize those two over there." She moved to stand beside the commander, placing her hands behind her back and trying to make her overt action seem normal.

"I see," he replied, clearly irritated at her rash reaction. He cleared his throat and continued his conversation. "Yes, well. Thank you very much for bringing us our supplies, Captain D'ara. I know this area is not the safest place to be for a hauling ship such as yours. You deliver much needed relief."

"Not a problem, Mister Craig. Always like to help out the Navy, since they're watching my skin for me half the time." She smiled a toothy grin. One set of eyes went to Craig, and the other to Linsey. "I can't mind the lass fer noticing those two, since you're short crewed as you say. I snatched them in order to get this caboodle out to you." She pointed at Darian and Max, and the feather in her hat became a warm orange as she tipped the brim of it. "Good at simple things but messed up my sail, that tall one. Ford." She grumbled. "Not too sure what the other one does."

"Is that right?" Linsey responded, glad that she had heard Max's name and wouldn't have to ask him for it again. "You say you... borrowed them?"

"Yep. I'm not really happy to see the engineer go," she chuckled openly, looking at Max. "But if you need the help, you've got first dibs. They be Navy."

Craig turned his head and called to the two young men. "Mister Ford. And..." he looked at D'ara for enlightenment as to Darian's name.

D'ara just shrugged in disinterest.

"Carver." Linsey offered.

Craig looked at her strangely, obviously wondering how she knew his name. "Mister Carver," he finished. He beckoned them with his hand. Both moved immediately, dropping the supplies they were holding so they could move to approach the cluster of officers.

Linsey smiled openly at Darian. "Nice to see you again, Mister Carver. I see your situation has improved since our last meeting."

Darian's face fell, and Max just stood stiffly – looking down at the deck as if he was ashamed. Neither of them said a word. Craig left it a moment, but then began to speak to fill the sudden silence. "Yes, well. Apparently, there are fewer strangers here than I had imagined." He looked directly at Max, "You are an engineer?"

"Sir, yes Sir." Max replied immediately in a bright voice. "Delta-Seti. Just posted to the... uh... the *Prometheus*, Sir."

Craig's eyes widened a bit. "Well, well. An engineer from the flagship. That is something special." He smiled and continued, shifting his gaze to Darian. "And you are from?"

Darian didn't answer. He looked like he wanted to as he opened his mouth once, but he just stared at Linsey – his face losing even more of its color.

Max let the question hang for only a moment – unaccustomed to having someone not respond immediately to the direct question of a superior. "He's... in supplies, Sir. Ground based."

"Oh." Craig's face went stoic. But only for a moment before it turned to a questioning frown. "What are you doing out here then?"

"I..." Darian tried to start, looking from Linsey to Craig, then back again. "I- I'm supposed to be here. I'm... delivering these... supplies. To her." His wide eyes alighted on Linsey, as if begging for an answer or direction.

Linsey's brows came down slightly, and her longer felid ears drooped unconsciously. *Supplies,* she mused to herself. *Well, I suppose there's a story here.*

Craig chuckled. "Well, you certainly take your job seriously, now don't you? Not too many supply boys come halfway across Zefphyr to the edge of the frontier." He smiled in jest, and Captain D'ara chuckled as well. "You must be scared half to death. We best get you back to your natural environment." He sniffed, and looked at Darian with what appeared to be morbid curiosity – as if expecting a correction, reply, or even slight protest.

Darian was speechless again, looking like his face was about to crack from strain – his teeth clenched and cheeks parched white. He licked his lips, and looked from Craig to Linsey, and back again.

Linsey didn't know what to say. She felt her curiosity boiling, and something else in the back of her chest - pressure to find out what had happened and understand it.

Craig was visibly irritated by still not having any sort of verbal response from the boy, sighing like he dismissed Darian as a simpleton. "Well! We can use Mister Ford in our current state - surely." Craig looked back at Max, and smiled. "I dare say an engineer from the *Prometheus* could teach what's left of our crew a thing or two on our way back."

Max bowed slightly, and smiled in recognition of the implied opinion.

"Sir, uh... Commander Craig." Linsey injected. "Speaking of Mister Ford here. Our... prisoners. On the *Archer*. The Mantarian..."

Both Craig and Max snapped their gaze to her as she trailed off the deliberately half-finished sentence. In Max's face was surprised curiosity – in Craig's studious interest. He looked at Max up and down, then turned his head to gaze at the *Archer*'s foredeck. There was no way he could see that far from the deck of the smaller ship, but he looked for a moment anyway, before turning back again.

"You do look familiar," he said bluntly to Max. "We have one of... your kind. On board. A rough we captured in the act of piracy."

Max's face showed shocked confusion, as if a racial slur was implied.

"Very familiar," Linsey added. "Do you have family that has left the Queen's territory?" It was the simplest and most common way of asking if someone had gone rogue.

"No, sirs. None of mine. I've never heard of a rough of my kind. What is its name, sir?" Max maintained his sense of propriety, but replied in a staunch manner – and with some note of aggression. He obviously did not like the implication that his people could follow a pirate's code.

"It is male. Uh..." Craig looked at Linsey to fill in the other details.

"Adam," Linsey said quickly.

Max's short facial hair ruffled and he felt the heat in his cheeks – his ears falling down on the back of his head so quickly there was almost an audible flopping sound. Eyes wide in surprise, he turned and strained to see across the distance between the ships towards the foremast of the *Archer*. He looked back and forth between Craig and Linsey, and his hands shook as if he was holding something very, very cold.

"A- Adam? What does he look like?" His incredulous query was without any sort of formality – his soft voice turned hard in a direct demand for the information. Linsey could literally feel the indignation radiate from him. Darian stared at Max, mouth slightly open in shock.

"Like you, Mister Ford." Craig answered curtly. "Very much like you. Perhaps you know him, or could help us identify-"

"I- I certainly don't think so." His tone suggested completely the opposite. "That is, Adam is a common name among my people, sir– sirs." Max gritted his teeth and looked at the deck, squinting as though he was going to tear a hole in it with his gaze. In complete disregard for protocol, Max started stomping away towards the gangplank to the *Archer*, crashing into several crew members transferring supplies. Craig flinched at the loss of control, and took a hard gaze out on Darian as if he were responsible.

Captain D'ara smiled – knowing that something interesting was afoot, but also that she had no business in it. She cut in.

"Well, I'll take the supply boy back with me, then. I can get him back in three days, easy. - so long as I keep him away from my sails."

Darian's shoulders slumped as he turned his face to Linsey and projected his desperation at her. "Uh... Sirs!" He spoke up with a yelp. "Uh... Uh Uh We.. we saw a battle! On the way here."

D'ara sighed heavily, the feather in her pompadour hat turning blue as she shook her head.

"A battle? Where?" Craig looked around, acting again as if he believed he could see it from where they were.

"Uh... yesterday. Out there. Um... near the crags at the Daedalus Mesa." Darian looked at D'ara, clearly wanting help with the explanation. Linsey knew he would get no help - he had undermined her authority. "We... that is, our ship did not investigate, sir."

"Don't know what we saw," D'ara intoned dismissively. "Heard some loud noises. Probably thunder."

Craig said nothing for a moment, considering Darian with his eyes. Linsey watched him. It was their job to make sure of situations – not to guess or ignore. Craig knew it just as she did. And she knew what Vrue would do.

"We should investigate, then," she stated flatly.

Craig looked over at her, his shoulders coming up taut as he bristled from having her make what sounded like a decision, without his approval. He gritted his teeth for a moment, then showed the best face he could muster. "Yes. Yes, of course. We should depart immediately." He looked at D'ara, then at the young human next to her. "Captain D'ara, you have charge of the stock boy."

"No." Linsey looked at Darian, staring. She felt trepidation in her stark denial of her superior officer's wishes – but her mind stabbed out with its reasoning.

Don't be afraid. Do what you know is right.

"We will take him with us."

Darian's eyes widened, but his face stayed pointed downwards. Craig looked at Linsey with first a furrowed brow, then lifted one of them to a questioning air.

"For what purpose? He is not a useful for-"

"For Captain Vrue's purposes, Commander." Linsey responded immediately, with a commanding tone. "He has specifically given me responsibility for the medical arrangements. Mister Carver is Navy, has the required first aid training, and can be of assistance." Inside she knew Vrue would approve – even though she was surprised at the bravado of her independent decision. To make her point further, she repeated Max's prior action and turned and started maneuvering back to the *Archer* without further argument.

Craig guffawed openly at her back. "Absolutely, *Commander* Linsey." He stressed the rank in a jeer as she passed by, and rolled his eyes. "Whatever you desire." He shook his head in mock wonder and looked at Darian, before beckoning towards the *Archer*. He then bowed to Captain D'ara. "Captain, we take our leave of you. I recommend an alternate course on your return – we will check on this... battle... you witnessed."

seventeen

Max's heart pounded in his chest as he jumped down off the gangplank and brusquely pushed around the last of the deckhands, to stride with a long gait onto the main deck of the *Archer*. His eyes were wide, and his expression had hardened from determined to angry. *Adam. A Mantarian named Adam. That's all. It can't be him!*

"Ahoy there, young one." Vrue's deep tone caught Max up suddenly, snapping him out of his inner musings as he reacted instinctively to the voice of command. "Are you hankering' to come aboard, then?" The Captain had stood just off to the side of the gangway, watching the actions of his two officers from afar. He was in perfect position to see Max's abrupt departure and to gauge his mood.

Max gaped at the size of Vrue – he'd seen a few Ursids in his travels, but none quite as massive. And one that was a Captain, he figured, must be rare indeed – Ursids were not well known for anything but brute strength. Max realized how far he had intruded onto a ship that was not his own and snapped to attention. He started to sputter an explanation for the breach in protocol. "Sir, yes sir. That is, sir, I- Ma- uh... Ford, Engineer First Class, Sir. I had no idea you were there, sir. I apologize, sir, for not..." Max caught his tongue for the slightest moment, counting the number of 'sirs' he had already used. Too many.

Vrue said and did nothing. He stood there with his usual good-natured half-grin, and his eyes belied no inkling of wanting to break in on Max's spiel.

A moment of silence hung in the air, before Max decided to try to finish his sentence. "Not... not asking permission, that is, sir." He winced and gritted his teeth. "To come aboard. I- that is, they- your- Linsey. Commander! Commander Linsey... and the first officer Mister..." Max trailed off, his breath not coming well as he tried to remember the first officer's name - the one who had told him to switch ships. He gulped once as he felt the lapse of his memory.

Vrue lumbered two steps closer to Max, staring down at him from his gargantuan height with a curious gaze mixed with a trifle of amusement. He pursed his lips, but still said nothing – which made Max realize that again he hadn't finished his statement.

"Your first officer. He commanded me to be here." Max finally stopped talking and clamped his lips together – almost to the point of pain.

"Mmm-hmph." Vrue pondered – but that was all he said for a moment. Slowly he leaned closer, his nose almost at the bridge of Max's. Then he very quietly whispered. "You've got a burr in your bonnet, Mister Ford. I can tell." He leaned back and his voice came up to a normal volume as he looked into the young male's eyes. "Why don't you just take a breath there, a moment, before storming onto my ship."

Max's eyes dropped, and he thought of his place – in the Navy, and especially on someone else's ship. "Sir, yes sir," he breathed, and focused on the floor planks. The cool wind gusted around them for a moment, and Max could feel the heat in his mind subsiding – reason creeping back in.

Vrue watched him simmer, and hypothesized as to the cause of the Mantarian's behavior. "I know my Mister Craig, he can get on some people's nerves. But what in blazes did he say to you to get you to stomp on over here like that?"

Max was confused, but only for a moment. Then he straightened and looked up at the Captain, beginning to explain the situation. "Sir, it- Commander Craig is... fine, sir. It is..." He swallowed hard. "You have a Mantarian prisoner named Adam."

"I do?" Vrue raised a brow. He then looked Max up and down, then turned his whole body to gaze up towards the front of his ship, towards where the pirates were lashed. "Hmph. Well, your kind isn't known for causing trouble, I know that. How do you know the rough we got?"

Max stood still for a moment, trying to fathom an answer. He couldn't believe what he was trying to explain to the enormous Captain. "I have a brother named Adam."

Vrue raised a brow. "And you think it's him, do you?"

"No!" Max blurted. "It can't be. I mean... Adam is at home, working. With the rest of my family. It is... possible that he could have been captured while delivering sails near the frontier. But my parents would let me know right away. He's not a rough! I-"

Vrue held up his hand to stop Max. "No, no. I can imagine why you're upset, then. I figure you're about to blast up there and see if it's him. If it is you can ask him why he's plundering the badlands with a bunch of rag brigands. Killing my crew."

With those words the tension in Max's body started to make him ache. The Mantarian had known some Captains to expound at great length about the fitness of one particular species over another. In the trying times of the Queen's expansion, most officers of rank were highly prejudicial. They used racial and familial references very commonly, and stuck to well known stereotypes when describing a person and his or her capabilities. They simply did not have time or energy for much more than that. Max braced himself for confrontation – but didn't know if he would have to defend himself or his brother.

"How're you expecting this to work out then?" Vrue mused with a grumble. "Got any ideas off the top of your head?" He gestured, and gently pulled Max in the direction of the forecastle.

"I won't know him, sir," Max said defiantly. "It can't be him. I mean.. I- I haven't seen my brother for two years. The year before my last at the academy at cycle break. He was- uh... is... younger. Headstrong like my mother, but he always wanted to know every detail about whatever I did. I'm sure he'd be in the Navy as well if we could have afforded it." Max shook his head as he listened to his own words. "It can't be him."

Their pace was plodding. In his state of mind, Max would probably have run right up the side of the vessel – on the edge railing if necessary to get around the other crew to where he wanted to go. Vrue was pacing him – giving both men a chance to think, and including Max in the process. Vrue looked at him for a long moment.

"Looked up to you, did he? Hm.. You didn't see him at your graduation then – where was he gone off to?"

Max thought for a moment. Only his mother and father had come to see him graduate and get onto the big ship that took them away for assignment.

He had understood that the rest of the family needed to work - to feed and clothe them until Max's Navy pay would start rolling in. Reflecting on the time, he recalled his mother had cried a lot during the ceremony. He'd assumed it was just her emotions of happiness for the completion of his training. A pang of fear swept up his back as the plausibility of the situation became more apparent to him.

"He was at home, sir. Working on power sails and... growing up."

Vrue started walking again. "Hmph. Perhaps he has grown up, lad. Faster than your ma or pa or you would like. Maybe got a little bit tired of hearing about what you were doing - and wasn't getting a chance to do it himself." He turned to look at Max again, and his eyes were hard. "If it's him he's done it now. He'll pay for it – the way every pirate from the rough should."

Max's heart fell, and his face burned as the reality sunk further into him. They came up the last set of steps to the broad forecastle, and Vrue stepped out from in front of Max, to reveal to him the prisoners lashed to the railing in front of the foremast.

Adam and the Drago were still tied tightly – whispering in low voices. Surprisingly, the latter had a grin on his face. Then he looked up, and did a slight double-take himself – glancing immediately back to Adam and then to Max. He shut up and his grin faded. Adam's was perplexed by the actions of his fellow pirate, and snapped his head around to look himself.

Max frowned, unable to speak.

Vrue moved to the side and swung his arms around his back to stand easy, sighing as the truth sunk into them all. His voice was one of quiet resignation. "You can pick your friends but you can't pick your family, boyo."

Like a fresh wound being assessed, in shock Max turned the situation over and over in his mind. The repercussions of Adam's actions sank in, and he felt the sickening drop of dread in his heart. Then the cauterizing burn of responsibility. His family, his blood. His mind flashed over how people would feel about him, knowing his brother was a traitor. Would he be branded the same way Darian had?

Max realized quickly the Captain was deferring to him, and he stepped forward. The barrier of his denial had burned completely away – and now he felt a core of cold anger in his gut. His voice reflected frustration and sadness.

"What are you doing here?"

Silence came back at him as the brothers stared at each other. Adam blinked once, his face reddening. The Drago saw the reaction out the side of his eye and immediately spoke up, his grin returning.

"Ah, so *this* is the prissy brother you were telling me about."

Max shot him a hot, baffled glare at the intrusion. The Drago smiled wider, knowing he'd easily hit a target. Still Adam said nothing. Max took a step forwards, and another – his closeness now making the difference in the brothers' height apparent. He ignored the Drago's comment, and kept his brother directly in his glare.

"How long have you been... out here?"

The Drago wasn't done, and continued his jibes to eat into the dialogue that Max was trying to establish. He looked at Adam, and his voice carried an egging, boisterous tone. "He's been with me just over a year now. Fancies himself a darling for the ladies. He's pretty good with 'em too. Especially the ones that like it rough."

Max's cheeks tightened, and he steeled himself from bursting out some of the rougher sailor curses he'd heard in his travels. He closed his eyes and came even closer to his brother.

Adam looked down, his eyes finding the deck in shame. But only for the merest of moments. As if splashed with cold water his head bucked upwards, eyes blazing with frustration and defiance as he stared.

"A pirate." Max stated flatly with sadness. "Stealing. Killing people. Good people. My friends. Adam- what... what happened?"

"He found out what he needed to do – something you wet-eared lackeys are incapable of. He grew a spine. Your parents apparently didn't want any-one in your fam- ErrAAKKh!"

The Drago gargled out the last word as the Captain's enormous paw grasped him tightly around his neck. Even with the thick plates of scale that covered him, the crushing pressure Vrue was able to apply made the male's eyes bulge. Adam jerked his head to look, concern flashing over his face.

"I asked you a question!" Max barked at his brother to get his attention back. His deep voice vibrated with new anger now – all of the softness gone and a growl coming up from inside of him as he showed his teeth. Together with the emotional weight of the past few days with Darian on board D'ara's ship, he felt more at the breaking point than he ever had in his life.

Adam turned back with a start, his voice becoming petulant. "What Vek said! I stopped living for you, and started living for myself." He grunted and unconsciously struggled with the tight bonds as he looked at the Drago again, still overtly worried.

Max was flabbergasted – it was as if he was standing in front of someone he'd never knew. Adam was looking at Vek with the same expression as he had when his mother was ill. At his father with those same eyes when he was injured. At Max when he'd left for the academy. All the solid memories Max had were twisted – curved backwards and pointed at this vile brigand.

"So what – this... Vek guy," Max threw another poisonous glare at the Drago that was steadily being choked by Vrue. "He came and told you how fabulous it was out here raping and pillaging? Hmm? No laws or rules?"

Adam considered for a moment, then ground out a tired, gravelly tone.

"What do you care? You had it made. You Navy guys are doin' the same stuff we do, anyway." His eyes glazed and his voice rose in volume as he gained momentum – as if he was fanning a white hot ember. "I know what really goes on in the world now! It's just like Vek says it is. Not like you and your stupid fairy tales." He started to yell loudly back at Max. "We were your dirty little secret hidden away! Dana, Angie, Vanessa, Robert and me. Mom and Dad. Working. Working all the time. Every day in the freezing cold till we'd fall asleep on each other. Working our fingers to the bones. Giving the Navy EVERYTHING we made to pay your *stupid* damned academy dues - so that you can do the same thing I'm doing now except with your high and mighty Queen's blessing. To hell with that." A gob of saliva dripped off the end of his mouth. He reeled himself in and looked at the boards of the deck again – the gravelly tone returning. "I got tired of living my life for you."

Max was speechless with guilt. The shame and grief he felt was overwhelming - all he could think about was the Captain watching them. Everyone watching them. *It's over*, he thought. *Everything we've worked so hard for.*

Vrue looked between them for a moment, then gradually released his grip on Vek's neck. The Drago wheezed and collapsed against his bonds – his face slick with sweat from the exertion of trying to stay conscious. Adam broke his stare with Max to try to assess his pirate friend's state.

"I hate you damn Ursids." Vek spat the comment about Vrue's race as his chest heaved. He twisted his neck to stretch it out as he hung from his bonds. "Glandular freaks. The women are a fine sight though, except for the inbred ones. Which is most of 'em."

Adam sniggered, obviously pleased his friend was all right and acting what was for him, normal.

Max felt like he was going to throw up. He gritted his teeth and turned away – right around before starting to walk back towards the stairs leading amidships. His shoulders slumped down at a steep angle.

Vrue's eyebrow just went up slightly. "Right," he sighed again. "Well, there it is then. Nothing quite like a family reunion."

eighteen

Darian watched Linsey stare at him across the desk in her tiny quarters. From the fingers of her right hand extended her felid claws – most notable of which was the index talon. She used the exposed six inches of natural hardened razor to casually scratch patterns into the wooden top of her tiny desk.

They had walked back to the *Archer* in relative silence, but the door behind Darian had scarcely closed before Linsey had sat down. The young human stood just inside the room, looking back at her as she scratched on the desk.

"You are not your father."

Her matter-of-fact tone made it hard for Darian to recognize if she was trying to tell him that he had disappointed her expectations, or if she was remarking at a personality difference between him and the kin she had known.

"You told the Admiral that," he nodded to her, as his head tilted downwards to let him look at the floor. "Two years ago, when you... kept me from getting kicked out. And you gave me a pep talk." He paused and scuffed the floorboards a bit with his boot. "Then you left."

Linsey remained silent. Darian didn't even know what he'd meant to accomplish by the last comment. But he spoke from his heart – and he remembered how he had felt abandoned. He looked up, into her face. She was pensive, not showing a hint of guilt. He decided that she was probably not judging him. Rather, she was waiting for him to explain to her to what he had become.

"I didn't know what was going to happen. They... they all changed. Everyone. Somehow they thought I was cursed. Like I'd... poisoned them." He thought for a moment, recalling the hard times as he took a step towards her desk. "Some asked what the mistake was,. that my father had made. Most didn't really care. They all just... stopped trusting me."

"What about... your friend?" Linsey responded, looking at him up through the top of her eyes. "The... engineer, he-"

"Max. Max Ford," Darian started, then sighed. "He... never changed. At least, not until now." His face gained color as his speech trailed off and he considered his own words. "I thought at least he would still believe in me, but even he's given up."

Silence gripped the room. Linsey did not offer another question or comment - she simply appeared to be waiting for him to bring it all out in the open.

"At least *he* is still on track – wind in his sails, all that crap. He's moved on, moved up. Accomplished what we... what I always dreamed of – get to the top and... live... there. Really live."

"He's living your dreams." Linsey's voice had an air of understanding as she shifted back in her seat, looking him over. "I know what it's like to want to be more than you are. But already we can both see... some regrets taking the place of your dreams."

Darian gulped softly. "My father - why did he do it? You told me he made a choice. One that cost nearly everyone's life. I thought he was a good man..."

"He was a great man."

"Then WHY?" Darian interjected. Any consideration of rank was gone from him. He needed to understand the decision. "How could he have been so wrong?" The human breathed in heated huffs for a moment, realizing the level of his outburst and reeling in his frustration. His voice was edged with disappointment.

"I... I guess you must not be allowed to tell me - even to help me understand why everyone turned against me. But, I mean... it's been so long now and..." he trailed off with a look of hope in his eyes, tempered by trepidation over what Linsey would say.

The commander was very quiet. Darian felt it was curious that she seemed to specifically alter her gaze so that she did not have to look at his face. Her words were dry and slow.

"He chose... what he wanted."

"What did he want?"

"He wanted to be able to live with himself." Linsey's face was reddened – there was no way she could hide it. "He chose from his heart. Death of the spirit is harder than death of the body."

Darian thought over her words for a moment, thinking back on every-thing he knew about his father's demise.

"You said he chose to save... some people. People he cared for."

Linsey's hot face held a hardened jaw as she nodded slowly.

"Who were they? Were they important?"

"They were Navy." Linsey answered quickly – expecting the question and clearly not wanting to dwell through a thoughtful answer. "They were like you and your friend. Others that do what we do. Our family." She sighed. "He made a hard choice - and an unpopular one. But no one but him can understand it."

"I... didn't have a choice," Darian continued – wanting to let out what he felt to someone who would listen. "For what I wanted or otherwise. The... last year at the academy – that was hard. But I had Ford - Max. He was al-ways there. Then graduation day came, and we got our assignments. Him off to a ship – me... salvage. Land based crew." He stared at her now – his gaze icy as he tried to convey the specific moment that he remembered. The day he had felt his heart wither and die in his chest.

Linsey's face changed subtly, watching him. Darian could almost feel her anger - she blinked once slowly, softly blew out her breath, and looked at the pattern she had carved into her desk for a moment more before respond-ing.

"Did you ever consider that you were handed a challenge?"

Darian's mind balked at her words. His experience had been insuffera-bly unfair – totally outside the scope of his capabilities and his intentions, and it had savagely curtailed the only thing he'd had left. Hope.

"A challenge?" he said sharply. It wasn't a question – it was a rebuke. "I was handed a sentence! To a... a- prison! To a place where I had nothing! Nobody! And no way out." He sniffed and growled out the words, rearing his head back as he rebuffed. "And you think it was just a chal- "

"HEY!" Linsey barked, cutting him off. Darian snapped his mouth shut and looked downwards. "Did you learn to speak to an officer like that at the academy? Did you speak this way in your first job? And to Captain D'ara?" She paused, barely reeling in her snappish voice. "To your friend? Mister

Carver you earn the respect of those about you. And they should strive to earn yours. But tell me - what is it you are giving them to respect? Hmm?" She paused, staring at him as she calmed down. She retracted all her claws as her hand came to her face.

"Have you nothing left in you of the man I knew?" she mused aloud.

Darian's face burned. *Why would I want to be like my father?* Everyone he'd ever met in the past two years had seemed to despise the man. Had inevitably mentioned the incident which had ended his life. But he'd never seen his father as an officer. He'd hardly ever seen him at all. "I never knew him," he responded quietly. "Or what was in him."

"Well I did. I served with him for three years." Her voice was just as quiet, and her eyes didn't blink as she addressed him - formally. "Darian Carver, you have been dealt a bad hand. It is unfortunate, but it is and has been your life. And strangely... it has brought you and I together. Again."

"Why did you want me here? Captain D'ara-"

"Captain D'ara is a supply ship Captain, and does what she needs to survive. Out here. I, on the other hand, do *more*. The question I have is – do you wish to?" She studied his face. "Do you still want to be more than what you have been? More than your... 'bad hand'?"

Darian stared back at her, his eyes burning and his throat dry. In his chest he felt a dead, wet weight - a pressure coming down on his heart. The same one which had been on him for two years. But looking at Linsey he found the answer to her question, and felt she would listen to it.

"I want to be more... for something that wants more from me. For someone that doesn't always expect less than what I know I can give." His teeth came together, and his jaw clenched. "Not like this... stupid... Navy."

Linsey's brows went up slightly at the comment, but the rest of her face remained set. Darian's mind was exhausted, and he closed his eyes – expecting once again to be chewed out for his tone.

"That's why I wanted you here."

Darian opened his eyes to look at her, and saw her face had changed, to appear compassionate and open. She smiled the merest bit, hoping he would know the meaning in her words.

"So what, you're going to... teach me? Is that it? You heard that other Commander. And Captain D'ara. I'm a stock boy."

"Argue for your limits and you will always stay within them," Linsey responded strongly, never breaking her gaze at him. "Do you want to argue, and have me send you to the storeroom? Where everyone can expect less than what you can give? Or...", she lingered. "Do you want to show me you can be more than that?"

Darian knew the answer inside of him – he felt rescued. Someone was going to believe in him, finally.

Craig abruptly opened the door to Linsey's small office cabin, jutting his head inside. "Ah, hello Commander. I thought you-"

"A gentleman doesn't knock at a lady's quarters?" Linsey cut in strongly, indicating her distaste for the first officer's insensitive behavior.

Craig bent his brows in annoyance and did not respond to her query. Darian could feel the charged energy between the two, and tried hard not to smile at being so close a spectator. Craig went right ahead, hammering his perspective through by repeating his sentence from the beginning. "I said- Hello, Commander. I thought you might like to know that we've departed, and are on our way to investigate the incident that was reported by Mister Ford and your... stock boy." He looked in at Darian for a moment, down his nose, then he continued. "If you would be so kind as to find the time in your... busy... schedule... to report to the Captain for briefing."

Linsey's tone didn't change a bit from the irritated abrupt level she had used when Craig had poked his head in. "Yes, sir, Commander Craig, sir. I do know the requirements of my post and I shall report to the Captain forthwith. *Since* it is such an urgent action for me to undertake, could you please do me a large favor and show Mister Carver here to the second level supply room?"

Darian was shocked, after what they'd just discussed. "The s- supply room-?" he sputtered.

Linsey bent her brows and continued her speech to stop his outburst. "He is going to repair our damaged auxiliary sail, then report to his engineer friend Mister Ford to have its fitness checked."

Craig sputtered and looked at her as if she had gone crazy. "I have duties to attend to, Miss Linsey, and as far as I can remember *I* am the one to give *you* orders".

"Oh come come now, Commander," Linsey dared, cutting him off again with a quick, sweetened tone. "Coming in here to tell me to report to the Captain was your most important job at the moment – so how could there be something more pressing than for me to get to him as soon as possible? Mister Carver does not know the way. Shall I report to Captain Vrue that you have deemed repair of our damaged sail unnecessary?"

Craig set his jaw hard and glared at her, then roughly threw his glance in Darian's direction.

"Fine. You're with me - hop to it."

Darian's eyes widened, and he jerked himself out of his attention position and through the door of Linsey's cabin. Craig had moved fast, not even looking to see if Darian had followed. Luckily, Craig was human – his stride not too hard for another human to match. Catching up behind the commander, Darian ventured a question at his back as they moved along the main deck towards the stairs.

"Uh, sir. Commander Craig, sir. I haven't mended sails before. Is that going to be a problem?"

Craig sighed and Darian saw his shoulders move into an exasperated slump. "How does she manage to do this?" he muttered. "Why I have to pick up her problems I'll never know." He strode on for a minute, down the first flight of stairs, without a glance back at Darian, much less an answer to his question.

Inside the ship the space was cramped, and they jostled past other crew as they went. Craig knew what he was doing, and slipped by each of them with barely a brushed coat-tail. Darian repeatedly walked almost headlong into each person in their path – feeling at each bump that he was falling farther and farther behind. He barely had time to offer curt apologies while they descended to the second level. The crew density was less further down, and there were only a few small rooms other than those absolutely necessary to live. There was a tremendous amount of damage near the outer wall of the ship. In almost pitch darkness, Craig stopped in front of a cracked door that looked like it was barely hanging together and half-lifted, half-dragged it open.

Darian squinted in, and saw what looked like a grayish bale on the floor of the small chamber. The space was otherwise empty – curiously dusty and hollow. He quirked a brow at the bale. "Uh, what.."

Craig's tone lost none of its exasperation. "That is our quarterdeck sail. It gives us stability. It is stored in this room because this chamber still has some energy field shielding. Commander Linsey, for reasons unknown to anyone but herself, has decided that you are to stay out of the way down here and repair it."

Darian gulped quickly, but smiled back at the commander. "Ah – yeah. So... you just want me to, like, sew it or...?" Darian was not thrilled about the nature of the job, but he knew Linsey was giving him a challenge. Something nobody had tried in years - he tried to maintain a positive attitude.

Craig paused, rolling his eyes and emitting another sigh. "Your first time out, right?" He looked down at the floor, and he spoke to himself in a whisper again. "Oh, I'm going to get her back for this."

Darian blushed as the familiar feeling of low expectations came at him. "Yeah. I been... busy."

Crag seemed to drag himself into the room and waved his hands over the bale, but did not make contact as he bent down. His voice followed a very slow but lecturing gait as he explained. "This is an auxiliary sail. Like all the other sails it has inside of it a lot of very sharp crystals tied with channel fibers woven into the cloth. They break through the strands very easily." As he slowly explained, he pointed at some of the parts of the sail, especially where some pointed crystals were stretching the fabric that contained them.

"Ah. Okay. So..." Darian lingered. He hated to be talked to in such a patronizing manner, but he still wanted to do a good job. To live up to the expectations that he knew at least Linsey now had for him.

"So, we need you to go over the sail and fix any portion that you see a big break." His tone then concentrated, and went even slower and waved his hands for extra effect. "*Don't* worry about small things. But the big ones, you need to sew up using the edges of the tear. With this." Craig held up a large gleaming silver needle that had been lying on the floor next to the sails. He handed it over carefully. "Let's say... anything bigger than your fist?" He looked at Darian with an exaggerated wide stare.

Fixing a sail. Wow. Fun. Darian thought as his face flickered into a depression – but something inside his gut hammered upwards. He forcefully righted the corners of his mouth, and tried to look brightly back at Craig. "Okay, Sir. Sounds good."

Craig bent a tired smile back at him. "Just go over it and patch it up. Then check your work with your friend, Mister Ford. He will be... elsewhere. Doing work which is actually important."

Darian tried to ignore the dismissive assessment of his task. "Uh... okay. Is there... anything else I need to know. I mean – so I don't hurt myself or... the sail?"

Craig stopped at the door, but did not look back at him. He began to close the portal, moving the cracked wooden panel back into place. "For some bizarre reason Miss Linsey thinks highly of you, so I'm sure you'll figure it out. If you don't, it's her problem. Unless you've got a battery in your jacket, you're not going to break anything. Thank goodness." And with that he was gone.

Darian smiled – glad Craig had left, and also that he didn't have to worry too much. *Why a battery?* he thought to himself as he got down on his knees to unbale the sail fabric. Right away he remembered what Max had said, up on the spar on D'ara's ship. A sail was something that amplified and channeled power. He regarded the one in front of him with curiosity and wonder, then spoke to it as he mused over the job it performed. "I guess wrapped up like this, you'd probably be a bit of a wild card next to something that pumps out power, wouldn't you?"

Unwinding his charge, he found out right away a few things that he shouldn't do. Most involved how not to grip the fabric – he cut his palm on a crystal, then scraped a portion across the fabric of his uniform so badly it ripped. He cursed quietly at these events, frustration coming easily. But he persisted in checking over the sail, looking intently at the workmanship and how the jagged crystals were attached. He realized that the sail could easily have been made by someone from Max's family. *All this work,* he thought, stopping to feel the intricate fabric. Then he looked at his cuts on his hands. *Man, why would you want to do this for a living?*

But he knew why - knew who the family were doing it for. Darian buckled down, and tried not to recall the last few words Max had spoken to him. He started to repair the sail in earnest. As if he was trying to fix the damage he'd done to their relationship.

The sail had five rips – three long and large ones, and the rest much smaller. Darian fixed them all. Painstakingly he used the needle he'd been given and a spare edge of the ripped portions to put them together, and make it look the best he could possibly make it look. Then he wound the fabric back into a bale again with extreme care and attention. Sitting back, smiling and wiping his brow, only then did he notice the volume of blood all over his hands from small cuts the crystals had made. He gritted out a curse – not at his hands, but instead worried he had soiled the sail.

Standing, he picked up his completed work, hoisting it over his shoulder. All the way up to the main deck, he smiled. He knew he was carrying something useful, necessary, important. He felt connected to it, and what he knew it was going to do. His hands didn't hurt at all.

nineteen

Max worked on the damaged wiring hanging from the ceiling of the first level's passageway. He concentrated, trying to keep his mind off his brother. *Whatever happens with him, it's not in my hands,* he thought. But he knew that something had to happen. He could hear his mother's voice in his head. She would want to strangle Adam, but she would still try to save him. Argue for him the way Max wanted to.

The large Mantarian moved purposefully and never made himself take more space than he absolutely needed to. The other crew depended on this – they stepped around Max easily, and he paid none of them any mind, used to the bustle of activity around him as he worked.

It was the soft clearing of a throat behind him that jolted him out of his concentration. An oral request for him to move so that someone could get by. He glanced down in irritation – to see Darian staring back at him with a baled sail over his shoulder, blocking the hallway. "Just go around. I won't bump you. Nobody here makes sudden moves unless they have to."

Darian blinked, then looked down. He'd obviously wanted something more as a response. Max shut his eyes, strained to the limit. He was already trying hard not to dwell on the failings of his brother, and having to deal with Darian's issues as well...

"I fixed the sail." Darian's voice was stiff and even. "You're supposed to check it. See if it's okay." He looked up again, his jaw set. "See if I screwed up again."

Max felt a drop in his chest - like he'd missed something important. His mind flickered over what Darian had done – that he was trying in spite of a lack of support. A lack of trust. "I... I'm sorry."

Darian swung the sail around, off his shoulder so that it stood on end in front of him. "Yeah, well. I did my job. Go ahead and check it."

Max looked at him, feeling as if the apology had only been a start. He'd been so disappointed back on D'ara's ship. But deep down he knew that it was training that drove Darian. He had been trained to be a disappointment. "I – I'm sorry about before. I mean."

Darian just stood, with the same expression on his face. After a moment, he nodded. "So, you're not giving up on me then?"

Max's eyes opened a bit wider, and he felt what he was sure was some of the hurt Darian had had. He swallowed hard. "No. You fixed that..." He pointed at the sail. "That's hard. I know."

"I know you know. I also know I'm not a loser."

Max sighed. He couldn't lie to Darian, and the quality of his field training flooded through him – experiences that had been the opposite of his friend's and from some of the Navy's finest. He took a step towards the human, and dipped his head to see him better, in the dim light of the passageway.

"You used to be the type of guy who did it right – even when nobody was watching. You were the first person I can remember who... who I could depend on like that. It's who you were." His throat tightened as he saw Darian's face blush. "Who I felt like I wanted to be."

Darian's reply was almost a whisper, as he stared up at Max. "It's nice to be asked to do it right. It's nice for someone to care."

Max nodded, smiling slightly. "That's what I'm used to, now. Every day. From everybody,"

"Max, that's all I ever wanted," Darian responded. Then he had to twist as another crewmember approached down the hallway, intending to pass them. He blew out his breath to get rid of the overt emotion, and Max nodded at the deckhand that slipped by them. Darian then picked the sail up again, both of them knowing Max did not really need to check it.

"Linsey's giving me a shot." He turned and started heading to the stairs to the main deck.

"Good," Max responded simply. "Good." He stared after him for a moment, before he turned back to his wiring panel in the ceiling. *You deserve a shot.*

twenty

In searching for evidence of the incident witnessed by D'ara's ship, Linsey expected they would find debris. Either that or a burnt out hulk of a slow merchant ship unable to outrun one of the more powerful bands of roughs. Instead, the crew of the *Archer* found one of their previous escort ships, the *Kristoff*.

The smaller airboat was not hovering - it had apparently been put down to rest peacefully on the ocean,. Bobbing just off a small reef in between two smoking volcanic islands, it appeared alone and undamaged. Its sails were loose on its masts and there was no sign of any people on board. The ship had a platform on each side of its foredeck to hold two small support skiffs, but one of the small boats was gone. The other was lashed tight to its deck, but seemed undamaged.

The weather in the area had turned rough, and the sea was up – blown by a harsh wind that kept the *Archer* from being totally steady as it floated in the air.

"Abandoned, Captain?" Craig queried as they stood at the edge of the boat and looked over the railing. As a drizzling rain started in earnest, a gust of wind blew and the Commander reached up to prevent his wide-brimmed hat from leaving his head. "Perhaps they took the other escort we lost, and were unable to crew this one."

"No." Vrue replied quietly. "They would've torched it. Or at least taken the other skiff. Don't need more than one person to crew that." Contrary to military tradition, Vrue didn't wear head covering – even in harsh weather, and his hair got more and more wet as he stood looking down.

A moment more of consideration in the breeze, and Linsey felt she had to make the obvious query so that they could move on out of the bad weather.

"Captain, shall we check it out?"

She could see Vrue silently puzzle over this as she stood next to him at the side of the ship. The *Archer* didn't touch down on the water – standard procedure when approaching an unknown. It came close, meandering about the smaller ship to give its officers a better look at what was going on. But the rain and wind made it hard to keep a steady position overhead.

"I don't want to spring a trap right now if I don't have to, Miss Linsey," Vrue replied. "We're short crewed in the middle of nowhere and if you'd noticed, the weather's not in great shape. Prime for an ambush I'd say." He sighed, a hard frown on his face. Then he looked at the atmosphere around them – trying to find the likely place that an attack would come from, if indeed the situation was a trap. "But we can't just leave it here, if indeed it's just been left. That ship can move faster than we can. And we don't know what happened to the crew. They might still be alive somewhere. Even down below, maybe." He stood back after a moment, and the wisp of a grin was on his face as a dribble of rain ran down it. His arms then swung around him to clasp behind his back.

"It's a toss-up. Mister Craig – you'll decide what we do."

Craig blinked, and he too drew away from the edge, mouth open in surprise. He started to sputter a question.

"No, No - don't you ask me anything. Imagine I'm not here. That I'm not going to see whatever it is you do. You decide and the crew does it."

Craig flushed as he considered.

Linsey glanced between the two men, her curiosity ablaze. *What would I do?* She knew she would have needed to make a decision quickly and confidently, giving anyone watching the clear impression that she had figured out all possible outcomes and chosen the best one instantaneously. In short, she would have had to direct the crew like she'd known this situation was going to present itself.

Vrue's testing him. Seeing if he can act like a Captain. Linsey was envious, but at the same time relieved she was not the one currently under the microscope.

"Uh... well. That is. We- we investigate... uh.." Craig faltered and scanned Vrue's face for any sign of positive or negative feedback on what he was starting to say. Absolutely nothing came back at him – the Captain was a blank sheet, standing in the rain and wind looking almost bored as he waited for directions to his crew to come.

"We go- find- I mean... evaluate. The ship's condition. To see if we can use it. Or... if we burn it. If that's what we- I-" he blinked and sweated, sounding like he was listening to his own voice to try to get guidance from it. He kept staring at Vrue as if he felt he was going to be interrupted, but the same blankness kept coming back at him.

"Sir. That is what I decide, sir." The final 'I' was said strongly, as if he was trying to show that he had confidence in his own decision. He finally smiled – mostly out of relief that he'd finished the process.

Linsey didn't quite snigger, but had to smile at the spot the Captain had put her fellow officer in. Craig's plan had simply pushed off the real decision for what to do until later - in effect, avoiding a plan. Linsey knew that sounding that way in front of her crew would not have brought confidence.

"Right. Well, get on with it then." Vrue simply replied, and turned to move towards the foredeck of the ship – apparently to get out of the rain. Looking down as he went he seemed to dismiss them from his consciousness, in all ways giving the impression he was letting Craig take over. Linsey felt a twinge of loss as he went. She knew it was a necessary learning experience for her fellow officer, as well as for her. But she noticed the sudden change, and inside she wished it could somehow have been different.

Craig coughed, visibly taken aback at having no further direction, but then caught Linsey looking at him with her amused smile. His brows came down and he talked quickly in frustration.

"Yes, well. Miss Linsey, you and I will take three additional crew over to the *Kristoff* to evaluate its condition. If it is abandoned, we will check the condition of its engines and weapons, as well as check for any supplies that may be on board. If it is not abandoned..." he trailed off, and looked over at Vrue as the Captain disappeared out of the weather into his cabin.

"Then... well, then I will decide what to do."

When Linsey responded, she sounded sarcastically impressed with his direction. "Very good, sir. I suggest we take the engineer, Mister Ford, to assess the engines and the support skiff. Miss Karthow and Mister Tukh in case we run into trouble." She paused, then bobbed a quick bow. "Sir." She started to turn away.

Craig coughed in protest as he saw her about to leave. "Linsey, I-" He took on a stern face, and wrapped his hands around his back as he stood straight – strongly mimicking the actions of his Captain. "Not Mister Tukh. Take Mister Redd instead."

Linsey felt her face show her exasperation, and fought to check it. He wasn't giving a reason - he just wanted to show that he could overrule her choices. She felt a growl coming up, but forced it into a smile by the time it reached her mouth, and continued her sweet voice of total compliance. "Of course, sir. As you wish." She did a deeper bow, adding an outward sweep of her arm. Then she turned away, unable to keep her eyes from pointing skyward.

Approaching the top of the stairs leading below decks, she saw Darian coming up with the sail baled up and hoisted over his shoulder. The wind and rain blasted him as he came into the open, and he winced against it – clearly surprised at the biting cold.

"Mister Carver. You are finished – excellent." She smiled at him. "Has Mister Ford inspected your work?"

"Yes sir."

"Good," she nodded at him. "You now know what a proper repair job looks like, and can check someone else's work when it is their turn. Please move up to the mid-deck and find Mister Tarok, one of our riggers." One hand held her hat, and she pointed with the other arm. "You can help him mount the sail – which.. as you can tell, is needed right now in this weather."

"Sir, yes, sir." Darian looked unsure. "Uh– sir? Mounting a sail..."

"Is something I trust you will be able to do. Mister Tarok is an excellent teacher." Her voice dropped in volume and she leaned closer so he could hear her. "Much better than Mister Craig."

Darian smiled and chuckled. "Yes, sir."

"Where is Mister Ford, by the way?"

"Uh.. down one deck – in the hallway. He's... well, it looks like he's fixing- uh.. wires."

"Ah. Excellent. Fixing the lighting for the privy. He will enjoy a break from that." Linsey began to move down the stairs, but her progress was stymied by several larger crewmembers coming upwards from below.

"What's he going to do?" Darian dared. He knew he should probably address her formally, and that whatever Max did was none of his business –

but he was intensely curious now. Excited, really, at the chance he was being given to learn what he wanted to learn.

"Mister Ford is going to help secure the *Kristoff*, which we have just located below us, resting on the sea. You have no field experience and will stay here." She saw Darian's face tighten in envy as a result of the order. "It is not a slight to be left out, Mister Carver. It is reality. Attempting to cope with reality gives you valuable experience. Your time will come. Deal with it."

Darian's face changed instantly at the words, and he nodded. "Ma'am, yes Ma'am." Linsey continued downstairs. *Well*, she thought, *at least I have HIS approval.*

twenty one

The weather got worse as the Navy crew quickly prepared. Hovering in the air allowed the ship to avoid being bounced around on waves, but the gusts of wind and rain did not help their situation. Coming down on strong rope lines, five Navy crew rappelled quickly over the railing at the side of the *Archer* in a controlled fall towards the deck of the *Kristoff*.

Each of them had lashed to their waists a single-channel short range pocket radio, a knife, and an electromagnetic spike pistol. The guns were extremely expensive, took tremendous amounts of energy to charge, and were therefore rare. They only had six of them for the entire crew of the *Archer*, and each weapon could only hold three shots at a time. Firing transuranic heavy pointed bolts, the weapons shot their payload at several times the speed of sound. Over short distances they were lethal - and messy.

Normally at least ten crew would go investigate an abandoned ship – especially one left at sea in the present conditions. When Max first saw the *Kristoff* from over the side of the *Archer*, he had half expected that Vrue would have simply ordered them to drop firebombs to burn it. If anyone had come out to stop the fire, they could see who it was then act accordingly. However, the loss or damage of a single Navy ship, even one as small as the *Kristoff*, was not something to take lightly. Also, if there were injured or trapped sailors aboard, they would not be able to free themselves to stop a fire.

Max landed first – crouching to lower his center of gravity and test the slickness of the deck in the rain. He'd done only a few excursions off his previous boat – usually to assess Navy outposts that had been lost and subsequently reclaimed, or to explore and assess captured ships. His eyes were wide and his ears were up, and he could feel his heart beating strongly in his chest. He much preferred the safe, warm, confined space of an engine room with its regular noises and motions. Max liked to think of his race evolved and distinct from what they once were, and he found the animal fear reaction welling in him distasteful.

The deck was clean and steady to walk on, and he noticed no other sound than the steady howl of the wind as they all fanned out over the empty space. Being on the wind-tossed ocean, the boat rocked roughly from side to side with an occasional shaking from wave impacts. Linsey landed near Max and found her footing, then came closer to the large Mantarian and gave him commands in a low voice.

"Mister Ford – take Miss Karthow and head for the engine room. Secure it, then get her to head back up top to me to check on the skiff that's left. Quietly and quickly please."

Max nodded, and looked to the striped Tebryn female at his other side. He cocked his head in a silent message to have her follow him, and started towards the stairs leading below decks. From behind him as he moved came a quick, hushed exclamation over the noise of the weather.

"Hoy!"

Max looked back. It was Craig – coming up on Linsey from behind with an irritated gaze in Max's direction. He whispered harsh words Max could not quite make out to Linsey. She glared at him, then spoke quietly back. Max stood still, and as the boat rolled he glanced at Karthow. She looked confused. He felt the same, and looked back at the two officers, who were now in a hushed argument.

Abruptly, in the middle of Craig's speech, Linsey turned and jutted her chin upwards at Max with a quick tilt of her head – a direction to proceed. He turned immediately without waiting for Craig's reaction, and moved forwards down the stairs with Karthow. He thought he heard a last protest from Craig, but he ignored it.

Give me an order or don't give me an order, he thought. *Just don't make me stand there and get my butt shot off in the breeze while you decide.*

Max headed in the direction he had been commanded – the inside of the ship masking the noise from outside and gripping them with low echoes. With her padded feet and light frame, Karthow's movement was quiet. Max had to keep checking behind him to make sure she was there. Whenever he did she bumped gently against him, then looked around him to see if there was a reason why he had stopped. He felt quite awkward just resuming his travel without a word. They had to keep quiet, especially with no cover noise. The ship seemed deserted - the floors were barren, and most useful items that normally hung from the walls had been removed. Its three decks made it seem bigger inside than it looked from the outside. The pair descended fast down the layered staircases and through the dark passageways.

The engineer in Max knew instinctively where the engine room was – right behind the ship's tiny brig. He found the door to it jammed shut. Trying quietly to push and prod at the lock, he could not make any progress. He backed off for a moment, and spoke to Karthow in a low voice.

"It's jammed. We can kick it in, but we'll lose any element of surprise."

Karthow looked at him, then quirked a black brow. Her tail flicked once, then she whispered back. "We're surprising them, or they're surprising us? At this point, I'm the one that's going to be surprised. I don't hear anything – I think the boat is empty."

Max made a wry face, concentrating. He knew that Karthow could see heat, and would have spoken up if she'd seen any of it. But they were right next to the engine room – a place where heat lingered for a long time. He knew there was no way she could be sure. "All right. Well, we'll kick it in then. Ready?"

Karthow nodded, and stepped back with him to get a run at the door.

twenty two

Craig bawled Linsey out. As part of it he had promised to tell Captain Vrue all about her indolence and her disrespect of his authority. He was adamant that she check any commands she wished to make with him before proceeding. Linsey just stood in the wind and rain and took it – waiting until she felt he was finished before responding with a quick and quiet "Yes, sir." She blinked and stared at him, not moving an inch.

"Now, Mister Redd shall stay here and relay any information back to the *Archer*." He looked up, blinking through the falling rain to the galleon above them.

"Out in the open?" Redd queried. He didn't look happy, and looked about with a worried expression as the wind blew strong gusts at them.

"Yes, Mister Redd. Right here. We can see you, and Miss Karthow will soon be returning from the engine room. Miss Linsey will check the officer's cabins, and I will head to the bridge to determine whether the ship can be piloted. Then we will check the skiff with Mister Ford and fly it up to the *Archer* deck. Clear?"

Linsey nodded. At least Craig seemed to be forming some kind of plan in his head. She doubted he would do more than report back to Vrue his findings and wait for commands from above, but that was his choice – his actions. Even though she wasn't really worried about the Captain's assessment of her behavior, she knew she really had overstepped by not getting Craig's consent for her commands. She did what she was told to do, and moved back on the main deck toward the doors to the officer's cabins. Craig moved further out to the stairs leading to the bridge, and Redd stood in the middle of the main deck – shivering and nervously looking around.

Linsey came out of the rain and up to the covered entrance to the officer's quarters. She took stock of what she remembered of the layout of the small escort.

This is Culley's ship, she mused. The only female Captain - someone every member in the Navy of her sex looked up to. She clasped her teeth together hard, trying not to let her mind wander.

Life on a ship riding the winds of Zefphyr was a razor's edge - to give up your liberty was to give up your life. Death was shockingly normal and occurred very frequently. Culley would only leave the ship in its present condition to barter for the lives of her crew. Linsey's face hardened more into an angry frown as she wondered if she could have made the same choice that Culley did. And wondered that if the Captain still lived, what pains and trials could be happening to her now, at the hands of her captors.

Drawing her pistol, she kicked open the door in front of her – crouching down at the entrance and scanning the room. It was empty. Or... almost empty. The first time Linsey glanced over the cabin, she missed the long coat. Laid over the desk chair, it did not present itself as important to her assessment of possible sources of peril. After a more thorough scouting of the chamber, she picked up the jacket and turned it over, opening it and remarking at the sturdiness of the fabric. Her own Lieutenant's jacket was similar, but not quite as thick, pristine, or regal.

Linsey smiled, remembering the woman who had worn it and how well it had fit her. But again the musings started to lead down a dark path. Linsey laid the long coat carefully back over the chair, and smoothed it out. "Don't give up, Culley," she whispered.

"What are you still doing here?" The hissing query came at her back. She whirled to see Craig crouched at the door. He looked around at the empty space, then stared at her. "Have you already checked the other cabins?"

"No, I-" Linsey started, but was cut off again.

"We are not here for your leisure and enjoyment, Lieutenant. If you're going to dally, then perhaps you should not come on these excursions, hmm?"

"Commander, I found some evidence of Captain Culley, and was inv-"

"She's not here. No one is here. That's all that's important. Let's get back outside, move that skiff and get more people down from the *Archer*."

She moved out into the hallway with him. "Is Mister Ford back from the engine room?"

"How should I know? Making them go down there was your mistake, remember?" He gritted his teeth and made a distasteful sneer. "I've been in here retrieving a little lost kitten."

Linsey's brows bent down hard as she growled at the racial barb. Instinctively her claws came out, and although she held on to her fury her reply to him was loud and firm. "Commander. I shall check the other cabins as you requested and meet you on deck." She turned away from him and went down the hallway.

"Fine. But don't waste any more of my time."

Linsey kicked the doors of the other cabins open much harder than she had Captain Culley's.

twenty three

Darian strained to see over the side of the *Archer*, trying to keep his eyes on the crewmember left in the center of the *Kristoff's* deck. As the boat he was on swayed in the air with the buffets of wind and sheets of rain, he had to change his grip on the railing – alternately pulling himself and pushing himself to stay steady. He watched for Max and Linsey; both of them had disappeared into different parts of the ship tossing on the ocean below. He glanced to his side to see other crew looking down, all watching and waiting.

It had only taken Tarok and him a few minutes to rig up the repaired auxiliary sail – much less time than he'd anticipated, even in the harsh weather. The Impalan male was lean but muscular, and did most of the work while giving him terse commands to assist. Linsey had not given him any other orders and unaccustomed to actively looking for work, he didn't know what to do with himself. The other crew seemed idle or far more interested in what was going on down on the *Kristoff* than on their own jobs, so he didn't feel out of place watching with them. He looked at the skiff on the deck of the escort. *I could have gone and flown that*, he grumbled.

"All right, all you! Don't just gawk down!" Captain Vrue suddenly belted out from a few feet away, close enough to startle Darian. "This funny business is going on for a reason. We just don't know it yet. Yell any marks as soon as you see them." The Ursid looked around to the thick low cloud about them for emphasis, then turned his eyes down over the edge again.

Darian looked around as well – squinting into random places off the side of the ship. He felt almost claustrophobic in the heavy wet air around them, not understanding how anyone would see any threat coming.

A brilliant flashing stab of lightning cut through the sky, making the human jump and his heart ram against his chest. He looked down the line of crew to his side – none of them even flinching at the blast of force. They all seemed to let the weather just roll off them.

He sighed – the people on the boat had been doing well without his involvement for a long time. His heart felt heavy in his chest at the depth of what he had been missing. *They don't need me,* he thought. *They do this every day. Exploring. Danger. Roughs.* The last thought made him look up to the forecastle of the ship where their prisoners were being held.

Max's brother was staring straight at him – his face suddenly blanched as he noticed Darian's attention.

The human got the eerie feeling he had seen something he was not supposed to see - as if he had caught a child stealing candy. Peering at the condition of the bound Mantarian, he noticed a hand. A free hand, working quickly and deftly in the wraps of twine at the prisoner's side.

The Drago beside Adam was furiously wriggling against the ropes. Some of his knifelike scales had already poked through the lines holding the two prisoners. They both stared at Darian, gritting their jaws in frustration as they wrestled against their tight bindings.

The shock of imperative drive thrust itself up to the human's mind, making him gasp for breath to sound the alarm.

"HEY! THEY- THEY'RE LOOSE!"

He took a step towards the brigands before his head snapped around to make sure the rest of the crew had heard him.

They had – most of them were starting to move in the same direction Darian was moving. Captain Vrue had also turned, and with an angry sneer on his face bellowed a command to his charges.

"BUST THEM DOWN!!"

Darian was overtaken by crewmembers rushing to respond to the bark of their commander. He had already learned that the Captain hated pirates - hated them more than anything else on the planet. The human jerked his head to look back to the front mast, suddenly worried about the ferocity that would be unleashed on the escaping men. But as he looked his eyes were distracted by movement in the air off to the side of the galleon beyond where the prisoners were tied. The emergence of a solid shape rapidly moving towards the *Archer* through the clouds.

Darian's eyes bulged and his chin dropped as he saw what was coming straight at them.

twenty four

Max and Miss Karthow slammed into the door to the engine room in unison, making the wood buckle and snap. Max grunted as the pain shot through his shoulder from the impact, and Karthow swore loudly. Any element of surprise now gone from the noise of the first hit, they reared back quickly together to lunge another blow.

The door seemed to disappear in front of them just as they were about to hit it, and they fell forwards together into the room. Max barely had time to bring up his forearms to protect his face from the floor before he hit it. Knowing instinctively they were in trouble, he jerked himself into a side roll after he hit, and tried to grab for his knife. As he did so something hard and black slammed into his face. He winced his eyes shut in pain, and heard loud raucous yelling.

"Welcome to the party! And ooh! You brought a girl."

Max was gripped by at least six pairs of hands. It was all he could do to slit his eyes open as his head rang from the blow inflicted on him. They were everywhere – all over him and Karthow. Holding them both down. Sitting on them, in fact. Max strained with his arms, grunted, and thrust himself upwards. For a moment he was able to lift up fully three of their attackers. His powerful legs kicked, and he felt a solid impact with one of them – something he knew the receiver would not soon forget. But another sudden hard bash to his head made him reel – dropping the three he had lifted as others joined in to beat down his protests. He felt blows to his knees and feet, and his own heartbeat thudded in his ears as he lost his equilibrium from the shots to his head. Dazed, he stopped struggling.

Karthow did not. She screamed again and again, writhing beside him. Hearing her terrifying cries invigorated Max to struggle again, and he let out a wheezing whinny of a yell. But almost immediately a boot was laid on his throat – a crushing weight that made him turn his head sideways just to breathe.

Loud laughter beat in his ears as he heard them inflict blow after blow on Karthow. She continued to scream. Continued to fight. Max knew she would fight to the end – with everything she had until they forced conscious-ness from her. Or life. Every member of the Navy knew that no female, re-gardless of race or age, could expect mercy from the bloodthirsty male that prowled outside the boundaries of the Queen's frontier.

Max lay under the crushing pressure, straining for breath as they broke her down beside him.

twenty five

Linsey came back to the entrance to the officer's quarters having nothing to report. One of the rooms had been the communications center, but all the equipment had been smashed and burned by the original crew. It was a clear sign that the *Kristoff* had been forcibly boarded.

The rest of the chambers were barren, with a turned over chair or table but stripped of all things of value. Craig was waiting for her inside the door to the main deck, and his mood had apparently not improved.

"Nothing? Right. Fine - let's get that skiff and get more people down here." Craig quickly opened the door to the main deck and beckoned for her to go first.

The wind and rain had intensified, blowing into the hallway and making Linsey grip her coat with one hand. A lightning flash lit up the corridor, and she squinted her eyes against it. Not wanting to seem deterred, she strode by Craig and out into the weather, looking for Mister Redd on the rolling deck.

He wasn't in sight.

Linsey looked left and right on the deck of the ship, then took a few more steps forward to swivel around and look above them. Still nothing.

"What is it?" Craig grumbled at her pause.

Linsey raised a brow, surprised Craig had not also noticed the absence. "Uh- Mister Redd?"

Craig flushed at the mental omission, and jerked his head around to look for the man. He was nowhere to be seen. Linsey looked up the lines that were dragging down from the *Archer* above them, expecting to see him on a rope. The lines were clean – and as she squinted upwards she could also see the side rail of the galleon. No crew were looking back at them.

"What's the hell's going on?" Craig muttered, raising a hand to grasp his hat and stride out onto the deck.

The sound of a rolling explosion suddenly came from the sky, causing both officers to instinctively duck their heads. Looking up in unison, they were unable to see beyond the bottom of the *Archer* hanging above them. All they could make out was a red glow reflecting off the rain and clouds.

"We've got to get up there!" Craig started, turning to the ropes still dangling from above.

"But – Mister Ford and Miss Karthow!" Linsey protested. She too felt the strong urge to rush back to their ship, but was firmly grounded in keeping their party together. "We've got to let them know something's going on, at least."

"Fine!" Craig barked back. "You go and get them. I'm heading up. Mister Redd is probably up there. Meet us on the ship when you're done collecting your flock." He started to hoist himself up, getting two full handholds up on the rope before it suddenly came free, sending him sprawling back onto the deck. He looked up into the rain, startled.

Linsey also turned her questioning eyes upwards – to see another of the five ropes fall, then another. Only two remained.

Craig cursed. "Who-"

"They'll be down in a minute," the high-pitched nasally voice came from behind them both. Eyes wide, Linsey hunched down and spun, bringing up her firearm as she scanned the deck behind her.

A stocky male human covered in gray-green wet clothing stood facing them both, seemingly unarmed with his thumbs hooked into his belt. His wide but relaxed stance kept him upright as the ship below them rolled. Linsey's eyes narrowed at the gall of the rough. He must have been hiding in the skiff.

"Hands up!" she commanded, standing as straight as she could and leveling her gun at the man's head.

Two more scraggly shapes emerged from the shadow of the midmast behind the brigand. Then four. Eight. None were armed, but Linsey still felt a hard knot dropping in her stomach. She'd dealt with bands of pirates before, but these ones seemed much more brazen. Confident and organized.

Craig was up off the deck, coming beside her and aiming his gun along with hers at the men.

"What, you gonna shoot us all before we get you?" the man's squeaking tone casually queried.

"No," Linsey growled. "Just you."

The man frowned, but nervously swallowed. Linsey had known none of them would jump at her alone – roughs were far too individual and had almost no sense of loyalty.

"That's enough," Craig broke in. "All of you. I appreciate your... surrender." Craig's tone was almost jovial, certainly patronizing. "Miss Linsey, if you would please shoot the first one of these bastards that approaches you, while I call up to the *Archer*?"

Linsey didn't answer. Internally, she balked at being left alone with the eight men. She shifted her footing nervously, but felt compelled to nod. Craig moved backwards out of her line of sight. She kept her eyes keenly focused on the men.

There was a loud jarring impact from behind her, combined with a grunting squeal. She couldn't help it – she had to whirl her head around to look.

They were on her before she could fire a shot.

twenty six

Darian had tried to do the right thing – to get out of the way. Loaded heavy with pirate roughs, the *Kristoff*'s missing skiff had headed straight at them. The brigand crew opened fire just as they became visible, bright red lances of the tracers from their guns streaking through the air and impacting both the ship and the people on it.

To protect himself Darian instinctively fell to the deck, where he was instantly tripped over by another crew member who was rushing towards the attackers. The man fell over him and landed with a crunch on his face. Barely was he down for a moment before he scrambled up to continue his rush to defend. He was hit by blasts from the pirates, red tracer lines hammering through is body and splashing Darian's crouched form with blood.

The human gulped for breath, wide-eyed in shock.

"BACK THEM OFF!!" Vrue's baritone hollered out from directly behind Darian. This was almost immediately followed by returned fire from the *Archer* crew – hammering sounds of compressed gas-powered weapons shooting their hard short spikes through the air to tear at the pirate skiff's sails. Dirty looking men of differing races jumped from the skiff onto the galleon, hunkering low to evade the returned fire and move to free their captured comrades.

Still in a daze from the blood splashing his face, Darian covered his head and tried to rid himself of panic so he could think and act rationally. He knew he could fight. But before he could move Vrue grabbed him by the uniform at the scruff of the neck, pulling him up and backwards. Darian's feet dangled in the air for a moment, making him feel completely helpless as the Captain took two of his huge strides and moved him out of harm's way. The Ursid deposited him quickly behind the huge center mast, looking at him only for a split second to make sure he was all right. Then from a box next to where he put down the human he grabbed a small studded silver orb, twisting it in his enormous hands. He turned and threw it back in the direction they had come from. A perfect toss – obviously well trained into the huge male. The orb landed right in the middle of the pirate skiff, bouncing once with a hard metallic thunk. To Darian the silence after the sound was deafening.

The sphere exploded in a red fiery blast that shook the *Archer*. Wood, metal, and people in the skiff went flying in all directions. The skiff itself was brutally cracked in two, and to Darian its halves seemed to hover in the air for a moment before they fell out of view towards the ocean below.

Vrue hadn't stopped – he'd just barely covered himself from getting perforated by thousands of tiny flying splinters that had been the skiff's hull. He bellowed a frightening deep-throated yell as he raced upwards towards the front mast, with no weapon or armor, to assault his ship's attackers head on. The first pirate he met he grabbed fully around the chest with an enormous hand, instantly squeezing to crush the breath from the man's chest. He then brandished the body as both a shield and a club as he waded into the fray towards the others.

Darian was breathless, eyes wide as he tried to take in the unfolding carnage. The pirates who had been lashed to the front mast were in the midst of freeing themselves. They were assisted by other brigands from the skiff that had made it onto the galleon before their craft had been taken out. Darian found it strange that the men lashed to the mast were not shot at by the Navy crew, while the ones coming off the skiff were fair game.

We won't shoot helpless people, he thought and set his brows in anger at the inequity. *I'm sure they would.*

For an instant Darian thought of Linsey and Max, and looked to the side of the ship where the ropes the crew had repelled on were still hanging over the edge. He was surprised to see Vek and Adam halfway over the side, holding tightly to the ropes and attempting to slip unnoticed from the main fray on the deck. They had cut the other lines, and were using the last two to descend to the *Kristoff* on the rocking sea below.

As Captain Vrue had, he shouted out a yell and ran headlong at the two pirates as they disappeared out of view over the edge of the boat. Running up to the side and grabbing one of the lines, he hoisted himself up and over –

immediately getting a shock of vertigo as he saw how far it was down to the other boat below them. It was the sudden visceral shock that made him realize that he'd acted without thinking. That he had just jumped at the chance to help his friends. A heat welled in his chest.

As he gripped the rope and started to slide down it, he barely looked out for his own safety. In his mind he saw himself sliding down the rope – landing on Vek or Adam and knocking one of them off before fighting with the other one. He didn't really care what happened after that.

He did slide down – too fast. The line had become almost icy from the rain and wind chill, and his hands burned trying to control the descent. He was about to jam his legs together to abruptly stop himself when his feet slammed hard into something. He heard a Mantarian yelp and a snarl, and looked down to aim further kicks more precisely, gritting out his own angry sneer.

Adam tried to defend himself for a moment, before Darian landed a solid kick into his right eye. Then he let go, falling freely the remaining ten meters towards the deck of the *Kristoff* below. Darian watched him fall away, a lump in his throat jumping up as he realized he may have just killed his best friend's brother.

Before he could see the Mantarian impact the deck, a stabbing pain jammed into his side. Beside him, swinging on the other rope, Vek had struck him in the midsection. A short spiky scale on the Drago's fist had impaled the stretched muscle of Darian's abdomen. It was all he could do to hang onto the rope as the wind rushed from his chest. Pain shot up his back, and he instinctively bucked his hips, freeing the small spike and causing him to emit a painful cry. He shut his eyes gripped his jaw tightly shut while he fought to hold on. He heard the wind rushing through the air around him and squinted an eye open to try to avoid being impaled again by the Drago's dangerous fists.

Vek was swinging only a few feet away, a fixed angry stare lanced in Darian's direction. He seemed to be positioning himself on the rope, trying to set up for a swing at Darian the next time the human drew near. Darian's side stung, and he could feel blood flowing over his skin. He gasped for breath and tried to avoid the man by swinging his legs in the opposite direction. For a moment his momentum seemed to be assisted by an unexpected pulling on his rope.

Despite his pain he glanced up to the edge of the ship to see if he was being helped, but did not see anyone. Then he realized - the *Archer* had started to move, either from being buffeted in the wind or because a Navy crewmember had taken control of the ship. Still looking upwards he did not see Vek swinging towards him until the last moment.

Unable to position himself to dodge the impact, Darian let go of his rope, grabbing at the Drago instead. Latching onto him and scratching at his face, Darian felt the desperation of wanting to pull his adversary down - to force him to let go of the rope and drop, meeting whatever fate they would far below. But Vek's scaly constitution resisted the scratching, and he head-butted Darian in the nose. Dazed from the impact, the human slipped downwards, scrabbling at the pirate's wet clothes. Then he fell.

The wind and the rain buffeted him as he fell end over end downwards in the storm, slapping finally into the icy black water of the sea.

twenty seven

Karthow's cries had long stopped. The laughing and grunting of the pirates had seared his mind, and he felt like a frayed string. Thankfully, very early on they had pulled a dirty, oily cloth bag from the engine room over his head and spared him from having to watch. Beaten and bound with his face inside the bag Max had been taken past his breaking point. He had snuffled and tried to hide the sounds he made as he cried.

They tied his arms tightly to his torso and moved him upwards, out of the engine room on what he soon realized was the direct path back to the main deck. Whenever he felt even the slightest freedom on one side or the other, he would try to buck free from his captors. Usually he was cuffed in the head or kicked in the belly in response, and pushed around roughly before he was shoved to move in the right direction.

In moments they were outside, and with his feet sore from being stepped on and kicked, Max found it hard to maintain a sure stance on the slick boards of the deck. The *Kristoff* was moving – even with the bag over his head he could tell by the direction of the wind and how it blew his open jacket.

They were just sitting and waiting for us, he thought. *We should have torched this thing when we had the chance!* He could hear some yelling and muffled banging, and then an angry voice he recognized - Vek's. *How could they get down here? There's no way they could have taken the Archer.*

"Just get us far enough away so that they won't follow us, then get low and head to the cove."

Max was glad to hear the confirmation that the roughs indeed had not managed to take the galleon. He gritted his teeth and waited for the familiar sound of his brother's voice to chime in after Vek's, but it didn't come. In-

stead rough hands stopped him and stood him up straight, holding him painfully by the hair at the back of his neck. Then a blow suddenly hammered
into his gut. Choking, he doubled over but continued to be held up by his
captors, who complained about his weight. As he fought to regain control of
his breathing through the stinking greasy bag covering his head, he heard
them laughing at his state.

"Oooh. Been wantin' to do that for a bite, I'll say." Vek's voice came
even closer. "Be much more of that comin' along, pretty boy." He was
shoved over and kicked several times from behind as he lay helpless on the
deck. There was more chuckling from all around him. Max just kept still and
tried to breathe. To endure.

"I heard you boys already had your fun with the other one." Vek's voice
was full of feigned reproach. "'Tis a shame she didn't last longer. Just so
long as this cog had a front row seat."

"He did." Another pirate chimed in with mock pity. "Cryin' in his bag.
Awwww..."

Max's face ruffled and he felt the heat in his cheeks. He forced his
breath out and clenched up his muscles, shoving the still-vivid memories of
below decks away before they could overwhelm him.

"Well, we'll make sure he's about when we do the cat, then. And no bag
next time. Heheh."

Linsey?! Max's mind screamed. They'd gotten Linsey somehow? He
found it almost impossible to believe. She would have fought as hard as
Karthow, if not harder. He was sure that the last thing any of the men would
be jovial about is a fight with Linsey. He moved his head around, trying to
hear any noise the felid might be making. But in the confine of the bag his
senses were useless.

The bag was removed with a quick jerk. Surprised, Max blew air out his
nose repeatedly to clear the grease fumes, and blinked to try to stabilize his
vision. He was outside on the top deck, not far from the door leading below
decks where he had been taken from. He was surrounded by ragtag brigands
all of whom had mean dirty faces and worn, torn clothing. Lying partially on
the wet deck, the wind and rain still came down on him. He smelled blood,
and realized it was his own – caked under his nose. One of his eyes was
swollen from having taken repeated blows.

But as he had guessed, the *Kristoff* was indeed moving. Fast. Through cloud after cloud and up and down – an evasion pattern.

The Archer's after us, Max thought. *We're not done for yet.* He squinted and looked around – not recognizing any faces. His brother was no-where to be seen. Maybe he had been killed.

"Oh, he's here all right," Vek grinned, as if he had sensed Max's unspo-ken thought. Folding his arms behind his back, he made a mocking imitation of Captain Vrue, and spoke in an imperious tone. "Inside with our two 'officers'. One of 'em broke yer brother's fall down here. Prolly saved his life." The Drago looked around at the other pirates, then put his hand over his heart. "Dear old Navy, always comin' to the rescue."

"Sick bastards." Max bit out. "You're running now. Vrue will find you – and when he does..."

"When he does we'll show him what else we got!" Vek barked back. "And he'll be the one running. You shouldn't be concerned about our wel-fare." He came closer again, bending down to whisper seething words into the Mantarian's face. "You've got your own to worry about. I hope your brother hasn't gone too far already. Hate for you to miss what he's gonna do to that felid trash."

Max steeled his teeth as he was forced to consider going through the same thing he had when they had taken Karthow. The images grated in his mind.

"Pick him up." Vek gestured curtly with his hand to a short, stocky man. They jerked Max to his feet, and he was led towards the covered area at the back of the main deck where the cabins were located. "Figure out who's next. And who's after that. And who's after that..." Vek's voice trailed off in a comical lilt. The other pirates guffawed and shouted obscenities at Max as he was led away.

Being able to see didn't make the shoving and prodding that forced Max around any more pleasant, but he felt a measure of relief at least from being moved out of the rain. Inside the short hallway to the officer's quarters, he was pushed roughly up against the wall. While Vek opened the door to the Captain's quarters, the other rough grabbed Max by his neck and threw him inside.

Adam was there, standing in the center of the room. Linsey and Craig were bound as Max was, and sitting against the far wall. Craig looked dazed, had a bloody nose and a large bruise on his forehead. Linsey appeared un-hurt, but was obviously very angry as she strained against her bonds. Behind Max, Vek dismissed the man who had thrown him into the room with a curt "get out", and the door was closed. In the silence that ensued Max could hear everyone's breathing, and feel the heat of rampant anger.

"So..." Vek started slowly, walking gingerly into the room with his hands once again behind his back. "Who's in charge here, then?"

Sitting against the wall bound tightly, Craig blinked his eyes and blearily lifted his chin. His response was slurred, as if he was in a dream. "I am."

Vek smiled. He drew out one of the Navy pistols from the belt around his waist and aimed it at Craig's head. "Oh really?"

Vek fired.   Sitting right next to the commander, Linsey was showered with bits of the man's flesh and bone. She squealed and spat, and could not help mewling while pulling up her legs in front of her in a fetal position. Vek stood over her, arm still extended pointing the gun where the shot had gone. He turned the weapon so that it pointed at Linsey.

Max winced his eyes shut, turning his head downwards. In the sudden silence following the blast, all that could be heard were Linsey's soft sobs.

"Now who's in charge?" Vek said softly.

Max looked up, to see Linsey seething breath, shaking. She gazed up, scared, through her brow at the Drago. "You are."

Vek sighed and suddenly relaxed, letting the gun lilt sideways as he ex-aggerated relief. "Oh good! We're learning." He turned and took a step to-wards Adam, then held out the gun and pointed at Max's head. Max just stared at him, fear leaving his body as he prepared to die.

But Vek didn't fire. He strode up to the Mantarian's side and grabbed Max once again by the hair at the back of his neck, then kicked out his legs from behind.

The sharp pain as he fell forwards onto his knees made him wince, and huff out a hard breath. Held strongly by Vek, through bleary eyes he looked up at his brother. Adam looked conflicted for a moment, then he glanced at Vek. But Max saw Adam's face muscles harden and the anger return. Through bent brows his gaze flicked towards his kneeling brother. "How's that feel, huh? Finally! Finally you see what it's like being shoved around. Put where you don't wanna go and being forced to do things you can't even imagine ever wanting to do. How's that feel?"

Max's breathing was labored, but he gazed steadily back up at his younger sibling. "You're sick," he growled. "Something's gone wrong with you-"

"Something went RIGHT!" Adam yelled back at him, then he showed a toothy grin. "Right for me. More right than it ever could have gone back home. I took what was mine – my life - back from you. And now I'm doing what I want."

Covered in bloody splatter, Linsey still shook in fear as she cut in. "I doubt you ever wanted to be a killer." She jutted her chin in Vek's direction. "I'm sure he made you do that."

Adam rolled his eyes and sighed, but then continued speaking to his brother. "He never made me do anything. He gave me a home where I could choose. A future."

"A family?" Linsey offered, looking down at her knees. Max stared at her, and wondered for a moment if Linsey was trying now to get herself shot. To end possibility of a worse fate. He felt a sinking sense of defeat as internally he tried and failed again and again to think of a way to reach his brother. How things could have gone so wrong?

Adam was quiet for the merest of moments, looking at the deck again and concentrating. "These people are more my family than you ever were. They know I'm an adult. I make my own choices, and I take what belongs to me."

Linsey piped up again. "You take what he lets you have."

"SHUT UP BITCH!" Adam roared to cut her off and turned to stride hard toward her. "Around here women are good for one thing only!"

"Leave her alone!" Max burst spoke up in his deepest booming tone. It surprised even him – and Adam stopped short of Linsey as if he were yanked by the ears by his mother.

Adam scowled at his own instinctive reaction to his brother's voice, and glared at Max. But then he quickly shifted his gaze to Linsey, looking down her body.

"The last three girls we had on this ship, all I got to do was watch. Next one was supposed to be all mine." Linsey's eyes narrowed, while Max's went wide with fear and anger. A look of disgust and revulsion started to form on his face.

Adam took a moment and slowly looked around at their reactions. He was actually a little surprised, and chuckled softly. Egged on, he continued.

"Come on, Max" he intoned, drinking in his brother's cold look of revulsion before turning to Linsey, "You used to hang up naked pictures of them in your room."

Max seized up in his bonds, the anger on his face impossible to hide. The treatment of Karthow fresh in his mind, he wildly bucked at the ropes holding him.

"Oooh. Hitting a nerve there..." Vek laughed, before pushing Max forward so that he landed hard on his face. "Perfect. I think you're not the only one who wants a crack at her, my boy. You've got a jealous brother. Sorry to mess her up for you with... well, with that guy's... brains. You put those two a bit too close."

"Mmm," Adam returned, licking his lips. "Close." His gaze lingered on her, and his voice became soft but menacing as he gazed at her body. "We're gonna get close. You and me." He turned his head, and shot a pointed gaze at Vek.

Vek looked back at Adam for a moment in silence, then his expression became quizzical. There was only another moment before a flash of insight passed over his face. "Hah! You wanna be alone? Fine. But yer priss brother stays here too. I want him to enjoy the show."

Adam swallowed hard, and flushed, but then nodded. He was going to force himself on her, audience or no audience. Vek moved back to the entrance of the room, and without a word opened the door and slipped through it.

The door had barely closed behind Vek before Adam moved down to straddle Linsey's bound legs. She had stopped shaking, and looked detached as he towered over her. Max was much less reserved, seizing up in his bonds and yelling imperatively at his brother.

"Get off of her! Get off!"

Linsey said nothing, looking sullenly up at Adam. Max was prone on the ground, helpless as he gaped in Linsey's sudden silence. He simply couldn't believe his eyes - her inaction at right angles to his view of reality.

Adam's grin faded slowly to fascination. He was a strong fifteen-year-old, but was still only fifteen. His hands came to Linsey's jacket, and he looked at her face. She continued to look at him, eyes large but expressionless. A total silence gripped the room as he pulled her jacket open, popping the three gold buttons apart and revealing the soft shirt clothing underneath. Adam's breath could be heard releasing as he let go of the jacket fabric. Max just stared at Linsey, mouth open in shock that she was not resisting.

Linsey's face, spattered with Craig's blood, was still a sullen mask – staring at Adam through even breathing as if waiting for his next action. Adam was completely lost in her emerald stare. His right hand came forward and found its way underneath her jacket, probing up over the soft fabric to her chest. His mouth opened more as his breathing deepened. Max's eyes were transfixed on Linsey's dead stare as his yearning to try to understand what was going on overwhelmed him.

Adam's left hand moved up, towards Linsey's face as he too stared into her eyes. His index finger slightly extended from his left hand, he touched her cheek, feeling its softness and deep warmth. He laid the finger against it and trailed it down her face. For the first time, Linsey's eyes closed and she uttered a slight moaning sound. She turned slowly towards Adam's finger. Adam smiled, and trailed his finger to her lips.

The world gone mad, Max's eyes jammed shut as he gritted his teeth.

Adam's harrowing scream pierced the metal room as his body convulsed backwards off of Linsey, clutching his bleeding hand. At the sound, Max's eyes shot open and he jolted his body, as if being woken from a nightmare. Linsey loudly spat, and a bloody severed finger dropped in front of Max's eyes.

Linsey's face had turned into a scowl, blood dripping from the right side of her mouth and down off her chin as she continued to stare at Adam, howling in pain a few feet in front of them on the floor. Slowly her gaze turned away to Max, and he struggled fiercely with his bonds.

"Mister Ford," she started, voice cold and even over Adam's painful yowling. The younger Mantarian was frantically trying to stem the flow of blood from his hand. He jolted up his head and glared at Linsey. She knew Adam was bearing down on her, but did not break her gaze at Max.

"You must take command now."

Adam came at Linsey full bore, an angry yell sounding through the room. His knees bearing his weight came down on her midsection and his right arm swung around, connecting his hard, curled fist directly with the left side of her face. The cracking sound of the blow shocked Max, and a high-pitched cry of pain escaped Linsey. The force of his blow and the follow-through made Adam lose his balance, and he swayed on top of Linsey, then stood up, grunting and swearing. Adam's weight gone, Linsey slumped over to lie on her side.

Hands against the wall and leaning over her, Adam held his wounded hand and cursed over and over through labored breathing. Shaking his head he glanced back at Max.

"I am going to take this bitch apart!" He kicked Linsey hard in the stomach, grunting as he did so. "I wish she were more special to you." Linsey groaned and tried to bring her bound legs up to protect herself, but Adam just kicked them away. "Then what I'm going to do to her would make us... square."

Max looked at Linsey. Tears of pain ran down her bruised face, and trickles of her own blood from her nose and mouth. Then Max looked up at Adam, and his brother broke his gaze at Linsey to look back.

"Say goodbye."

Max's face was a mask of helplessness as Adam moved over to put his hard-toed boots directly in front of Linsey's face. Linsey looked in delirium and pain at Max, and closed her eyes. Adam raised back his leg and sneered. "Shame about the face".

The door to the room opened.

"Dammit!" Adam cried out as he rolled his eyes and looked up at the ceiling. "Give me some more TIME will you?" He sighed and rocked his head sideways, looking in frustration at the doorway.

Just in time to take Darian's lunging punch squarely in the jaw.

twenty eight

Darian had opened the door intent on simply surprising whoever was in the room, hoping in fact that it was empty so that he could scavenge a weapon. Then he'd seen Max bent over with his eyes jammed shut. And Linsey – a moaning bloodied mess on the ground with Adam towering over her.

He'd practically flown across the room, slamming into the younger Mantarian with all of his weight behind his fist. The cracking pain of his knuckles hitting the dense jaw bone shot up his arm. Adam's legs caved in and he dropped to the ground. But Darian didn't stop – with crazed eyes he screamed out a yell and hammered overhanded blows twice more onto the brigand.

Adam was out cold, the first blow having jammed his jaw hard enough sideways to short circuit a nerve to his brain. Gasping for breath and red faced from his exertion, Darian looked back behind him at Max. The Mantarian was wide-eyed from Darian's sudden appearance.

Linsey whimpered in the sudden silence. Both young men whipped their heads around to stare in concern at their commander. She let out a slow, shaking cry, and moved her bound arms upwards towards her chest in a protective motion. A huge bruise was already showing through the thin hair on her face, and there was blood streaming from one of her ears.

"Comman- Linsey!" Darian stumbled on his knees off of Adam and came up beside her, his hands reaching out to her bound wrists. He was sopping wet and icy cold. At his touch her claws instinctively flashed out and she swiped at him, growling deeply from her chest. Darian snatched his hands back in surprise.

"The door. Get the door!" Max's urgent call came from behind them. He was still bound and on his chest, but was struggling earnestly again against his bonds.

Still taken aback, Darian's stark worried face was locked onto Linsey, with drips of seawater coming from his hair down onto his face. He'd never seen anyone so badly beaten in his life. He felt a hard pull in his chest as he thought of how she must have gotten to this state.

"Darian! The door! They'll come back in a minute!" Max pleaded, trying hard not to raise his voice and alert the other roughs. "Shut the door and lock it!" He grunted, struggling still with the ropes binding his hands. "Then come get me out!"

Darian jumped, skittered up off the floor and stumbled over to grab the edge of the door and jam it shut. Then he fumbled with the lock and engaged it, turning to rest against its inside with a deep breath.

"Great! Now come ge-"

"I know! I know!" Darian shot back, face red as he took two soppy strides to his friend and bent down. "I got myself this far," he grunted in frustration as he untied the knots holding Max's hands in place. It didn't take long to get him free. "I thought you guys were dead for sure."

"We were." Max muttered. His eyes looked very tired to Darian – face weary from tears and exertion. "They already killed Commander Craig over there. And... Karthow."

"Your brother killed her?"

Max gulped, frowning hard but not responding verbally. At that point his legs were free and both young men started for Linsey. She had stopped whimpering and was simply lying on the floor with her eyes closed.

Darian was worried about trying to free her. "Careful, I think she's a bit freak-"

"I am fine, Mister Carver. Please release me." Her voice was soft and even, and her breathing had calmed significantly.

Max moved forward and gripped her lithe wrists, using his dexterity to quickly pull and release the knots. As the commander was released she sat up, then leaned against the wall and started to stand. She brushed some of the gore from her chest and put her other hand on the bruise welling on her cheek. Her motion was unsteady and she started to lean to the side, teetering on one leg.

Darian jumped to grab her, supporting her weight by holding her elbow and giving her something to lean against. She pulled away, apparently surprised by how cold and wet his hands were.

Her face turned to look at him. Inches apart the two stared at each other – Linsey's deep green irises searching his face in dizzy confusion for a moment. She seemed to be disconnected, gazing back in time. Seeing someone else.

Darian's own wide eyes were full of concern, and he just stood still for a moment and held her up. She closed her lids for a moment and did a slight shake of her head to clear it.

"I can see why Captain Vrue hates these brigands so much," she sighed.

Max wasn't with them – he was a step away standing over Adam's crumpled form, a deep frown on his face and his brows set in painful loss. The younger Mantarian's face was bruised as well, but devoid of tension as he lay unconscious.

"What happened? How did he change - to get like this?" he said softly, closing his eyes. "What did they do to him?"

"I can only imagine," Linsey offered, standing up more fully as she appeared to shrug off her grogginess. "He probably went out to find himself, and got lost. Among these spoiled men. They taught him he had to be like them... or else. That their way was the only real way to survive. To get what you want." She sniffed and took a step towards them, coming away from Darian's support. "And so he gave up his liberty to purchase his safety."

Max turned his head to look back at Linsey with the same sad frown. He appeared completely at a loss. Linsey reached down to the floor to pick up the ropes that had previously bound her. Then she tossed them at the larger young male, her brows knit.

"He deserves neither. Tie him up."

"But then what?" Max protested. "He'll wake up in a minute and start yelling. Then the rest of them will come in here and we'll be back where we started."

"We either tie him and gag his mouth, or..." She lifted her right hand and the long forefinger talon flashed out – sharp and gleaming. "Which would you prefer?" She paused a moment to let the choice sink in. The claw retracted slowly, and she tipped her shoulders backwards to shrug out of her blood-soaked jacket. "Here – tie this around his mouth and eyes."

Max grunted and took both the rope and the jacket. Stretched out, the fabric would provide a good gag and blindfold. He started to work on his brother's limp form.

"I set a fire." Darian suddenly offered.

Max looked up and quirked a brow. Linsey turned and gave him a half smile, although it appeared to hurt her face to do so. "Oh, did you now? Creative."

Darian wiped his wet hair back from how it dangled in front of his eyes, and nodded. "We're going to steal that other skiff on the main deck. They'll be fighting the fire and won't notice us."

"Oh are we?" Linsey smiled at his direction. She looked pensive for a moment as she considered. "Good plan, but that skiff cannot outrun this ship. Our escape would be momentary." With her ruined jacket removed, Linsey had pulled her arms about herself to conserve warmth. Darian reached to his lapel to offer his own, but realized he was still soaking wet and cold. Oddly, he'd barely noticed the effect of the elements on himself.

Max yanked tight on the improvised gag around Adam's mouth, then dropped his head roughly back to the floor. He stood and looked at Linsey and Darian. "Give me thirty seconds in the engine room and I can kill at least half their power. For a good long time. They won't be able to catch us."

Linsey rubbed her arms with her hands in an apparent effort to warm them. She was still shaking from her ordeal with Adam, and Darian wondered if she was actually in shock. He glanced about – noticing the desk and the chair, and what was hung over it. It looked like a navy jacket - a good, thick one. Darian took a step and grabbed it, turning to offer it to Linsey. "Here, put this on."

Linsey paused, looking at it tentatively and not extending her hand. She sighed as if she was about to refuse it, but then logic seemed to get the better of her and slowly her arm came out with fingers extended. She held the heavy fabric gently for a moment, staring at it – then she quickly slipped into the garment. It fit her perfectly.

Darian tried a smile. "Great. Looks good on you."

"It's not mine," Linsey said bluntly, and turned to start for the door.

"We need to take him with us," Max spoke up. Darian looked back to see his friend contemplating his brother's form, still with a pained expression. "I can't tell my mother I just left him here."

Darian was taken aback. "What?! Are you kidding me?" While looking at Max he cast an arm backwards to point at Linsey. "You saw what he did to her, Max. And you can bet this isn't the first time. We... I mean- you guys fight people like him every day. I know he's your brother, but-"

"He's my blood." Max started, cutting Darian off and turning his sad eyes up to meet the argument. His face softened and he glanced back and forth between Linsey and Darian. "You're my brother. Up here." He pointed a finger towards his head, then slowly moved the hand down to rest on his chest. "In here." His eyes and hand dropped down as he regarded Adam again. "He was once. Not any more. But he is my blood."

"You can't help him now," Linsey said stiffly. "And you can't very well carry him to the engine room with you."

"No, but I'd rather have him hate me from prison than be out here hurting more people." Max argued.

Linsey looked to be steeling herself to give a command that would make her decision final. Darian broke in just before her mouth opened.

"I can carry him. I'm strong enough."

Linsey looked doubtful. "He's almost twice your weight. And what about when he wakes up?"

"I can do it. I pack supply boxes bigger than him around. And if he wakes up I'll pop him another one. Or drop him on his head. Anyway – I'll shut him up."

Max looked at Darian and he seemed to brighten for a moment, cracking the hard mask that had been worn into his face.

Seeing a familiar expression emerge, Darian felt something he hadn't for a long time - trust.

Linsey sighed, but still gave a slight smile. "Fine. It seems I'm not going to be able to convince you two it's a bad idea. But, if they see us and we have to run, you will drop him Mister Carver. That is an order."

As Darian and Max lifted Adam over Darian's shoulder, Linsey opened the door a crack. Sounds of angry yelling came in from outside on the main deck.

"I think they've noticed your fire, Mister Carver. Let's move."

twenty nine

Coming out onto the main deck, Max was surprised at the chaotic mess of brigands trying to fight the blaze that was spreading on the left side of the vessel. Men of various races and sizes were yelling at each other and pointing, but hardly any of them were actually doing anything about the flames. Max shook his head and smiled as he moved, the black comedy of it all breaking through the horror of the last few minutes.

They moved as inconspicuously as they could around to the other side of the ship. Max looked back when they got to the platform that held the skiff to make sure the other two were all right. Adam had apparently woken up and was beginning to struggle and issue muffled grunts. In response Darian heaved up and dropped the young pirate on his head. Adam's body landed with a heavy thump at the base of the skiff platform, and went limp. The human looked up at Max and smiled.

"Don't kill him, or you'll answer to my mom," Max grumbled in a low voice. He looked over at Linsey, who was already quietly untying the small boat from its platform. "Commander, I suggest you lift off and drop aft. I'll come through the emergency vent and hop on from there."

Linsey nodded. "We can't hang around – they'll know the moment I lift off. You have two minutes before we're gone." At this Darian jerked up his head, looking worried.

Max looked as confident as he could back at the human. "Thanks for saving our asses. You did good."

Darian smiled, the fear of the danger for his friend seeming to dissipate. "Just cripple this tug and meet us so it wasn't for nothing, ok?"

Max nodded, turned and quickly moved towards the stairs leading below decks. He tried not to think of what had happened to Karthow, and whether he would find her body in the engine room when he got there. His heart started to thump loudly in his chest as he turned at the bottom of the first flight of stairs. He wondered how many roughs he'd have to fight on his way through the bowels of the ship.

Max almost never got to fight, almost never had to. There was a reason his family had chosen him to be the one to go to the academy - his physical size put off even those with a hefty amount of bravado. The navy kept him fit and lean, and the work in the engine room kept him strong. But when it came to combat, Max just tried to end a fight quickly - he just didn't like hitting people.

Luckily, it seemed as if all of the ragtag crew were up on the main deck telling others to fight the fire, or watching from a distance so they wouldn't have to get involved in the distasteful hard and dangerous work. Coming up to the door that he and   Karthow had crashed through earlier, he pulled up in his steps and stared at it for a moment, gulping.

What am I going to find? he mused as his face became taut with anxiety. He knew she was dead – but the pictures he'd tried so hard not to form in his head when he'd been forced to hear them...

Before he could move, the door opened in front of him. He flinched instinctively, and his heart jammed itself up into his throat.

Vek blinked, a surprised look on his face settling only for the merest of moments before his trademark toothy grin settled in.

Max scowled and dropped his shoulder, springing on his back legs to try to crash into the Drago, expecting his weight to bowl the spiked male over. As he flew through the air towards the open door, Vek seemed to vanish in front of him. Max felt a sharp forceful kick in his side, one hard enough to abruptly alter his path through the air. He slammed into the side of the hallway and fell to the floor, his momentum having carried him only to just outside the engine room door.

Vek stood over him, laughing loudly at his failed attempt to attack. "Okay," his gravelly voice ground out, "I'm curious now." He eased down to his haunches.

Max tossed himself onto his side and kicked out his powerful legs in Vek's direction. But the Drago twisted sideways and grabbed the Mantarian's upper leg with a taloned hand, before smashing the pointed elbow of his other arm down onto the meat of the muscle in the upper calf. Max screamed at the impact, an intense pain shooting up and down his leg.

Vek chuckled and let go of him, seemingly unconcerned at giving Max the freedom to strike again. His tone was slow and even, almost jovial.

"You got out of that room, somehow – and I'm not surprised with how useless your brother is. And then you come down here. Just so I can kick your ass. Now why would you do that?"

Max pulled up his knees, starting to get up. Vek made a fist, and tiny sharp spikes extended from the knuckles of his fist. He punched into Max's soft belly just below the ribs. The wind rushed out of the Mantarian's chest and the muscles in his midsection cramped down at the stabbing pain, refusing to let his lungs work properly. He wheezed and collapsed again. Vek stood up.

"How you think I got where I am?" the Drago grumbled. "Survival of the fittest, my friend. And that's me. All you've done is piss me off." His arms went behind his back and he quickly shrugged his thick jacket onto the floor, exposing his and thick muscular arms. "I'm not even sure we should take you back to put you with the others. Maybe I should just solve your brother's problem right now." He gritted a smile at Max, then extended his arms. Along the outside of his forearms sharp curved scales extended themselves like knife blades.

Max tried the only thing he could think of – he pulled his knees up under himself again and somersaulted forward, through to just inside the engine room door. He sprang up, turning to show his fists.

Luckily, Vek hadn't moved this time. All he did was quirk a brow, his smile fixed despite his description of his mood. He shook his head slightly. "You don't honestly think you can beat me."

Max huffed, finally able to pull some air back into his chest to respond.

"I'm not trying to."

His hand flashed out – grabbing the edge of the door and slamming it shut in Vek's face. He spun the lock mechanism and stood back, wondering if the Drago was strong enough to break down the door himself. But all Max heard was muffled laughter.

"What are you going to do?" Vek said through the door.

Max ignored him. He turned and came up in front of one of the engine panels, stabbing out a finger and concentrating on the lights and readings that flashed out at him. He pressed a few buttons, then looked around, searching the familiar layout of the room. Vek continued his jibes through the door.

"What? You're gonna blow up the ship? With your brother and your precious commander on it?"

Max found what he wanted – a hydrospanner. Small and shaped in a half curl at one end, it was extremely dense. He stepped over to the right, and pulled a lever. In response a panel on the far right of the ship shifted and opened – letting in a gleam of light from the outside and making the atmosphere in the engine room suddenly cooler.

Vek smashed into the door. It held, but the wood around its metal hinges cracked and splintered from the impact. "You think you're making me any happier pulling this stuff?" Again the door bucked as the Drago crashed into it from the far side.

Max jammed the spanner into a small hole in the engine, ducking to the side as he did so. A jet of flame blasted from the opening, and the sound of grinding metal shrieked out. Black smoke puffed from the wounded machine and started to fill the cabin.

Vek's third attempt at breaking down the door was successful – its top hinge popped off and the heavy wooden panel slid sideways then thumped onto the deck. The smoke in the engine room billowed out the door. Max was already gone, having moved quickly over to the emergency vent. He held his breath as he attempted to squeeze through.

Linsey and Darian were right there – barely a half meter from the side of the ship. Max toppled out the opening and fell into the skiff, right beside his brother's wriggling form. As they pulled away Max swore that he saw Vek's angry face staring through the smoke that had followed him out the emergency vent.

thirty

With Vek engaged below decks and the fire that Darian had started spreading quickly, the roughs were almost powerless to do anything about the skiff's liftoff. Two of the ragtag men ran over to the side of the ship and each fired single shots at the trio in the skiff, but they seemed reluctant to waste any more of their ammunition. It was very hard to find or improvise shot for the Navy guns they had stolen, and it was obvious there was little chance of stopping the escapees by that point.

Linsey had dropped the skiff back behind the *Kristoff* and sided up to the emergency vent. When Max had made his presence known by having opened it from inside, she'd felt a swell of relief.

Darian had looked back at her with a grin, and she hadn't been able to stop herself from responding in kind. Their situation was desperate, but at the same time they were working together seamlessly. Linsey knew that feeling connected to others for a common purpose was what grounded her - it was the part of her life she loved the most. Once Max had fallen into their craft beside his brother, Linsey steered the skiff away. With thick smoke coming from the emergency vents, the *Kristoff*'s speed suddenly and drastically dropped. Linsey flew their much smaller boat off at an angle and through some thick clouds to further discourage pursuit. "Great job, Mister Ford." She called to Max.

Max got up from his prone position to nod slowly at her – but he was not smiling. A hand went to his ribs and he grimaced as he looked at the blood that oozed through his white shirt when he pulled it away. Linsey could tell he was in considerable pain.

Darian leapt to his side. "Max! What happened – did you get knifed?"

Max shook his head, swallowing hard as he shut his eyes. Linsey evened out the skiff's attitude and engaged the throttle and control locks. She left the rear of the small craft to come up and help assess Max's condition. As she came forward Adam's body started to shift and move, his covered head lifting itself up. She barely resisted the urge to kick him in the head to knock him out again.

"It was that Vek guy. He's... sharp."

"Yeah. He got me too, but not too deep. Looks like he swiped you worse. But... you gave him some, right?" Darian jibed. Linsey could tell he was trying to gauge Max's reaction, to see if the Mantarian was able to return the jest and demonstrate that he was going to be all right. He didn't – he just looked at the both of them, then shook his head. Darian gulped, looking more worried.

"I'll be fine," the large Mantarian grunted. "Nothing deep. Just some cuts. I heal fast."

"I should have gone," Linsey muttered in frustration. Instinctively she looked down as she pondered how the fight would have gone if she had been the one to go to the engine room. In doing so her eyes could not help but take in what she was wearing – Culley's red Captain's jacket. Linsey frowned with anger, feeling the heat of shame in her face and the itch to extend her claws. She forced herself to look back at the pair of young men. Linsey could tell Max's spirit had somehow been affected by his run-in with Vek.

"He's a Drago, Max," Darian offered. "You're not going to beat him that easily."

Max looked back, visibly depressed. "That's what he said. He knows it." He blew out his breath and started to close his blood-stained jacket, tying the two buttons on the front to keep it tight to his body. "All of them know it. Just makes me wonder what the point is."

"The point of what? Of fighting them?"

Max nodded. "They're not going to stop. They believe in something different than us. Their... philosophy. It works different from ours."

"Whoever's the strongest wins?"

"I don't know. I just don't see how we're going to... change them." He looked over at his brother lying in the bottom of the skiff. "Prove to them why our way's better than theirs."

Linsey tried to think of a way to lift their spirits. After a moment she gave up, deciding to think through it rather than show any kind of false bravado.

"You can't," she sighed. "They understand simple rules. Strength. Intimidation. They think they're the fittest."

Darian seemed to mull her words for a moment. "What if they are?"

Linsey felt her red hair blowing around her face and heard the wind whistling in her sensitive ears. As she stared at the young men she felt Captain Vrue talking to her. Through her.

"Strength is only one attribute, Mister Carver. Compassion, Courage, Intelligence, Integrity..." She paused. It felt comforting to be able to lean on the teachings of her mentor. She knew they were part of her now, easily feeling the truth in the words. "How many of those traits do you think Vek has?"

Max looked up at her, and took a deeper breath as he closed the last button on his jacket. His face seemed more relaxed. Darian was watching him, and smiled a bit seeing his friend's relief from pain.

"No one has all of them," she continued. "But together – you, me, Mister Ford, Captain Vrue. Our... society. What we all want, together. We can achieve far more than they can."

She turned around to go back to the skiff's controls. "Now, we need to find the *Archer*."

"No. We can't," Max's objected.

Linsey quirked a brow and looked over her shoulder at him. "Mister Ford, you are not invulnerable and you may have internal injuries that ar-"

"I'm fine! I got cut and winded. The bleeding has even stopped. I just needed a minute." He huffed a breath and swallowed again, before jutting his chin in Adam's direction. "He knows where the others are."

Linsey was confused, and looked down at Adam for a moment, before returning her quizzical gaze to Max. "What others?"

"The crews. From the *Kristoff*. The *Raven*. And probably any other ships the pirates have taken. He knows where they are."

Linsey's eyes widened. "How?"

"Vek said he was going to put me back with them. I'm sure he wasn't lying. I think they've got a base of some kind. A... pirate's den."

"What would they want with the crews?" Darian protested. "Why wouldn't they just kill them all?"

Max shook his head. "I don't know," he admitted as he continued to stare at Adam. "But I'm sure he knows where they are."

Linsey's head spun as she considered what they should do. Both Max and Darian turned to stare at her, searching for direction. She clenched her jaw and shut her eyes, trying to think despite the attention.

What is the right thing to do?

Except for the soft grunting noises that Adam made as he struggled and the wind of Zefphyr blowing past the skiff, there was silence. She knew what she wanted to do - follow the direction her heart pushed her in and help their comrades. But she felt the weight of the jacket she was wearing around her, and knew the fear of making the wrong decision.

"We've got to go back," Darian interjected in a pleading tone. "Ford is hurt and it's too dangerous. Captain Vrue would-"

"Captain Vrue isn't here." Max protested, even though his voice strained through obvious pain.

Captain Vrue isn't here.

Something clicked inside Linsey, and in her mind she felt comfort. The same confidence she'd had when speaking a moment before. She had been weighing her decision and now she'd made it. She opened her eyes, almost smiling from the release.

All right.

Without looking at the two young men she turned and took a step towards Adam, reaching out to pull the improvised blindfold and gag from his head. The younger Mantarian huffed and blinked for a moment from the change in brightness to his eyes. When he could focus he snorted and spat bloody phlegm at Linsey.

She didn't flinch. She simply held up her right fist and curled her index finger. Her long primary talon suddenly jabbed out from her paw, unsheathing like a stiletto knife. In a macabre mirroring of the way that Adam had sat on top of her on the *Kristoff*, she slowly shifted her weight down on his midsection. Leaning forward, she put her razor claw to rest at his throat.

Adam's eyes widened, and he glanced past her in Max's direction. Linsey did not look up. She did not smile. Her jaw clenched and she started to push the sharp edge of her talon into his throat, until she saw a trickle of hot blood run over it.

Adam squawked, and started to convulse and kick his bound legs as Linsey continued to push forward. She stared squarely into his terrified eyes.

"Max!-" Adam gurgled in desperation and strained to see around her.

"Where are they?" Linsey growled softly. She gently grated the tip of her claw over the large artery that strained out in his neck as he gasped for breath.

Adam gulped – the motion making her claw poke into him again. He winced and tears trickled down the sides of his face. Linsey forced herself to stay still – to push as far as she needed to push. After a moment Adam's breath quieted as he relaxed, shutting his eyes. He gave in.

"They're... at... Crag Cove."

At the admission Linsey withdrew her claw the merest fraction of an inch. She'd come close to giving up herself, knowing how difficult she must have been making it for Max. But she'd also known that Adam had been conditioned to be controlled. To fear for his life and to capitulate to a stronger presence. To Vek.

"You're going to tell us where Crag Cove is," she responded to him after a moment. Her voice was only slightly higher, but her razor talon still pressed into his neck. He had already been beaten.

"263 West, 125 North," he wheezed.

Linsey withdrew her claw, and wiped the blood on it onto his shirt. She put her other fist into his breast bone and pushed herself up to standing, turning to look at her comrades. Max's face was directed down at the deck, eyes closed as he held a hand to his injured abdomen. Darian just stared at Adam with a clenched jaw, a look of pity on his face.

"There's no point. You'll never get them out," Adam called to Linsey's back, growling as he recovered. "There's too many of us! We've got weapons - ships!" He looked around, as if trying to spy the *Kristoff.* "You're going to try to beat them there in this thing? They'll get there first! They know you're coming. They'll kill every one of them we've captured. They've probably called back to the cove already."

"Hm. Not with smashed comm gear and broken engines, they won't." Linsey countered confidently. She stood in the middle of the skiff and looked down at Max for a moment. "We're going for our people. Mister Ford, deal with your injury as best you can."

"I'll be fine, Captain." Trained to respond, he acknowledged her command without thinking.

Linsey's ears perked, and she stiffened knowing his response had been natural. It was the first time anyone had addressed her at that rank. She stoically watched the clouds move past them for a moment, etching the memory of the moment in her mind.

"Mister Carver, do you know how to drive this skiff?"

Max rolled his eyes. Darian just grinned.

thirty one

Darian finally felt cold. His clothing was still wet from his dunk in the ocean, and the stiff breeze that blew by the skiff cut into him like icy razor blades. He held his teeth tightly together and concentrated on his piloting, leading them over and around treacherous rocky terrain. They had come much further inland from the areas of the archipelago and oceans, and now the ground under them became ragged, barren and empty.

At the front of the boat Linsey kept her keen eyes out for any other ships. Adam sat in the bottom of the skiff out of the wind, his eyes clamped shut and a scowl on his face.

"If there are Navy people there, how are we going to get them out? On this thing?" Darian asked over the rush of passing air.

Linsey didn't turn around, she just kept her eyes on the terrain and yelled out so that they could hear her. "We improvise, Mister Carver."

"I hear that stock boys are good at improvising," Max added after a moment with a smile.

Darian felt a stab in his chest at the comment. His cheeks burned and his heart sank. While he was glad that his friend was feeling well enough to jibe, the comment still hurt. "I'm not a stock boy any more," he said with a frown, staring at the Mantarian. He knew inside he was where he was supposed to be now. Doing what he was meant to do. How could he be wrong about that?

"Look, it was a joke, ok? I told you I was grateful for what you did." Max stated flatly.

The two young men locked eyes for a moment. Darian could not help his anger at Max's comments. He'd done so much, but now felt like an impostor.

"Mister Carver." Linsey's head and eyes stayed pointed forwards - she had yelled out to be heard. Darian felt a sinking in his chest, assuming she was going to make a point of agreeing with Max.

The felid let the sound of the air rushing past them intercede for a moment more. "You are only a stock boy until you believe you are not."

Darian took a breath, calming himself through the flush in his cheeks. Then he looked Max in the eyes. "I'm not."

Max sighed. "I'm sorry. Look- I'm serious, I-"

"Mister Carver, reduce our forward velocity, and bring us down within three meters of the ground." Cutting off Max, Linsey's command was given in a stiff, staccato sentence.

Darian responded immediately to the directions and did as she said. Cutting down through the air between rocky outcrops and out of the blowing winds, Darian could see a large lake of dirty polluted brown water in front of them. In the distance on the far side was an angular gray and white shape – something that he realized after a moment was a ship's sail.

"We're here." Max said, having turned to look forwards himself. Then the Mantarian grunted and swiveled his body around to move closer to Adam. "Aren't we?"

Adam said nothing. He maintained his position in the bottom of the boat, with jaw and eyes fixed shut.

"I can see one sail, but that's it," Darian stated as he brought the skiff to a standstill just above the craggy ground. "Can you see more than that?"

Linsey was quiet for a moment before answering. "There are two ships there – a hauler and a corvette. Tied up to a dock with three shacks and a turret. There's space for a third boat that's not there. Probably a berth for the Kristoff. And... there's a..." she trailed off.

Darian stood up and squinted in the direction of the pirate's den, trying to see what the felid saw. He blinked his eyes repeatedly, knowing he could probably never see the distance she was able to. "A what?"

"A... hangar. Or... closed off building. Something like a dock. Partially over the water, with doors that are closed right now. Big doors." She made a puzzled face, half frowning at her inability to comprehend the arrangement. "There's also a black building on the right – very dirty. Another smaller one is built halfway into the ground. Must be a bunker or storage facility. This group appears quite organized. I'm surprised."

"Why? You think we can't figure stuff out?" Adam said from his place in the bottom of the skiff. His eyes remained closed and his voice was full of anger. "We can't make our own rules and organize ourselves? That we're perfect idiots?"

All three Navy members were silent for a moment.

"No," Linsey answered. She came forward to stand over him. "Nobody's perfect."

Adam grunted, fuming.

Max shook his head and smiled. Darian ignored the jibe and pressed with the question that had gotten them here. "Can you see any Navy people? Ships? Or... debris?"

"No." Linsey answered immediately. "The black building has bars on the windows, so it could be a prison. If they captured Navy ships they've either scuttled them or broken them down." She pursed her lips and thought. "That would be hard work, which these men seem to be allergic to."

"What if they used the crews to break them down?" Max queried. "The crews would know how the ships work and how to make the most out of the parts. If they had an engineer like me, they could-"

"Well, they probably do. I know there was at least one engineer on each of our escort ships - the Raven and the Kristoff," Linsey confirmed.

"If they need to break down Navy ships for parts, and they have at least one engineer, they'll use them to do that. Killing them would be stupid."

"Until they're finished," Linsey stated. "Then the period of their usefulness will be over." She sighed, and turned to look across the ruined lake at the pirate's den in the distance. "Let us hope that they are doing something in that hangar that they need the crews for."

"What are we going to do?" Darian asked.

"We're going to come in from the east," Linsey said confidently. "I can see some cover and we can get close without being seen. Then you and Mister Ford will check out the black building and see if you can free any prisoners you find without alerting the roughs to your presence," Every statement was made matter-of-factly, as if she'd seen this precise situation before and was reciting from a textbook. Inwardly she praised herself on learning the technique from Captain Vrue. "I will examine the hangar with the large doors, then assist you."

Adam jerked up from his position in the bottom of the skiff, trying to right himself. His bonds strained and he grunted, swearing at them.

Darian smiled at the reaction. "Sounds like the right plan."

"Yes, apparently" Linsey agreed, and sat down beside Adam. She picked up the trailing end of the piece of rope he was tied with, and began to affix it to the seat she sat on. "We'll have to leave him in the boat."

"What if they find him?" Max protested. "They'll free him and he'll tell them where we are. What we're doing."

Linsey sighed. "We kill him or we leave him in the skiff. You have a better idea, please let me hear it."

Max frowned and seemed to think hard for a moment. Darian knew it was pointless – the only options were those already on the table.

"Right. Mister Carver, take us around to the east edge of the cove."

thirty two

It was easier to hide the skiff than Linsey had anticipated. Coming in at an oblique angle to the brigands' base had given them enough cover, and Darian had proven his skill in keeping their vessel low to the ground. Touching down amid thick brush, they made almost no sound as they stowed the vessel's small sails and jumped over its sides onto the ground.

Tied up and with his mouth securely gagged once more, Adam's protests were hard to notice.

Linsey had immediately sent Darian and Max off on their assignment to investigate the imposing black building. Her own interest was fixed on the large hangar-like structure protected by the enormous wooden doors.

Fascinated at the idea of well-organized roughs, she crept closer to the structure using the craggy rock outcrops and thin bushes as cover. Every few feet she would stop, watch, and listen for signs of a guard patrol.

Coming up to the side of the building, the felid exploited shadows as much as possible to complete her reconnaissance in relative safety. While scanning the outside of the structure for portals or windows, about halfway along the exterior wall she found a door. The only access seemed to be from a clearly marked pathway that trailed in a roundabout fashion the direction that Darian and Max had gone.

She agonized over whether to do the obvious – go up to the door and open it – or to wait for something or someone to exit or enter the portal. She knew she didn't have a lot of time - Max and the Darian would follow their orders and return to the skiff. Setting her brows, she slunk closer and closer to the side wall, having only a few small barrels to crouch down behind.

A noisy shuffling came up from the bushes behind her and she froze, trying to make herself as small as possible in the tiny shadow afforded by the containers around her. Gritting her teeth she peered out to watch the approach of a single dirty male Impalan. The squat horned male was grumbling and seemed preoccupied, kicking the ground as he moved slowly towards the hangar structure.

Only one, Linsey thought. A vicious grin came over her face. *This won't be that hard.*

"HOY!" the Impalan yelped at the door in a loud bellow. Nothing happened. He sounded angry and frustrated as he continued to grumble under his breath. He moved closer to where Linsey was crouched beside the building and yelled again.

"Well...?! I'm here!" He raised a flat hand and slapped his buttocks with it, grinning stupidly for a moment. "Mooooove-em out!" Linsey quirked a brow.

The Impalan reached behind himself to pluck a Navy-issue heavy metal spike gun from the small of his back. Whipping it around he pointed it randomly at the sky and fired. The bright flash of the muzzle imprinted itself for a moment on Linsey's retina, and her shoulders hunched down instinctively from the loud crack of thunder that erupted from the weapon. The brigand chuckled as the echoes of the blast faded.

The door to the hangar next to the containers swung upwards on hinges at the top of the door. Bright light from inside sprang from the hole in the wall, making the angry male outside squint and curse as he shielded his eyes.

Linsey could not see around the containers. She wagered that even if she could, the light from inside would have hurt her eyes as well. Gritting her teeth, she puzzled over the brigand's bizarre remark. Shadows came into the light cast from the portal. Then the scraping sound of dirt being moved by tired, shuffling feet.

"Move it! Move it! Move it!". The angry rough outside the door waved his gun around indiscriminately in the direction of the figures coming out of the door. "No lollygaggin' or talkin' today, or I'll put another one of ye into the ground!"

Beside Linsey on the other side of her cover several people staggered tiredly outside, casting long shadows in the lee of the streaming bright light. Two came out in a line. Then four. Then four more – ten in total.

They were Navy. Still in uniform. Ragged and dirty, with hands bound – but Navy. All men.

Linsey's teeth clenched and her razor claw instinctively deployed from her right hand. She tried to see as best she could the ranks and races that had been captured.

The raised door to the huge structure suddenly fell closed behind the ten prisoners with a loud bang, cutting off the blinding light. The hoodlum and his charges blinked again and shook their heads as their eyes adjusted. Linsey just closed her own to let them clear, knowing they would quickly do so. Thinking and listening to the sound of the prisoners' shuffling feet, she resisted the urge to leap out and attack their captor. There was no question in her mind that if he was alone she could have killed him quickly and silently. But she knew he would get at least one shot off. He did not seem to be drunk, simply angry. And there was nothing between him and the prisoners.

Ten. How was she going to rescue ten? She struggled to place them in the skiff in her mind. A couple of them were larger than a Mantarian – certainly enough weight by themselves to slow any escape. With only Linsey, Max, and Darian in the skiff it was fast and agile. But with thirteen on board, it would barely move and be nearly impossible to steer. Any pursuit from the pirate vessels she had seen tied at the docks would end quickly – and not in their favor.

Improvise, Linsey recalled her own comment from before and sighed, frustrated at its simplicity.

She started to move after the line of bruised and disheveled men as they wound their way into the trees separating the black prison building from the hangar. Then she stopped, looking back. She knew where they were going but she didn't know where they had been, or what they had been forced to do. She turned back, coming up close to the door the captives had come out of.

There was a point at which Linsey knew she could not remain hidden and at the same time gain entry to the building. She had to take a chance – and she did, coming right up to the portal and examining it closely. A small indentation in the right edge of the panel was visible. Stepping to the side of the door she worked her fingers closer to the crack and then finally into it.

The door sprang open, swinging upwards silently and allowing the brilliant glare of light to splash out onto the ground again. Linsey slipped through the hole, crouching down to try to be as inconspicuous as possible.

She forced her eyes to stay open, which caused her irises to shrink further than was comfortable. But even then, she could not see for a moment after entering.

Moving sideways, she bumped into a large solid box and slid her shoulder down its side to rest on her knees on the floor. Her heart pounded in her chest as she waited for her vision to clear. Waited to feel the impact of a gun butt on her head, or a to hear a shout of discovery.

Her eyes finally adjusted, although she still had to squint. The brilliant light was coming from everywhere – up above and from the sides. But she could see that she was in a corridor formed by boxes on either side of her – scattered containers with small spaces between them. Moving up off her knees she jammed her body into one of the crevices – pushing hard to get out of the immediate line of sight. Just as she was sure she was concealed, the door she had come through slammed shut with a bang.

She winced at the noise and jammed her eyes shut again, listening. She heard and felt nothing.

The prisoners certainly weren't here on their own, she mused and redoubled her efforts with her keen ears.

After a few more moments of silence she peeked out, letting her eyes take the time they needed to fully adjust. Brilliant spotlights were everywhere, pointing down and towards the center of the enormous building - towards a gigantic steel-reinforced wooden hull.

Linsey looked left, then right. Resting on floating joists, the hull ran the entire length of the hangar and had a characteristic sweep upwards at its rear. She couldn't see all of it, but she knew what it was.

A ship. A vessel bigger than any Linsey had ever seen. Even bigger than the *Prometheus*, somehow. All the markings and styling of the wood were Navy – right down to the rivets which held the hull boards in place. But the shape was... Wrong. Too big. Too mottled together. Masts where they wouldn't normally be. Odd patterns of bulges everywhere.

How in the world did a bunch of brigands build something like this? She swallowed hard and tried to deal with her sense of incredulity. They were organized, and much more sensible than any she'd ever run across before. *They must have the engineers*, she thought as she gritted her teeth.

"The engines are ready. Started up fine. Those fancy self-righteous wet-necks did what they were told to do at least." The voice came from Linsey's left – slightly muffled but becoming louder as the figure which owned it approached. A chuckle followed. "They follow orders pretty well."

"Now we just get rid of them?" A weasely second voice responded.

"Yeah, Psssh. I mean, not me. I'm not going to be the one to do it. Vek is supposed to be back by now. I'm sure he'll do it. Probably enjoy it too."

"What? Just line 'em up and shoot 'em?"

"Shoot 'em? No way. You kidding? You know how much that ammo we got is worth. Naw – I think we're just gonna have a big bonfire."

"A fire?"

"Yeah, you know. Where we're keeping 'em. The... bedding. You know. The straw they're using to sleep on. That'll go up pretty fast. Whoof!"

There was silence for a moment. Linsey's eyes were wide as she thought of the scene of all the prisoners being burned alive inside the black building.

The owner of the second voice spoke again, and seemed to be just as taken aback. "I don't wanna be there for that."

"What? You mean to... watch? Psssh- Me either. Vek gets off on it. Me, I don't like screaming. If I can sneak off I'm going to."

"What? Like Brittan did? You don't think that Vek'll notice?"

There was silence for a moment.

"Brittan was an idiot. He got told to stick around when they passed out the girls, and took off anyway. Did you expect anything different to happen after that?"

"Yeah, well, Vek's pretty good at knowing who's where. I'm not takin' a chance. He wants me to watch, I watch."

There was only a grunt in return.

The sense of urgency that welled in Linsey was difficult for her to control. They said they were finished with the prisoners – did that mean they were going to kill them right away? Right now? *Vek is supposed to be back by now.* She knew he wasn't – but he was coming. Coming fast. The *Kristoff* had been slowed, but not disabled.

If the two men said anything else, it was lost on her. She hunched down behind the her box and crammed her eyes shut again, and for a few long minutes tried to think as terror welled up in her.

There was no time. No resources. No way she could fathom to stop the slaughter. She brought her arms closely around her chest again, hugging Captain Culley's jacket to herself as she tried in vain to find an answer.

Behind her was a snap and a creak as the doorway opened again. Linsey winced and tried to conceal herself even more behind the array of large boxes. The sound of heavy scrabbling feet came from the entrance area.

"Hey! Hey!"

Adam. He was free.

Dammit, Linsey cursed to herself. A tightness in the muscles of her back increased to almost a painful level. How could he have gotten out so fast? *He's apparently very good with ropes*, she gritted.

She could hear the two men upon which she had been eavesdropping move quickly to Adam's calling voice.

"Oh. It's you," the first man replied. "I thought it was someone important."

"Look, dumb-ass, they're here – alright?!" Adam wheezed, trying to sound commanding. "There's three of them. A human, a felid and a Mantarian like me. They're gonna-"

"Whoa-Whoa-Whoa! Who's here? We don't need anybody else. We got barely enough food as it is."

"No! Idiot! Navy. Three Navy here. Probably more coming. Where's Vek?"

"I thought he was with you."

"He's not back yet?" Adam's query was pleading.

"I dunno. I guess not. He'd probably come here right away, you know. Check on progress, so-"

"We've got to get to the docks. Get people together right now. Come on."

Linsey's mind screamed at her. The brigands knew. Every rough would arm themselves and brace for an attack. They would scour every inch of the cove to find the three Navy infiltrators.

She tried desperately to think of a plan. What she could possibly do. She could get out - run to reach Max and Darian to warn them. But then what? Even if they were able to get inside the prison, they would still have to break out at least the ten that she'd seen being led from the hangar. Ten that were guarded by at least one gun. Probably more. All before a simple fire was set. And what if there were more prisoners than the ten she'd seen?

What have I gotten us into?!

BLOOD AND BROTHERS 179

She knew she was responsible – she'd made the decision. And she knew they couldn't just leave the captured personnel to die - burned alive. She knew they had to try something – but what?

The sinking sense of defeat in her stomach made her feel sick as she cowered in the shadows. All she could see was the end. It was if it were already over – that she was defeated. That Vrue had been wrong about her.

Vrue.

What would you do if you weren't afraid?

Linsey began to relax. She took a long breath and unwrapped her arms from around her. Slowly and purposefully she rose and slipped between the crates back towards the door to the hangar.

Whatever happened she knew who she was - what she had to try. What she had to do.

She wasn't afraid any more.

thirty three

"Crap. They're here already."

Max's head turned around and he peered over Darian's mottled hair towards the docks in the distance behind them. They could see the *Kristoff* slowly siding up to the furthest dock tower, black smoke streaming from its emergency vents.

"They didn't even stop to fix the engines," Max responded, blowing out his breath. "Well, you heard Adam back on the skiff. Once they get the word up here that the Navy knows about this place, they'll kill all our people."

Darian nodded in response. "How many you think there are?"

They had found a small hole in the side of the stained prison, covered by a patch of thin shrub. Sneaking up to the wall had been easy, although they had to kneel and bunch up close to each other to get completely out of sight. Max turned back and looked through the hole, trying to see which of the cells that were visible were occupied and which were empty.

"Four bad guys inside. There's probably others around the other side at the front. At least forty Navy in about nine cells. I can't see any officers, though."

"You think they killed them already?"

Max's face muscles tightened and he felt a sinking feeling in his gut. "Probably. Either that or they're being held somewhere else. Separated." He turned again to look at Darian.

The human's face was equally strained. "I hope so." He looked downwards for a moment, towards Max's midsection. "Are you up for this? I mean... with your..."

Max frowned, snorting. "I'm fine. Stop trying to take care of me. You have to deal with pain sometimes." He turned back to the hole to size up the situation one last time. "I've been doing this a lot longer than you have."

"Yeah, sorry about that." Darian's angry voice gritted back at him, almost loud enough to penetrate the hole and be heard inside. "I've been busy paying the price for the epic screw-up of my father. So sorry to let you down like that."

The words stung in Max's ears. His shoulders slumped, face tilting downwards. They'd both been acting more like their old selves, but Max still felt this was the last place and time to be dealing with their feelings. Unable to speak, he just turned his eyes to look at the human.

"What you going to do now?" Darian continued to bite out at the same volume. "You know what to do? You know how to handle this? Being in ships for a couple of years sitting in engine rooms taught you all you need to know, huh?"

"Ssssh," Max hissed silently. "Look, Darian, I-"

"Don't call me that. My friends call me that. People who don't think I'm a loser call me that. You going to tell me what we're going to do here, Mister Ford?"

Max's chest constricted in anxiety. He really didn't know what to do. He was hands-on at fixing things and making machinery work, doing things in ways that could be perfected. This was a situation where there was no perfect solution – no matter what they did. No procedure to follow. He gulped and just looked back at Darian's glaring eyes, inches from his face.

"Maybe I'm worth more than a stock boy, then, huh?" Darian queried, lowering his voice to a whisper.

"Ok, I get it, ok?" Max's stressed reply pleaded in defense. "I'm... sorry."

"We're gonna save these guys." Darian stared his icy glare for a moment more. "I'll apologize myself when we're done, ok?"

Max knew that Darian had been angry, but also knew that some of the things he had said were true. Some been justified. He did want Darian's apology – and did want to earn it.

"Now, you gonna stay here and die, or start being my friend again?" Darian stated flatly.

Max blew out his breath, grumbling. "Oh gee, let me think on that one."

"Fine." Darian stood up, partially exposing himself. Max's eyes widened, and he had to resist the urge to grab the human by his jacket and yank him back down behind the shrubs.

Darian saw his reaction and stood his ground, staring back into the Mantarian's face as he stood just out of reach.

Max stood himself, even though his instincts screamed at him to remain hidden. After a moment he realized Darian had done it on purpose. To see if the Mantarian was going to react instinctively or was going to trust him.

"We're going to get caught," he sighed.

"If we do, it's your turn to take the heat," Darian chuckled as he walked out into the open. "We have no weapons, no backup – I mean, except for Linsey and she's got that..." he made a claw motion with his index finger and displayed a toothy sneer.

Max looked around nervously. Did Darian intend on just walking out right to the front entrance? They were at the side of the building, but he was coming up fast on its front. The light of day was fading and the shadows that were cast by the side of the building had become deeper.

Right next to the corner of the building, Darian edged up to the wall and peeked around. Max sided up to him quietly in the slight shadow, relieved the human was showing at least some sensibility.

"There's four out front," Darian whispered as he peeked around the corner. "They're playing dice and drinking... Killeagh!" He chuckled at the familiar sight of the electric blue bottle, his mouth curling into a grin. "Some of Brad's magic..." he trailed off.

Max was baffled at the words. He gulped and tried to imagine how he and Darian could handle four drunken armed bullies. "Well, unless you're planning on asking them for some, you're stuck. We can't attack them."

"No, we can't attack them," Darian agreed. "Their friends inside will hear, then we'll be dealing with eight. And some of them probably have guns."

"We don't know what we're doing. We should wait for Linsey."

Darian turned his head to look at Max, scowling as he took a hard mocking tone. "Look – this isn't just pushing supplies from place to place. These are *people*."

Max heard the words and remembered saying each one of them to Darian, back on D'ara's supply ship. He felt the patronizing sting of each syllable. "I don't know what you're used to, but when somebody gives me a job I get it done."

The human turned back to look around the corner once more, making sure nothing had changed about the situation. Then he knelt down and drew a simple box in the dirt.

"This is the building. I'm coming out here, where we are. You go around. You're fast – it won't take you long. Then catch your breath and follow my lead."

"Carver – follow your lead?" Max pined, knowing all too well where Darian's leads used to go when they were in the academy. "What are you going to do? Tell jokes?"

Darian looked straight back at him, obviously very frustrated at the lack of faith he had received. "They're drunk and they're mangy, undisciplined roughs. That means they'll look out for their own skins first. Pumped full of Killeagh they'll listen to suggestions – I say it, they'll think it. Like I said... Magic."

"Well, ok... They attack you, I'll be there," Max sighed reluctantly. It seemed too far fetched.

"You be there anyway," Darian said in a commanding tone. He stood, smoothing out his almost-dry jacket. Stepping out into the open in the front of the building, he smiled. "Just like old times."

Max's neck muscles strained in anxiety as he stepped forward to peer around the corner after Darian. There were four burly brigands sprawled around the doorway to the prison, playing dice and arguing with each other over who's turn it was. One of them stood unsteadily and backed away, cursing – obviously the most recent loser. He took a long swig from a bottle, letting cast-off dribble down and over his sweaty chin.

Darian strode right up towards the group of them, not bothering to soften his footsteps or try to conceal himself behind any of the various broken empty crates lying around.

The ragged man that had stepped out of the player's circle spotted Darian first. A look of stunned surprise covered the rough's face as the smiling young man in naval uniform strode in a relaxed gait towards him.

"Hey!" the pirate called. "Wh- Where did..." He cast an arm around and banged another man on the back to get his attention. The other three men quickly turned their heads and stared wide-eyed up at the human.

Darian kept his smile put his hands out, palms down in a calming gesture. "Relax, relax, it's ok," he said using an exaggerated, patronizing voice. "You're fine. You're fine."

Max gritted his teeth and winced his eyes shut. These were *roughs*! Darian was treating them as if they were underclassmen at the academy. The Mantarian had seen men like these kill for less. Kill brutally.

"Aye, we're fine," the burly loser called. He turned his half-empty blue bottle over in his hand, and abruptly smashed the base against a container box next to him. Glass and Killeagh sprayed over the men who had been squatting on the ground behind him. All four of them formed up in a wide line facing Darian. "Yer not doing so good, though."

He kept walking, to within ten paces of the men before he slowed to a stop and crossed his arms easily on his chest. Max's heart sunk – this was it. There was no way that the human could defeat all four. And what about the others inside the building? So far, the only thing that Darian appeared to be right about was that everything had been relatively quiet.

"You're all going to jail."

The men laughed – all four of them, loudly.

"Oh, are we now? Ye come to take us away?" The largest one took a step towards Darian and brought up the broken bottle.

"No. I'm just here to tell you to surrender."

The smiles wore quickly away from the brutes. The remaining three started walking towards Darian.

Max's shoulder muscles clenched and he squatted down. He could take two of them, he figured. *As long as they don't have guns*, Max thought.

The lead bully pulled a long blade from his trousers with his free hand, using his fingers to wag it menacingly for a moment as he grinned a black-toothed smile at the human.

Or knives, Max's teeth steeled. He stood on the precipice of jumping out to defend Darian, but also knew that if they failed Linsey would be the only one left to possibly offer help to the prisoners.

"Oh, we'll surrender," the leader gritted. "Once I'm through with you."

"There's four hundred of us," Darian said calmly, never breaking eye contact as he idly toed the dirt in front of him. He sighed and his voice became dismissive. "I'm sorry but there's nowhere for you to run to. We're going to catch you now, no matter what."

The men laughed again – the leader first and then the others.

Max cringed. There were no Navy ships in sight, and no other apparent way into the cove.

The lead pirate did stop approaching for a moment, but continued to grin at Darian – apparently enjoying the joke.

"Well, maybe we'll just gut you while we're waiting for them to show, then, shall we?" The dirty man mimicked the same patronizing tone that Darian was using. "No harm in playing while your Army is on the way."

"Navy, not Army." Darian corrected. His voice didn't show the merest hint of concern at his situation. "And murdering me will just get you to the gallows faster. Right now I don't think we really know what any of you have done." He shrugged and raised one corner of his mouth. "You'll just be taken in for having known Vek. Being in the wrong place at the wrong time. Pretty hard to prove otherwise. But..."

He leaned forward for emphasis.

"Kill me and you will hang, anyway. Some of my friends will be here in a minute, and they'll see what you're doing." Darian pointed past the men at the other corner of the building behind them.

All four men turned their heads to look in the direction Darian was pointing. Max's eyes bulged – there was no faking the reaction on their part. A part of them, however small and however inebriated, was considering the possible truth of the drivel Darian spewed.

If Darian was buoyed by this reaction, his voice did not show it. He just easily kicked the dirt in front of himself and waited for the men to turn their faces back to him. "Plus, you guys will turn on each other for sure when they start to question you."

One of the three men behind the leader looked very nervously at the other two. He turned his head and strained through bad eyesight towards the docks, where the *Kristoff* had just come in. Its rear end was still belching black smoke. "Vek's ship's on fire or something," he blurted in a high, strained voice.

"Vek's dead," Darian quickly chirped up, smiling and confidently rocking on his forefeet. "He was pretty hard to kill. Captain Vrue had to drop him – from about a thousand feet over the Daedalus Mesa." The human's smile slowly faded. "Splat."

"I'm sure." The leader said with a sarcastic edge. He brought up his knife and took a step towards Darian. "You're full of it. And I'm gonna gut you and prove it."

"Hey, Carver" Max said in casual greeting as he came around the far corner of the building behind the pirates. His voice was even and relaxed, and the tone of his voice was quiet and sure. Running as fast as he could around the building had certainly raised his heartbeat, and quelling the noise of his labored respiration was difficult.

I wish he'd told me what he was going to do! Max's mind yelled. It didn't matter now – he was committed. This had to work or they were both dead.

"They rounded up the rest of them yet?" Darian boredly asked Max.

The brigands heads swiveled back and forth between Darian and Max – looks of incredulity on their faces. Darian did not smile. Max watched him and continued to try to show a normal face.

"Not yet," he sighed. Relaxing his shoulders he strode within a few paces of the men, seemingly unafraid to come very close to them as he walked towards Darian. "The hangar's done and all the boats down there have been cleaned out. But there's this place and the turret. They're all giving up, though. They said there's eight up here."

The leader of the four men showed wide eyes.

"Vek's dead?" his high-voiced companion squeaked loudly. Then he started nodding to himself. "Dropping him like that's probably the only way you could kill him. And they got the hangar. The ship-"

"Bullshit!" the leader gritted. But his three compatriots' eyes showed their terror as they looked at each other.

"Ok, fine." Darian sounded annoyed. "You just remember this moment when the trap door lets go and you're dancing on the end of a rope. I'm just trying to do you a favor. We're not supposed to hurt you guys – heck, I'm not even armed. They sent us up here first to talk to you, so it's not messy. There's a lot of paperwork when somebody dies."

"Mmm," Max agreed with a low noise. He couldn't help but nervously lick his lips, though. To hide the tell, he spoke loudly and pointed in the direction of the docks. "You boys can walk down to the docks now, turn yourselves in. Or you can give us trouble. Just...", he put his own hands out in the same calming gesture he'd seen Darian use. "Think. Think hard for a minute," he finished, wanting them to do the exact opposite.

The three terrified pirates backed away behind their leader – leaving a significant gap between them. One of them turned and ran around the building to scramble up the hill behind it. The other two looked at each other, then down off to the docks.

"You. think they'll let us off? I mean – not hang us? I didn't kill anybody," the high-voiced one started. He pointed casually at their leader "L-Leam did-"

"SHUT UP!" Leam barked back at him. The leader gritted his teeth angrily and held his knife pointed at Darian. His hand began to shake slightly, belying his own indecision.

"Well, it sounds like you should try to get away like your other friend there did, then." Darian countered. "We're not going to chase you. Our job is to come get our friends out from here and take them down to the docks."

"Nobody's coming," the man seethed through his teeth. "You're lying."

They all stood in silence for a moment, Darian's face rock solid. Inside, Max's stomach turned over as he waited for the men to act - he knew they couldn't hold out much longer with the ruse. Taking a step back, he bowed and made a beckoning motion with his arm towards the docks. "Make your choice then. You can walk down on your own, or wait for them to come up here and teach you a lesson for not listening to us."

The two nervous men looked blankly at each other, then turned together and started to move past Max, walking down the sloping hill towards the docks. They looked left and right in curiosity for signs of the takeover, but kept moving.

When they were more than twenty paces away Max looked back to the leader, who had sweat running down his brow.

"Look - kill me or don't, ok?" Darian said impatiently. He uncrossed his arms and put them on his hips. "We've got work to do."

The man's hand wavered in the air with the knife for a moment more before he dropped it and backed away. Turning, he scrambled around the far side of the building and up the hill, fleeing after his compatriot.

Max looked at the ground and blew out his breath, knees shaking from how long his muscles had been clenched.

I cannot believe this human.

He was incredulous that the ruse had worked, but happily surprised. He was also immediately worried at what this would do to Darian's ego.

"I love Killeagh." Darian stated in deadpan.

Max looked up and took a step towards Darian. "Don't ever do that again," he growled.

"Well, sheesh. What do you think we're going to do with the other four we know are inside?"

"Not that!" Max balked.

"Why not? I mean, it wor-"

"We're going to get caught! That's why!"

"You always used to say that."

"We always got caught!"

"*I* always did. *You* manag-"

"HEY!" A voice yelped at them from behind.

Both young men whipped their heads around to look. In front of them stood a column of ten ragged Navy crew and one angry Impalan rough holding a gun. Max's heart rammed itself up into his throat and his cheeks burned.

"I think we just got caught," Darian murmured.

thirty four

"What the hell's going on?!" The Impalan yelled at them, whirling his gun to point it at the nearest captured Navy crewman's head. "Who the heck are you two? Where's Leam?"

"Why? Does he owe you money?" Darian jibed, chuckling. Max winced.

The hard-headed male seemed baffled for a moment by the impertinent comment, but then his sneer deepened. He turned the gun to aim it at Darian and cocked its hammer.

"You're gonna tell me what's going on, smart-ass, or I'll blow your face off I swea-"

His arm was rammed upwards from behind.

Eyes bugged out, he reached up quickly to his throat to stem a rush of blood that spewed out from his jugular. The gun went off – its heavy transuranic spike blasting through the air to slam into the side of the black building. The Impalan gurgled and fell to his knees, dropping the gun as he clutched at his slashed windpipe.

Linsey stood behind him, a hard frown on her face. She kicked the dying male forwards onto his face, then wiped her claw on her pants. She looked around at the shocked Navy crew – then at Darian.

"They'll have heard that shot. Block that door and hold them in while I free these men."

Max jumped at the command – taking the four steps to the door to the building and jamming his shoulder up against it just as it started to open. A gruff yelp came from inside as the first rough through the door was shoved backwards. Angry cursing ensued.

"How many?" Linsey growled as she rushed from crewman to crewman and slit the bonds around their wrists and hands.

"Four inside, four outside," the prisoner in the lead responded in a croaking voice. Linsey could see that the ten men were weak and dirty – but all of them had stunned, elated expressions that made her own face flush in hope. They'd freed ten. Forty more inside, and only four more guarding them.

"Four inside, that's it." Darian countered as he formed up beside Max to hold the door shut. "At least two of the ones that were outside aren't coming back."

"Good job, Mister Carver. What did you do?"

"Uh, I improvised."

Max rolled his eyes. "He nearly got us killed."

The door they were holding shut surged from an impact from inside. Confused yelling voices from inside offered complaints and jibes.

"Nearly," Darian chuckled as he braced for another impact. "Not quite."

By the next impact, Linsey and all ten crew were ready beside the door. The felid held out the gun straight in front of her.

"Ok, we're ready. They think that we're their friends screwing around. Having fun. Let them come."

Max took a step back in unison with Darian, and together they poised for attack.

The door burst open with a loud bang – two of the burly men from inside having slammed against it together. However, since it was no longer being barred they flew through the portal and fell on their faces to the ground. Max leapt up and tucked his legs underneath him, landing with his full weight on his knees on the back of the larger of the two. With over three hundred pounds of Mantarian impacting on his spine, the man squawked a high-pitched wheeze. Max took no chances – he followed up the crushing blow with a punch to the back of the neck.

The other brigand through the door was grabbed by three of the Navy crew and pummeled. Linsey, Darian and four other crew rushed through the opening. Immediately a large shape lunged at Linsey, and she instinctively swept out with her razor talon. Her arm was blocked in mid-strike and a heavy weight slammed into her, bowling her over to the side. Another shot from the powerful spike gun rang out, blowing the man's body up off of Linsey and sending it flying through the air to hit a wall.

It was over. A single cowardly pirate had his hands stretched as high as they could go in the air as he was surrounded by the angry Navy crews. Linsey did a side roll to get up, then took a step towards the male and stretched out her arm, making the muzzle of the spike gun rest gently on the tip of his nose.

"Mister Carver, Mister Ford," Linsey said loudly. "Help free the others. We have a lot of work to do."

The crewman who had croaked before appeared beside Linsey, looking her up and down now that the excitement of the moment had passed.

"Who are you people?", he asked.

"That's Ford, that's Carver." Linsey jutted her chin in the direction of her two cohorts. "We're from the *Archer*," she added, still pointing the business end of her weapon at the last remaining pirate. "Some roughs tried to capture our ship, and we got away. Found out where they were keeping you."

"Bo'sun Ceres Hall," the man introduced himself. "From your escort, the *Raven*. How many more of you are there?"

"None."

The man looked at Linsey, then Darian, then Max. "J- Just you three? Where's your ship?" he asked, dumbfounded.

"We don't have one. We'll have to try to take at least one from the docks. More, if we can manage it."

"More? Are you crazy? They're armed to the teeth, and their leader-"

"We saved your ass, didn't we?" Max bit back. The man outranked him, but for the moment the Mantarian didn't care. "Now we've got- what? Fifty?"

Hall swallowed hard, then nodded slowly as he stared Max in the face, clearly still afraid of the odds. "Fifty six. Unarmed."

Linsey looked over at Hall and then lowered the gun she had held on the pirate. The man breathed a sigh of relief, but kept his hands raised towards the ceiling. She extended her hand and offered the weapon to Hall. "Almost unarmed. I'm sure we can find some knives and some fire. If they're armed, then they're vulnerable."

The backwards statement even made Max quirk a brow.

"Excuse me?" Hall returned as he took the gun from the felid.

"Armaments explode, Mister Hall. If they captured Navy ships, they've got Navy arms. Explosives, cannon packs and lob detonators."

"Aye, they took all that off the ships," Hall nodded, looking thoughtful about her plan. "Made us pack it in crates and take it to the turret. Then they towed the ships to the hangar."

"There's more than one ship in there, then." Linsey nodded. "From what I saw it looked like one big one."

"It is one big one," Hall grunted in frustration. "At least now it is. They built them up together. Strung the engines and the power couplings. Made us do it all – or else. There was another fifty here when we started, you know. Ones that couldn't work they got rid of. And the women, they-"

"Yes, Mister Hall. I am quite aware of what roughs do with women." Linsey gritted her teeth and looked back at their sole pirate prisoner.

"Any officers left?", Max asked Hall.

"They took 'em all over to the bunker. We haven't seen 'em since we got here. I think they're dead."

Linsey's face became a staunch frown. She took a step towards the rough and her razor claw flashed out. She laid it against the man's throat for a moment, staring into his face. He looked worried, but not scared enough to talk. She quickly moved it downward, towards his crotch and pressed it menacingly against him while he stood, still with arms raised. The change in her target made his eyes widen, and he swallowed hard.

"Are they over there?" she growled into his face.

"Y- yeah. I- I guess," the brigand stammered. "I don't know. I never been in there." He winced his eyes shut as she pressed the point of her talon forwards. "Look, I didn't take any of the women, even when I could I - Rrrrrk!"

It took every ounce of restraint in her to not eviscerate the man where he stood. She felt fiery burning in her cheeks and the animal rage mustering in her chest. Even with the weight of the red coat around her she still wanted to strike out, to free her body and mind from the confines of what she had been taught was morally right.

No-one would care, her mind seethed. *No-one would miss this scum.*

She pulled her talon away, turning back to the rest of the Navy crews and held onto her right hand with her left as she forced her claw to retract. The men around her were looking at her – some in disappointment and some in fear. Darian's eyes were clouded, his face conveying his own mixed feelings.

"We take all the men we have up here and attack the docks," Linsey commanded to get their attention. "In creating confusion among the roughs we stand a good chance of taking over a ship."

"A fast one," Max added. "No use getting away if they're just going to catch us."

"Yes, true." Linsey agreed. "Mister Hall, you said fifty-six?"

"Aye, we're about the same number they are, Captain..." his leading tone requested she fill in her name. Looking at the styling and markings on her coat he had inferred her rank.

"Linsey," she responded without a clarification of her rank. *Not enough time to quibble or explain.* "Get everyone out and set the building on fire. Then Mister Ford will help prepare you for your attack."

thirty five

The prison building burned – red flames licking its stained window portals. The smoke wafted up in the gathering darkness, leaving a pillar of black that pushed its way into the sky.

Darian and Linsey had to cross a small foothill to get to the bunker. The human turned back for a moment and watched the freed Navy personnel organize in the shadows of the flames. Max was with them – helping to improvise weapons and provide support to those crew weakened by their experience as captives. Darian could see him picking people up, slapping them on the shoulders, and peering into their faces to reassure.

Fifty-six in total, Darian mused. Enough to crew at least two of the boats they had seen down tied to the towers at the docks. With what they had accomplished so far, defeating the brigands on the docks to steal back the vessels did not seem so far out of consideration.

"I hope setting that on fire was the right thing to do," Darian mused aloud, lost in thought as he gazed at the spectacle they left behind them.

"They were going to burn it anyway – with our crews inside," Linsey explained. "All we did was make sure that doesn't occur. It can't happen now." She put her hand on his shoulder and pulled him away from the view to walk forward with her again. They entered thick brush on the side of the hill to stay inconspicuous.

"Yeah, well.." Darian muttered. "Now if they catch us Vek'll think of something even worse."

"No matter what happens I don't think they'll take prisoners," Linsey sighed. "Something we should all be prepared for, if the situation looks bad for us."

Darian considered her words for a moment as he moved around branches and shrubs beside her. She had specifically told him to come with her to investigate the bunker. It was hoped that the officers associated with the freed crews were being held in the more secure location. Darian felt a small degree of pride in being her selection as an assistant.

"I don't know what it's like, to look at death." he finally replied, glancing around to make sure they he felt they were still headed in the correct direction. "You've seen it more than once, I know. With my father. Today on the *Kristoff*. I can't even imagine it."

Linsey was very quiet, looking carefully at where she placed her feet as they moved from bush to bush towards the structure built into the hill. Her silence at the mention of his father made Darian intensely curious – she acted as if she was trying to find a way to tell him something.

"Mister Carver, your father-" Her voice was quiet, quieter than he'd ever heard her speak. She stopped talking abruptly, but continued walking. Darian couldn't see her face, but after moment she stopped and turned to him. Her voice stayed quiet.

"The parts of us that matter... can't die."

Darian was confused, and it showed on his face. Linsey took a deep breath and continued.

"I knew your father. My moments with him... changed me – had to change me. Your moments with him changed you. It's in those changes where life lies. You can't stop it. Can't un-do it. Can't kill it." Linsey looked straight into his face, and put her hand on his shoulder.

"Sometimes... the changes are ones we do not like or would not want. It sounds strange, but those pirates I killed, back there. They are part of my life, who I will be from now on. As they are part of everyone they ever met." She paused, sighed and looked downwards as Darian listened. "Vek has changed me. And you... Max... a lot of people."

"A lot of people who didn't want to be changed," Darian injected.

She nodded slowly in agreement. "And some who did not know he was changing them. Like Adam."

Darian swallowed hard, then looked over in the direction they were travelling. "I know how I want to be changed. By people like Captain Vrue... Max... you. I've been waiting a long time to have the chance."

Linsey smiled and turned to start walking again. "I know you have. I promise you, I won't let you be ignored again." She continued walking while Darian stopped for a moment, looking at her back.

What does that mean? Darian thought. The hope welled in him. Hope that this adventure was not just an excruciatingly detailed dream. She knew he could be something more - could overcome his father's mistake. "Mister Carver?"

"Y- Yes, Captain?" He stumbled to follow again, almost losing sight of her among the brush. When he caught up he saw that his unconscious mention of rank made her look down at the red jacket she wore.

"Do try to keep up. We *are* in a hurry."

Within moments they reached a short stone wall built around the bunker. Unfortunately, moving closer put them out of the line of sight with the burning prison building they had just left. Darian realized that they would have no way to gauge the progress of the rest their comrades. They'd simply have to catch up later. They examined the structure from just inside the short barrier, crouching in the long shadows of the late evening. There were no guards outside, and only a small amount of light flickered from the sole window. It did not appear that there was a door – just stairs into a hallway leading inside.

"Looks simple to get in," she sighed. "Which is strange. This place is built to be defended. If there are officers, they're being held here. I'm sure of it."

"Great," Darian responded, equally frustrated. "There's nobody outside to bluff or... steal keys from or anything."

"No." She steeled her teeth and hissed. "And we don't have any ti-"

A hissing sound made Linsey cut her sentence short. She jerked her head left, then right, then up. Darian just followed her stare, knowing that her felid ears would do much better at locating the source of the noise. A bright burst of light came from the sky above them, almost immediately followed by a loud rolling bang. Darian's brows went up as he stared at the incandescent light that hung in the air far above them.

"It's a signal flare," Linsey explained. "They know what's going on."

"How? How could they know so quickly?" Darian's voice wavered on the questions. Having the element of surprise had been one of their chief advantages to even the odds. Now they were surely outnumbered and outgunned.

"I didn't tell Mister Ford this, but his brother managed to free himself."

"Again?! He did that back on the *Archer*."

"Mmph," she mumbled slowly. "He has a way with ropes, then."

"Yeah. Max's whole family does. They do sails. Rigging."

"It was probably he who raised the alarm. And Vek is there." She fixed her gaze back on the bunker. "By now every pirate on the docks is armed. They'll be bracing for an attack from the freed prisoners – and getting the word up here to kill any Navy they see."

"What do we do?" Darian's brows hunched as he tried to think of a possible solution.

Linsey didn't respond verbally. She got up and started to move towards the bunker, staying low but looking away from the structure to be aware of the approach of any brigands from the docks. Darian scrambled to keep up with her. They got within ten feet of the main doorway when the felid held her right hand away from her body, letting her primary claw slide out soundlessly. Darian gulped as he stared at it glinting in the light from the flare. He realized he was scared – they were going to attack, and Darian hadn't had the guts to force a physical confrontation since the last year at the academy. He made fists with his hands, but even his usual bravado felt false.

"Uh, I don't have one of those."Darian stated in a nervous whisper. "Any idea what I should do?"

"Watch my back," Linsey gritted without turning to him. She surged forwards and came up to the side of the hallway housing the stairs that led into the bunker. Darian kept close to her – continually glancing towards the docks. He had no idea what he was supposed to do if someone came running up.

Linsey slipped inside, tiptoeing down the stairs. It was silent. There was no murmur of conversation, no snoring, no sound of revelry and no moans of pain or calls for help. Following her, Darian felt slightly better being inside out of plain sight. But he could also feel a cold emptiness coming from the structure built into the ground. A lifelessness.

At the bottom of the short stairway the hallway split to the left and right, each way leading to short corridors that ended at the side walls. There was only one door off each corridor that appeared to lead to rooms carved out of the hillside. The structure was drastically smaller than it appeared from the outside – obviously simply a tiny housing complex.

Or a torture chamber, Darian frowned.

Looking left, the human could see the doorway on that side was open, with no light coming from inside. On the right the door was closed – offering at least some hope of discovering captives that were still alive. They turned right and tiptoed down the short hallway, illuminated only by flickering light from lanterns at the end of the corridors.

Linsey came close to the wall near the closed door to examine it. Dim flickering light came from underneath it. There was no window in the portal – it was just a simple flat wooded door, with a rusty blue steel latch. A well-worn lock rested on the dirt floor in front of the door, unused. Linsey looked at Darian with a quirked brow, then moved to stand in front of the barrier. He could see she was worried.

She lifted the latch. Darian's heart hammered in his chest and he clenched his jaw as he prepared himself for a fight. He leaned close against the wall next to the door and watched Linsey step back to get her weight be-hind a hard kick.

The door slammed open with a bang.

Linsey just stood there – staring into the room.

Having expected her to leap into the room and attack, Darian felt the live wire of tension painfully ebb into his body as he watched the felid's face. It drained of color. Confused, he stared at her for a moment before jutting his head around the corner to look.

What he saw took him a minute to comprehend.

Then he threw up.

Falling to his knees the queasiness overtook him - his face felt like it was on fire, and his hands shook as he brought them to his face to wipe his chin. He rolled to the side and kept his eyes pinned on the ground.

Linsey strode past him into the room, her back stiff as a board. She walked up to the body that was sprawled there, and moved one of its legs into a less shockingly grotesque posture. Darian could hear her struggling to breathe properly in the stench that wafted from the room.

"She- Wh- what... how could they-", he sputtered, red eyes clamped closed trying to shut out the vision he had just witnessed. "What would make these people... able to do something li-"

"They are lost, Darian. In many ways they are no longer people."

Linsey's voice was stiff and strained – she was trying hard to maintain her own composure. Darian looked up and through his bleary eyes saw a tear trailing down her cheek and off her chin.

"Vek changed them. Took away their.. ability to even think about their own choices. And he reminds them constantly of what will happen if they try to choose for themselves."

Her hands came up to her chest and she unclasped the heavy red jacket she wore. Shrugging it off she moved in a fluid motion to cover most of the body with it.

"I'm sorry Culley," she whispered. She raised her hand to wipe the moisture from her face, and to cover her sensitive nose. Backing away, she turned and came close to Darian, squatting down at the doorway to look into his face.

"How... How can you do this?" He sobbed as he gazed at her somber expression. "Be out here- do this... when this is the kind of thing that happens to women? He gulped and rubbed his eyes, trying to deal with it the same way he saw her dealing with it. But it didn't feel right to push it away and detach himself. He found he couldn't. It was right there in front of him – not a scary story. Not a memory he could push himself to forget. "You look like you're... used to it." He coughed, an edge of anger in his voice.

"No," she said, still staring into his face. Her eyes were wide, but she was trying to connect with him – to keep his mind with her. "The first time... was the worst. I was petrified. I believed my end would be the same as theirs. So I asked to be reassigned to ground crew."

It just didn't seem possible to Darian. He spat to clean his mouth, wiping his chin again and looking back at Linsey with hollow eyes. His heart was heavier in his chest than it had ever been. How could she face this? Getting captured by these pirate roughs – even once – was a sentence worse than death.

"Your father fought against my request."

The human looked at her in shock, and she responded by turning her green eyes down at the dirt floor, almost as if in shame.

"He told me that the Navy needed me. Our society needed me. Not someone else – me." She wiped her own face again, and blew out her breath in what appeared to be an attempt to settle the situation in her mind. "He asked me if I would every truly be free - safe. If I just let the men do it all. If

I didn't make myself part of the solution." She mulled her own words for a moment, before raising her face to lock her glassy eyes on his again. She reached out and clasped his upper arm, pulling to raise him up to standing in front of her in the corridor.

"Many people expect women to run away when faced with this. To withdraw. Not take the risk," she stated in empathetic tones. "To earn freedom, to defeat evil like this you need to go beyond what is expected of you. I may not survive, but I'm here. When we finally have our victory, our safety, there will be no question that all of us have earned it. Not some on the backs of others. All of us. Earned it together."

"I don't know if I could face that," Darian responded slowly as he turned away from the room to gaze across the hallway.

Linsey simply nodded. "You have to choose. I have chosen. Your friend Max chose." She echoed his gaze across to the featureless wall of the hallway, but only for a moment.

"Captain Culley chose."

She let go of him, and started to walk out of the building. She did not look back.

Darian knew his own choice. As he walked behind Linsey, the image of Captain Culley's lifeless body cauterized in his mind.

thirty six

Max moved quickly through the dark, running from the cover of one tree to another down the slight incline. His comrades behind him rushed forward as well, fanning out wider and wider.

They had a simple plan – show themselves, then run away. Based on how they were followed, they would split up and come at them from two directions. The first group able to blow something up would do so. After that it would be a straight fight, with trained Navy members who knew they would be given no quarter against simple roughs with nothing but their fear for their own lives driving them.

And Vek, Max thought.

The Mantarian finally came out of the trees, turning to slam his back up against the post of a water well. He made only the smallest parts of himself visible in the flickering light coming from the docks. Peering around the edge of the structure, he tried to gauge the situation as best he could.

The pirates were getting ready. He could hear them move noisily on the wooden planks near the boats. Occasionally he caught sight of one of them running through the light cast from the turret that stood at the base of the hill they had come down. Cold sweat came out on the back of his neck, and he could feel the tension mount in his shoulders. But he forced himself to stay where he was - to cut through the welling panic instinct and hold onto rational thought.

"You think this is going to work?"

Max jerked his head around to look at the owner of the whispered query. Ceres Hall was beside him, huffing out a breath.

"Of course it's going to work. Linsey said so."

"She's not even here. If she thought this was going to work, why would-
n't she be here?"

Max frowned at the man.

"She doesn't need to be. We got an order. We're going to make it work
- one way or another. Got me?"

Hall looked Max up and down. After a moment he sighed, nodding.

Suddenly high-pitched yelling came from his left and right – screaming
battle cries of Navy members rushing noisily towards their foes. Max kneeled
down and grabbed a rock. *This is it*, he thought as a sinking feeling flashed
through his brain. *Here we go.*

The large Mantarian broke cover and started to run, weaving left and
right as he quickly covered the ground between the well and the docks. The
first group of brigands showed themselves almost immediately, brandishing
the spike guns they had stolen. At least two of them had stepped up in front
of the rest, pointing their heavy weapons at the rushing men. As Max saw the
end of a muzzle point his way, he reeled back and lofted the rock he had.

Any concentration the rough who was aiming at him had was shattered
by the obvious impulse to avoid being hit by the rock. The scruffy man
yanked back the arm holding his gun and his wide eyes watched the arc of the
rock - gauging how much he had to move to get out of the way. In the time it
took to do this, Max dug in his feet to the ground and slid to a stop, turning to
run backwards into the shadows. All around him, his comrades were doing
the same thing. As he rushed back to cover, he pleaded with fate that he
would not receive a pointed metal pinion through his back.

Four loud shots went off behind him as he raced back from the first rush.
He did not hear any screams of pain – just continued hollering and yells of
anger, both from the attackers and the defenders. Having reached the well, he
came behind it and squatted to grab another rock. Heaving a few quick
breaths he came back up to standing and turned to peer around the rock pillar
and check the effectiveness of their efforts.

Adam.

Adam was at one end of the line of the brigands, brandishing one of the
handguns and yelling in earnest back at the people rushing the docks. *How
did he get free?!* Max's breath caught and his face burned in fury. *I taught
him every knot I knew*, he thought regretfully. *And he learned them well.*

Bo'sun Hall came back from his own run and stopped beside Max, bending down to grab another stone. The yelling and the occasional crack of a spike gun continued in front of them. Hall looked Max over as the Mantarian gazed in scorn at his brother.

"What are you, scared? Come on – it's working. They're getting angry and moving further out. Spending their ammunition"

Max felt his hot face and clenched jaw must be giving the air of cowardice to the man beside him. There was no time to explain – he consciously tried to release the pressure of the anger in his face and ready himself for another run.

Adam's made his choice, his conscience spoke to him. *I can't help him any more.*

Max ran. Tearing out from his cover, his powerful feet dug into the ground and ripped up clumps of dirt. His velocity steadily increased as he came into the dim light of the docks, he saw Adam in front of him. Something inside him fell away and was left behind as he charged. He didn't care if he was seen now.

He abandoned the rock he was carrying and poured on the speed as he flew over the ground. The air howled in his ears as his gaze fixed on his brother, his heart ramming fiery blood to his extremities.

He saw Adam's eyes move and lock onto his own – a look of shock in his face. In the short moment the brothers stared at each other it seemed as though Adam did not understand what was happening. As if his sense of time and place were muddled and he was pulled somewhere else. Even through he swung the gun around and pointed it at his brother, his face was perplexed.

Max didn't flinch. At tremendous velocity he slammed into the younger Mantarian near the end of the line of defenders. With angry snarling they rolled over and over while striking each other with powerful kicks and punches. They bowled over the two pirates to either side as extremities flailed outwards.

In the jarring tussle the gun in Adam's hand was dropped, and fell onto the wooden planks of the dock underneath them. With a thunderous crack it expelled its payload sideways into the array of thugs, hammering the spike completely through one man before impaling another in the head.

The distraction this wrought was enough – the rest of the Navy crews attacked head on, buoyed by Max's lead. Rushing up in intertwining groups that weaved and turned the men buckled the pirates' line, grappling and breaking through to fight hand to hand. Rocks still rained down from a few of the weaker and injured attackers that had held back. But it was immediately apparent that the fight was lopsided – many roughs came up from the dark near their ships and began to overwhelm the smaller number of lightly armed Navy crew.

Max punched and kicked his brother – again and again in the head and in his gut. The younger was no match for the strength of his blows and seemed to try to simply back off. To move away and get his bearings and retrieve a weapon.

As Adam rolled away from a kick, Max realized he was next to the wall of the turret. The entrance was only a few meters away, marked by light streaming out of the doorway. All the pirates were out on the docks next to it, engaged with their attackers. Max twisted his body to get his legs underneath him.

Adam scrambled to grab the gun he had dropped. He was crazy with anger now, and barely had the weapon in his hand before he swung it around and fired.

Max leapt just in time – the spike from the gun impacted the stone wall of the turret in an cracking shatter of hot metal shards. He felt the searing heat of a splinter bury itself in his lower back as he was thrown further to-wards the door of the turret by the force of the blast. With a somersault he collapsed at the entranceway.

Adam set his feet firmly, then stood and braced himself. He pointed the gun more steadily as his eyes seethed hatred.

"You going to shoot me, little boy?" Max yelled out in a loud, command-ing voice. The same voice he'd used a long time ago to intimidate his brother. But rage had overcome any of Adam's reason – he jutted out his arm in a straight line and pointed the muzzle of the gun straight at Max's face.

Max turned onto his haunches and gazed into the mouth of the gun.

"I'm glad Mom and Dad can't see you now."

"SHUT UP!" Adam screamed back at him, his hand shaking with the weight of the pistol in his hand. The sweat crawled down his face and the muscles in his neck were taut enough to make him shudder.

But Max had seen the side of the weapon, where a small red light winked on and off to indicate the total expenditure of the pistol's power. Until it recharged itself, pulling the trigger would just dissipate any energy it gained. *Stop the charging*, Max thought. *I need to get him to fire. Get him mad enough to kill me.* He raised himself to his feet.

"Vek thinks you're useless. He told me that himself. Anyone can see you're just a scared little kid who needs someone to take care of him."

Adam pulled the trigger.

The gun emitted a harmless spark as the small charge it had built up was expended. Adam's eyes showed an incredulous disconnection with reality as the brothers locked eyes. As if he couldn't believe that what he had just done, and also that it had not ended the way he had thought it would.

Max sighed sadly, and stepped backwards. As he had back on the stolen Navy ship, he reached out and grabbed the door to the turret, slamming it shut on his brother's shocked face.

thirty seven

"It's all or nothing now," Linsey whispered to Darian. The two hid behind a large rock just past the far end of the docks. It was almost pitch black, and the rolling gusts of wind off the lake water had helped mask the sound of their approach. Luckily all the commotion of the battle further down had drawn away most of the roughs.

"The ships are fairly unguarded," Darian jutted his chin in the direction of the two large boats rocking on the ocean waters near them. "We should try to take one."

"Not without at least three more crew. There's no way we'd get it away before being noticed. And besides, we need to help them out – it looks like they're outnumbered and outgunned. They won't last long."

Darian gritted his teeth and looked at the ground. Bringing up his left hand he chewed nervously at his thumbnail as he pondered her words. He tried to mask his concern, but found himself looking at Linsey for reassurance that Max would be all right.

She stood up from their hiding place and gazed for a long, slow moment at the action near the turret to size up the situation. It seemed simple to Darian – either they added themselves to the fray or they try to launch some other kind of effective action. Most of the Navy personnel they could see were mixed up with the roughs and fighting hand-to-hand. But there also was a group of roughs trying to break through the door to the turret.

"I think Mister Ford has managed to get himself into a situation," she frowned. "I can not see him, but at least four of those brutes are trying to break down the door to the turret. They would not do that if one of their own was inside. So he is doing his job."

When Linsey looked back Darian she was smiling. He couldn't help but return the grin.

"Let us help him out, shall we?"

"Aye, Captain," Darian returned as he came up to standing beside her. He didn't waste his time trying to see the details of the carnage, and instead looked over the vessel closest to them.

"That's not a Navy ship," he said as he pointed at a boat's hull. "Looks like a Gamean hauler. Not federated. A free trader that would have its own rules... procedures."

"Yes," Linsey answered in curiosity. "And?"

"When they first got boarded they might not have followed Navy procedure and burnt their comm gear. Which mean-"

"Brilliant!" Linsey cracked a wide smile and slapped Darian on the back as she moved quickly around him and up onto the docks. "We shall call for help. Captain Vrue is probably out looking for us."

Darian rushed to keep up with the fast-moving felid, looking around nervously as their footsteps could be clearly heard on the wooden planks of the dock arm.

"What about Max? He's not going to be able to hold out long against those guys. And we can't move the ship by ourselves."

"You are going to help him, Mister Carver." Linsey said matter-of-factly. She came directly up to the side of the large Gamean ship and grasped the rope used to climb to the main deck. Turning, she pointed past Darian to the shadows of the other side of the dock arm.

Darian swiveled on his heel to look into the dark. It took a moment for his eyes to adjust, but he could finally make it out – a tiny dinghy, bobbing up and down in the wind-swept water. It had a only a shred of a power sail, no seat, and what appeared to be a scorched battery pack at its rear. Except for the faded green light showing a power charge, the vessel appeared more like driftwood than like a serviceable craft. Darian's eyes widened and he looked at Linsey with incredulity.

"I don't think that thing will make it into the air, Captain. And I don't have a gun."

"Mister Carver, by the power vested in me by..." she looked around for a moment, then shrugged. "Me... I hereby promote you to field Captain and assign you to that ship – her majesty's royal airship the S.R.S. ..."

Darian's jaw dropped.

"Asskicker."

Linsey turned and grabbed the rope, hauling herself up quickly hand over hand.

He couldn't believe her levity, but even in their dire situation it felt right. Felt normal. When the felid reached the top she took one last glance over the edge at Darian's blanched face.

"Go get your friend. Don't get caught."

And she was gone.

thiRty eight

Darian's original plan was to use the weight of the boat to bowl over or at least frighten some of the men on the ground. However, he soon realized that the only way into the turret would be through its high roof. If he landed beside it he would be in the same situation as the roughs trying to break in.

He rode the wavering dingy into the sky, nearly tipping it on its side as he tried to figure out the limits of its control. They were severe – it simply did not want to turn. The engine whined from the strain of energizing the lift mechanisms, and only Darian was aboard. *This will get me there*, he thought. *But there's no way this thing will hold Max's weight.*

Employing various curses at the boat, Darian rode his craft as it dropped and rose and dropped again, weaving back and forth towards the fighting that was going on less than half a mile away. Teeth gritted, he twisted the handle to the side to alter his course. The craft tipped quickly, and over too far for the human to maintain the center of gravity he needed for the turn. The front of the boat dipped and swung out wildly, which caused the engine in the rear to scream at the abuse placed on it.

Just as he thought he had recovered some modicum of control a hole was blasted through the base boards, showering the human with hot splinters. Jerking his head to look over the edge, he could see a keen eyed rough down below squinting at him over the barrel of a pistol.

Darian yanked the control handle and pushed the throttle lever at far as it would go. Expecting another loud whine or a heavy shudder to accompany an increase in speed, he was surprised that the craft responded smoothly. It gained altitude quickly and swung around to the lip of the turret's flat, round roof.

I guess you like being manhandled, he thought with a grin as he glanced back at the greasy engine. As if it knew his thoughts, the battery's light went red.

Then it burst into flame.

Wide eyed, Darian yelped and let go of the controls. He took a quick step to the edge of his craft and breathed a sigh of relief as he saw that he had come over the edge of the roof. As the fire from the engine flashed up over the oil-soaked boards, Darian crouched and leapt from the burning craft. Unfortunately, his motion to get to the edge and the airship's momentum changed its attitude as if it wished to follow him.

His feet hit the roof boards and went right through them. Falling a full story's height he landed on some weak boxes, crushing them and scattering their contents over the floor. His heart pounded in his ears as he rolled to the right and brought up his arms to shield his head – sure that the S.R.S. Ass-kicker was going to place its flaming bulk right on top of him. It slammed into the upper floor of the building right beside him and bounced, careening off of the central support pillar before coming to a sliding halt against a pile of steel-reinforced crates.

Darian uncovered his head and watched for a moment in disbelief as the wreckage burned. *My first command,* he sighed inwardly. *Oh well.*

The trap door to the lower level beside him on the floor burst open with a bang. A Mantarian head thrust up into view and jerked around quickly to survey the source of the noise that had accompanied Darian's arrival.

"Max!" Darian blurted.

His friend twisted around to look at him in shock.

"How the hell did you get here?!!"

Darian came up to his knees. The audacity of the situation made it impossible for him to hold back a smile as he pointed at the spreading flames from the remains of his dinghy.

"You looked like you were in trouble. I came to get you out of here."

Max didn't smile back. He stared past Darian at the wreckage, his face turning to a staunch mask of fear.

"What? I'm all right. Linsey and I we-"

"Can you read that?" Max cut him off curtly.

"Read what?"

"Read what's written on the crates that you just set on fire."

Darian looked. The boxes were stacked at least four wide and five high. The edges of them were burning, but he could make out the lettering on the front of them.

T-4.

Darian's head whipped back to look at Max.

"I think we should leave."

thirty nine

Max pulled his head from the hole and dropped quickly down the ladder. He heard Darian right behind him as the human urgently scrambled across the floor and jumped headfirst through the trapdoor.

Max didn't have a chance to move out of the way before Darian crashed into him. Both young men ended up in a heap on the floor. "Oh yeah, that was helpful!" Max muttered as he rolled to get up.

"They stacked the crates of it!" Darian exclaimed, his eyes wide. "You can't stack the crates! It's on fire! It's gonna explode!"

Max had blocked the turret door with heavy boxes which had so far managed to keep the pirates from entering. The thug roughs were immersed in battle with their comrades, but still made concerted efforts to break the door down by brute force of impact. They even shot it once.

When he had heard Darian crash into the roof Max had felt like his time had run out. He'd decided to move up the ladder to see if he could fall back to a more defensible position in the loft. In the time he had been gone from his improvised rampart the pirates outside had managed to wedge it open a few inches, and a thick arm stuck through. Max and Darian could hear grunting as their foes tried to increase the size of the crack in the entranceway.

The Mantarian lunged at the wooden door and slammed into it, making the owner of the arm squeal in pain as it was pinched between the wood and the brick edge of the portal.

"We need to get out!" Darian yelled in high anxiety. "All that's gonna be left is a big glowing hole in the ground. Any minute it'll go off!"

"I don't think we have any options!" Max shouted in response as the pirates slammed into the obstruction again. "We both can't get far enough away from the blast even if they weren't there. I can make it, but there's no way you can run that fast!"

"You go! I can distract them and you can run."

"I'm not leaving you to die."

"But it's my fault!" Darian protested with a strained voice. "I crashed the-"

"Shut up!" Max retorted. "I'm not leaving."

The roughs slammed into the door again. Both Darian and Max could hear the flames in the loft above crackling and spreading.

Darian stared into Max's eyes. For a moment the Mantarian wondered if this was it – that the next moment all they would feel is a hot wash of flame and see white light. There was no way out.

Then Darian swallowed, and his face flushed as his voice dropped to a whisper.

"Either we die... or... you carry me."

Max's heart shook in his chest. He stared back at the human, amazed for a moment that he was being asked to do the one thing that made him feel the least like Darian's equal. Like any sentient creature's equal.

But at the same time Max knew it was the answer. There was no-one else who would have asked him. No-one else he would have done it for.

He jerked his head back to face the blockade, and took a deep breath. The brigands crashed into the door again, and it opened a crack. Max stepped back and jutted out an open hand.

"Lets go. We're going to run right through them."

Darian nodded and quickly put his far hand in Max's. The Mantarian's arm twisted around to haul the human easily off the ground and bump him clumsily into his back.

Max reached out and grabbed the base of the top three crates blocking the door, grunting as he shoved them over to the side. Then he took a step back and bucked his shoulders once to adjust Darian's weight.

The pirates crashed through the door. No longer reinforced on its top half, the wood snapped and splintered as two brigands fell through it.

Max charged and leapt, brows set hard and teeth gritted as his hands hit the ground. A fire lit in his eyes, and with all his energy he blasted through the broken doorway and shot past the fray of fighting men.

fORty

Darian felt the Max's powerful muscles contract and release rhythmically under him with terrifying intensity. He gasped breath and jammed his eyes shut as his fingers gripped his friend's neck, clinging desperately as he ran. The pair tore towards the docks, weaving left and right through the fighting crowds to avoid collision.

"RUN! IT'S GONNA EXPLODE!" Darian yelled as he heard the clash and yell of angry voices around him. He knew the Navy officers had to disengage - if they didn't get away from the turret they'd be consumed in its explosion. "RETREAT! GET OUT NOW!"

Max was grunting from exertion at each spring from his back legs, sweat coming out on his thin fur. Darian squinted his eyes open to see that he'd been carried just outside the edge of the battle – already more than the length of a galleon in less than six seconds.

It was dark but he could still make out the dim shadows of their surroundings. Max bucked and jumped over a railing and fell the short distance behind the raised wooden walkway.

White searing light filled Darian's vision.

Even partly shielded by the walkway, the concussion of the blast threw Darian head over heels. His fingers dug into Max's lightly-furred shoulders, but he could not hold on as they were slammed into the ground and tumbled onto the short grass next to the dock boards. Fiery debris flew by and fell all around them as the cracking roar of the explosion rolled over their heads.

The world spun around Darian and he felt silent numbness for a moment, before he could feel himself roll up and get his bearings.

"Max!" he yelled, dizzy as he fumbled over himself to get up. The Mantarian just lay on his back, chest heaving and mouth open to gulp breath.

"A... a second... longer and... we would have been dead," Max gurgled as he turned his head to spit a thick gob of phlegm that had worked up in his mouth. He rolled onto his side away from Darian and moaned out a shuddering breath.

"Are you hurt?!" Darian continued as he dropped down at Max's back and gripped his shoulder. "We did it- You! You did it!"

Max chuckled under him, slitting opening an eye to look sideways up at Darian. The human was elated to see the curl of a smile on the edge of his mouth. Max's breath still heaved, and he lay the side of his face against the cool grass as he recovered. "You did it. I would never have thought of blowing up the building with us trapped inside it," he sighed. Debris was still raining down around them. He grunted and moved to start to get up. "It takes your kind of brilliance to come up with a plan like that."

"Hey! Watch it!" Darian barked. But he grinned down at his friend. "I'm a Captain now. You've got to watch out for career limiting statements like that."

"Career limiting?! Hah!" Max came to his knees and looked back at the flaming carnage they had run from. "Being around you is *life* limiting."

Darian saw Max look in his eyes - the smile was still there on his lips. For a moment they just sat there on the grass in silence, neither one of them needing to speak. The flickering of the fires from where they had run danced on their faces.

"With you around I'll always make it out of a jam." Darian felt himself smiling, with a lightness in his heart that he hadn't felt a in a long time.

"What in blazes did you do?!!" a coughing voice sputtered from the edge of the walkway they had jumped behind. Darian's smile left him and he jerked his vision upwards. The owner of the voice stood in front of the brilliant glow of the turret's burning hulk, making it impossible for Darian to indentify them. He brought his hands up to his eyes and tried to cut down the glare.

"Hall!" Max called. "Good. At least somebody other than us made it!"

"WONDERFUL plan!" The Bo'sun blurted as he held his head. "Next time do you think you could give us notice that something is going to blow up?!"

"Sorry about that," Darian called back, loud enough to hear over the crackling of the flames abound them. "We, uh, didn't know until we... had to get out."

"Yes," Max chirped. "*Captain* Carver here made the executive decision to crash a boat in-"

"The Asskicker..." Darian muttered.

"What?"

"Asskicker," Darian repeated quietly. "That dinghy. Linsey made me Captain of it."

Max quirked a brow at the human. But the edges of his mouth came up, belying the levity they both felt. He responded to Darian still in muted tones that Hall could not hear.

"Well, you're not a Captain any more then, are you? I mean, if your ship blew up."

"See, there you go again with another career limiting statem-"

"HEY!" Hall yelped. "When you're done with your private banter there maybe you could help us out up here with the injured?"

Darian got up and jogged across the grass towards the walkway to climb back onto it. Max was right behind him.

"Did we win?" he asked as he climbed over the railing. "Are they still fighting?" Once he got over he turned to grasp Max's hand and help him over as well. The Mantarian looked just as curious as Darian was about how effective the detonation of the turret had been.

"No and No." Hall answered, gesturing with his chin for them to have a look around.

Navy crew were running around frantically, rousing downed comrades and pulling the injured towards the dock. Darian didn't see any live roughs. The vessel that had been nearest the turret was heavily damaged and burning, fire spreading quickly through its sails - a write off.

"Your Captain is over there," Hall turned and pointed to the dock arm where the ships were tied. Far down from where the battle had been fought was the Gamean hauler that Linsey had been investigating. In the dim light Darian could see scorched and smoke-stained Navy crew limp and stumble the line of their retreat to the ship, helping each other up its sides. The tie-lines had already been cast off and the sails unfurled, flapping in gusts of wind as they started to catch power.

Darian swallowed hard as the hauler started to move up out of the water. The only other usable ship was the *Kristoff*, sitting even further down the dock.

"We're loading everybody who's left onto those two ships," Hall continued. "About thirty. In a hurry - get out while we can."

"What about the roughs?" Max queried, confused.

"The ones that weren't killed by your amateur demolition job? They ran. All of them. Off that way." He pointed in the opposite direction of the docks, back in the direction of the spot where Darian, Max, and Linsey had first landed. Towards the enormous hangar.

"Vek!" Darian blurted. "Did we get Vek? Was he here – near the turret when it blew?"

Hall shook his head. "Never saw him. I can't imagine why he wasn't here. That's probably why we did so well against them this time - when he's around they fight really hard."

Max started walking back towards the carnage. Just as Darian's sergeant in the supply house had predicted, there was a huge glowing crater where the turret had been. The ground all the way up to the hole was flattened and covered with debris. Darian followed behind him, and could see Max's eyes were large as he searched for signs of life.

"The one like you," Hall called after Max. "He ran. Just like you did – your... people. Way faster than the rest of us. I don't see his body, so he must have got away."

"Adam?" Darian queried, incredulous as he looked at Max. "Adam escaped?"

Max didn't answer.

"Soon as Carver yelled it was gonna blow, all them pirates took off." Hall explained with a slap and a stiff jutting out of his hand. "That told us they knew what was coming. We'd barely gotten started running ourselves when..." Hall's voice trailed off and he raised a hand to gesture around at the burning and smoking wreckage.

Max stopped walking.

"He's still alive."

Darian looked up at him from his side. He could see his friend's teeth steel themselves and the facial muscles go taut and his ears move back.

"We've got to go, Max! Help Linsey get the others onto these ships. Vek, your brother – they ran. They're going to keep running. We know where their hideout is now. Vrue – Captain Vrue can come back with an armada. We don't need to follow them now. We've got what we came here for."

Max just stared at the flames, seemingly unable to look away.

fORty one

"Mister Carver!" Linsey watched their approach with a smile. "I see you found Mister Ford - and improvised a solution to our problem with the roughs."

Darian returned the grin and glanced sideways at Max. The Mantarian appeared upset, his shoulders drooping and his face showing strain. Darian put his hand on his friend's back and rubbed for a moment.

"Yeah, he was in trouble. I saved him."

Max rolled his eyes, but did brightened slightly.

"I see," Linsey chuckled. She looked from the ruins of the turret over to the half-destroyed ship that had been unlucky enough to have been next to it. "Not the safest of methods, but effective."

"Yes, well.. improvise, like you said."

"But we are all still in need of saving," she continued. "We have to get out of here quickly. I managed to send off a coded distress signal using the comm gear on the Gamean hauler. However, the equipment could only transmit – which did not allow me to listen for a reply."

Darian nodded. "So we have no idea of whether somebody's coming."

"Someone will come," she responded in a definite tone. "We just do not know when. So we must take what we can, be thankful for our lives, and run. Just like our enemies have."

"Wouldn't everyone have fit on the hauler?" Darian asked. He looked off after the departed ship, where it climbed towards thick black rain clouds. "That thing was huge. Why did they leave already?"

"I told them to leave as soon as they had control of the ship. These roughs have another large boat, and there is no ti-"

She was interrupted by a huge creaking sound that erupted across the sky. With a flash the dim light of the atmosphere increased and became steady.

Darian, Linsey, and Max all stared across half the lake cove at the hangar doors as they cracked open. Linsey's breath caught and she jolted out her arms to grab the two young men by the backs of their necks. With a strong shove she pushed them towards the *Kristoff.*

"Move!" Linsey felt a tingling of too-late in her spine. She saw several of the former captives still struggling to the dock. Even though he'd been shoved, Darian stumbled sideways and grabbed a pair of injured men to help them move more quickly.

We don't have time for them!

There was no time to explain. Linsey ran quickly around the others and up to the side of the *Kristoff.* She grabbed the boarding rope and swung herself up two handholds before she looked back at the hangar to see how far the doors had been opened. They needed all the time they could get.

Just as she held the building in her eyes, its entire top half exploded outwards.

The huge heavy doors at the front shattered and splintered as a salvo of six cannon blasts punched through them. The roof buckled inwards for a moment, then blasted out as it was pierced by seven enormous masts. A pitch black flag sprang into view above the disintegrating structure, clouded only for a moment by the wash of dust and insulation as the yards cracked through, followed by enormous humming sails.

The lights that had brilliantly illuminated the inside of the hangar now streamed their energy upwards onto the bottom of the emerging ship's hull. In Linsey's eyes it appeared to her as if the vessel was buoyed suddenly and powerfully up out of its confines on a carpet of white fire.

"Mister Carver!" She shouted as she began to pull herself up the side of the boat. "WE - ARE - LEAVING!"

She knew at least ten crew were with them – four were already on board and six more were close enough to reach the ship before it had to pull away. *Carver and Ford with them*, she thought thankfully.

"Loose the sails and taut the braces!" She yelled to the four who were standing on deck and helping others board. "Let those below push the rest on! Leave the side! Get me engine primer and Nav power! Now!"

She turned and ran, in the process taking a glance over the side in the direction she knew the pirate ship would be. It was pointed straight at them, coming up to a level attitude and stabilizing. Bulging out at different angles, three ships were mashed together. It bristled with guns and support sails that sucked power from the air.

Linsey swore and continued her race up the side towards the command console. Reaching it, she yanked up a lever and pressed down the shielded button next to a dark indicator light. The whole ship shook roughly for a moment, then became calm. A high pitched whine filled the air as the batteries deep in the ship primed the engine core. Linsey looked up to the center of the boat where others were still climbing on.

One... Two... she counted in her mind.

Although she tried to stop herself, tried to let the fear wash out of her and concentrate on her job, she was compelled to look towards their attacker again. Her eyes widened as she saw the twin intertwined smoke trails of a cannon blast streak at them. The sound reached them first, a cracking boom that rolled stiffly above them.

"DOWN! INCOMING!" She whirled and screamed at the crew in the middle of the boat. But she did not duck herself – her eyes were glued to the console in front of her. She couldn't miss the signal.

Three... Four...

In her peripheral vision she saw Max Ford pull himself up and onto the ship. Right behind him at the edge was Carver. The cannon round from their foe streaked over the deck, low enough to decapitate anyone unlucky enough to be in its way. The passing blast wave was still enough to knock several men over.

Five! That's it! Her mind screamed. *Come on!* She watched the for the primer light on the console to illuminate. It would blink only for a second at most before it would go out again. If she missed it, there would be a full two minutes to wait before the mechanism came to the cycle point that allowed the engines to be started.

What if the light is broken? What if it doesn't turn on? Did I miss it already?

The light glowed red. She hammered her finger down on the button again to release it, and in response the whole vessel lurched. Immediately, smoke billowed from its emergency vents.

"Mister Ford!" Linsey cried as she took the helm and shoved the controls forward. The *Kristoff* bucked and rose, pushed forward and upward by her blunt actions.

"Yes Captain?!" Max blurted as he came up beside her at the bridge. Linsey looked past him to see that Darian was still running in their direction.

"Engine room! Fix whatever it was you broke before!"

Max's face blanched, and Linsey felt her heart drop as she took in his reaction.

"Captain, that- that's not possible. Starting the engine again will have filled the room with carb fiber smoke. I can't work in there. I couldn't breathe. And we have no masks, no air tanks."

Linsey swore.

Darian jostled around Max as the human came up the narrow stairs to the far end of the bridge. Breathless and bewildered, he looked back and forth between Linsey and Max. "Captain! There's still a couple of men on the docks! We can't leave yet - we've got to give them mo-"

A second cannon round streaked between them, blasting them all backwards with the force of its passing. Linsey covered her face with her arms and staggered into the back wall of the bridge area. Darian was blown off his feet to land at the top of the stairs he had just finished climbing. Only Max was able to stay where he was, instinctively crouching to lower his center of gravity and stay on his feet.

Linsey jumped forwards to grab the controls again.

"You were saying?"

Darian scrambled to get up himself, leaning on the boat's edge and peering back the way the cannon blast had come. "They're almost on us!" He ran towards her. "What do we do? What do you want me to do!"

"Stay alive!"

As Linsey intensely worked the controls, the large ship staggered into the air on fiery jets, its bow pointing steadily upwards. After only a moment it lurched and tilted at a rapidly increasing angle to the port side. Blown by the wind, the thick black smoke belching from its rear wafted across the bridge. There were loud cries of dismay from their comrades amidships as they realized the extreme to which their Captain was pushing the crippled craft.

"What's left of the engine can't take you pushing it like this!" Max shouted. "It'll seize. All the lube is burnt. I can hear it."

Linsey gripped the edge of the console to maintain her footing, but Darian lost his and slid. As he bumped across the deck he flailed out his arms, latching onto Max's leg. With a yelp the young Mantarian went down as well, and they both tumbled to the far side.

Linsey stared past them, gauging their distance and velocity as the ship rotated at an extreme angle. She saw Darian jerk his head up over the side to look. When his face turned to her again, his expression had become one of sheer terror.

"What are you doing?!! This is crazy! You're going to ram them?"

"Not quite!" she growled in return, all her senses focused on the task of piloting the ship. "We can't outrun them. We can't fight them. But we are smaller and lighter."

Suddenly a cannon round grazed the rear of the ship, its partial impact making the deck jump suddenly under their feet. Splintered wood and shards of metal flew by them on the bridge.

Linsey didn't move.

She felt the blast and the intense searing of a piece of hot metal as it bounced off the console in front of her and rebounded against her leg. She let out a yelp, but concentrated on maintaining her turn and her lift angle.

"Dammit!" She screamed at her ship. "TURN, you COW!"

Somehow, she allowed herself the thought they were going to make it. She jerked her head to look at the last second. The huge misshapen bow of their attacker flashed past the rear of the *Kristoff* as it rose and turned. She could see Darian gaping at the ship's bold name brazened in jagged burnt lettering along the front quarter.

BLACKAVAR. The ancient felid god of pride.

Linsey's heart dropped and she felt an icy tingle across her back – a reaction she could do nothing to quell. It had been burned into her mind and heart in childhood and the childhood of every felid in the Queen's domain. The only male felid god, Blackavar was the one that would come for you, if you had gone too far. If a child strayed where it was not supposed to go. If you forgot your fear of the world, Blackavar would remind you.

Linsey looked, and she knew. She knew as she knew up and down, or light and dark. Vek had chosen the name specifically for the Queen. To send her a message – put a stake in the ground and stab fear into the hearts of all of her people.

"They're turning!" Darian yelled at her as the ship leveled out. Both he and Max had retrieved their footing, and came quickly across the deck behind her. "They're going to follow us - get us in their sights again."

"Precisely," Linsey responded curtly. She carefully adjusted the controls to put as much forward momentum into the ship as possible. Craning her head around backwards, she frowned as the only thing she could see was the black smoke that still billowed from the rear of the ship. "And where is the Gamean hauler?"

Darian looked at her, confused for a moment. "Uh, I don't know - it... it's the other way. Behind us." He pointed in the direction she was looking.

"Good. They will escape."

Darian's brows hardened for a moment, and his teeth gritted. He glanced sideways at Max, and couldn't seem to stop a flush from coming to his cheeks.

"We're not going to make it," he said in monotone. "But the hauler will get away."

"Yes."

In silence they stood there for a moment, the wind picking up as they rose into the air. Linsey steered the ship in the direction of the biggest cloud she could see in the gradually lightening sky. The crew amidships had done all they could do to make the *Kristoff* as agile as possible. As she looked forward, Linsey saw them all turn towards her, faces pleading for direction.

Every eye on me.

In that single moment she felt the crush of their hope on her shoulders. Her shoulders ached. Somehow, she could feel every injury she'd had in the past days. All of them fresh, gnawing at her mind with their sting.

I will not break.

The wind howled in her ears, raking her face as it tried desperately to crush her will. Eyes surrounded her, babbling their questions and tearing apart every thing she thought she was. Demanding she give the proof she could meet her impossible ideals.

I will not break.

forty two

"Why aren't they firing?!" Darian yelped as he ran to the side railing on the main deck of the *Kristoff*. Leaning as far as he could over the side, he peered around the black smoke billowing from the rear of their ship.

"They've got at least six bow cannon. We're right in their sights!" He looked back to the bridge.

All eyes were still on Linsey. She had not yet said anything, and stared forwards with the gaze of a thousand miles. As Darian watched she bit her lip for a moment, blinked hard, and blew out her breath. When she spoke it was barely audible.

"Vek wants us alive."

Darian's felt his heart jump in his chest, ramming its way to his throat. *Alive? Why?* Then he thought back to Captain Culley. He knew why.

To show the other pirates. Show them what happens to those who defy him. No easy death. No fiery fall from the sky to the sharp rocks under them. Vek would make it painful. Long.

"We should pile in," Max spoke, his voice wavering from the suggestion. "Straight into the ground. If he gets his hands on us, it will be far worse than that."

"No," Linsey stated flatly, much louder. She took a deep breath, and her voice rose and she looked over at Darian, holding him still in her green eyes.

"All of you listen to me!" she yelled. "We earn freedom, all of us. We are out here – going beyond. Doing what others fear to do. What others will not do. So we can know that our children - our brothers, sisters, mothers and fathers – one day they won't have to do these same things. Over and over again. Because we love them, we are here. In this place. Right now."

She paused for a moment, and took another deep breath, seeming to convince herself with her words, just as she was trying to convince her crew. "I am proud to earn my freedom with you. I am not afraid. I am not afraid to do what is needed to rid the world of people like Vek. To stop the cycle."

Linsey broke her gaze at Darian and looked around at the others. Darian felt his face flush with pride that he knew her. That his father had known her.

"I am asking you all to let go of fear with me."

Darian turned his head to look at Max. The Mantarian was looking straight back at him, his face flushed as well, but his gaze steady. Darian felt himself being sized up – considered. Just as he had been what felt so long ago, on D'ara's ship. But this time Max softly smiled, and nodded at him. Then he turned to Linsey.

"You are my Captain. I will follow you."

Linsey looked back at him, her expression unchanging.

"I will follow you," Darian echoed, taking a step back from the edge of the boat and coming to stand beside his friend.

Ceres Hall stood still for a moment. Stiffly, he saluted Linsey. Then the others did the same – one after another. None of them wavered. All of them stared at her with conviction.

Darian saw Linsey's cheek muscles harden cheeks and her brow furrow. She swallowed hard, but her shoulders came down as if a weight had been lifted from her. She relaxed. The curl of a smile come to her mouth – fear gone, a the spark of a plan came to her eyes.

"Brace up! Two each to a sail! Get ready to cut the lines. They want to catch us, by rights they will catch us! Right in the nose!"

All the other crew started to scatter, but Darian was caught up, realizing he had several conflicting ideas on how he could assist but no experience to help him choose. Standing in front of Linsey, he looked sideways, to see Max still standing right beside him also appearing as if he was seeking direction. Or confirmation.

"Mister Ford, we cannot escape them, or let them survive to wreak havoc in the future. We are going to ram their ship."

Darian could see her bear down on him with her eyes, keenly concentrating as if trying to memorize the features of his face. Burn him into her memory. "In a moment I am going to force a flat stall and pitch up - hard. If they are as close as I think they are, they will collide very shortly after that."

Max nodded. "I know what to do."

"What?" Darian blurted, feeling lost.

Linsey did not look at Darian. She still had her searing gaze fixed on Max.

The Mantarian glanced back at Darian, but he spoke to Linsey. "You gave him back his sense of who he can be. I thank you for that."

Darian looked, at a complete loss, between the two of them. *What is he going to do?*

"Go to it, Mister Ford."

Max turned and moved quickly, jogging down the steps from the bridge to the main deck. Darian's wide eyes stared at Linsey for a moment, pleading for an explanation. She did not give it. She seemed to have no direction for him, staring past to watch the crew prepare.

"Wh- What is he doing?" he yelled at her again as he backed away. "Ford? MAX!"

Darian turned and jumped down the stairs, yelling again at his friend just as the Mantarian was about to disappear below decks. Max stopped short and looked back, eyes haunted.

"What are you doing?!" Darian yelled angrily.

A small metal orb suddenly flew down from above and struck the deck in between them. It bounced once before the short spikes on its outside had a chance to grip the wood planks and bring its progress to a quick stop.

Darian looked at it quizzically. The last time he'd seen something like that was on the *Archer*, when Captain Vrue had thrown something like-

"GET DOWN!" Max screamed at him as he ducked inside the doorway.

The deck in between them exploded in a fiery shower of wooden and metal shards, blowing Darian off his feet. His ears went numb for a moment from the noise of the blast, and with his eyes jammed shut all he could sense for a moment was the taste of blood. He cursed and slit his eyes open, spitting the red-tinged bile that had jumped into his throat from the shock. He looked around, dizzily trying to get his bearings and find out what had happened. *Is this what it feels like to die?*

"Carver!"

It was Max's voice. He bent down over Darian, but then snapped his face up and turned his head as if to track an object above them. Darian struggled and leaned back his head on the deck to look.

A skiff full of brigands was flying over them, swerving on an aggressive path to the *Kristoff*'s main deck. A glimpse only, but Darian could see a familiar figure standing in the middle of the craft. *Vek!*

"Boarders!" Max shouted to the other crew. "They're going to try to take us!" Then he looked down at Darian again.

"Carver, I have to go. I have a job – one nobody else can do. Stay alive as long as you can. Stay close to Linsey. Whatever you do, don't let them take her. Your responsibility. You're in charge." He got up, and moved again towards the covered stairs leading below decks. He did not look back.

"Max!" Darian protested. His legs screamed out in protest as he tried to move them. Looking down he realized that several large slivers of wood had rammed through his pants and into the muscle of his leg. Gritting through the pain he raised himself to standing and wiped his bleary eyes. He wavered and knew immediately that he could not follow Max, wherever he was going. He ground his teeth against the pain as he stumbled back towards the bottom of the stairs to the bridge.

"THIS IS IT!" Linsey screamed from above him.

The ship bucked backwards and shuddered as if it had rammed into a wall of water. The bow lurched upwards and the stern downwards while their speed rapidly decreased. The sails above him flew loose, cast forward by the wind as their restraints were severed. As the world twisted under him Darian lashed out with his arms and caught the stair railing. He clung to it at its base and let out an instinctive howl, while he kept trying to gauge their rate of turn and their acceleration to allow him to brace properly against the wood of the stairs. He held his breath and fought against the inertia the *Kristoff* was suddenly forced to suffer.

Then they hit. It was harder than anything Darian had ever experienced. The bone-jarring force of impact rammed its way through his body. His head hit the meat of his forearm that was laid against the stairs, compounding the mild concussion he'd already received from the bomb blast. The wind rushed from his chest and his ears cringed from the deafening sounds of the *Blackavar* careening its bow into and through the *Kristoff*.

There was a loud banshee screech and the snapping of huge bulkhead timbers. Wood fragments flew past Darian and the air filled with puffing clouds of black dust. The *Kristoff*'s energized sails collapsed downwards, their power sparking as they alighted on the ruined masts.

Rendered numb immediately from the blunt trauma, the parts of his body that had lain over the stairs felt crushed. He squeaked out a cough and a groan as he strained to regain his breath.

I'm still alive.

For a moment he didn't know whether to feel grateful of the fact. He just sat still, heaving and trying to relax his stomach muscles that had convulsed and pushed all the air out of him. Around him wood fragments dropped and bounced. Looking up, he gaped as he saw the huge spike that sat at the front of *Blackavar* coming straight out of the *Kristoff*'s deck. The angle of the staircase was now level with the angle of the ground far below them.

A scream came from above him. He craned his neck around and squinted along the stairs to the bridge.

Linsey!

Amid the carnage after the collision, the skiff had landed. Seven brigands had jumped down - Darian saw Adam. And Vek.

Linsey was crouched in a battle stance, green eyes blazing. She had managed to kick off her boots, and the short claws on her feet dug into the deck boards. Her razor talon fully extended from its ugly sheathe in her hand, Darian's eyes caught the gleam of its naturally perfect edge.

"You think you can take my ship down by ramming it?" Vek snarled at Linsey. Then he snorted a rough laugh. "Look around. We're still in the air, sweetheart. *Blackavar* has come for you."

The pirate to Vek's right drew his pistol, but let it hang in his hand at his side.

Linsey was silent. She shifted her weight from foot to foot, and her hair seemed to stick out as if it were frayed with raw energy. Teeth gritted, Darian could see she was readying herself for battle. Focusing in on the moment. What she probably understood would be her last, defining moment.

"Now...", he said slowly, nodding as he gazed menacingly at her. He bucked back his shoulders and shrugged his heavy coat off, so that it dropped in a heap behind him. "We're going to have some fun. I'm gonna take you back – put you on display. Give everyone their turn."

"Where's my brother?!" Adam interjected.

"Your brother is putting an end to all this," Linsey seethed. "To all of you."

Vek stared at her hard, brows crunched downwards as he examined her face to coax out every nuance of what she had said. He crossed his massive arms, then an amused look came onto his face and he nodded again, as if he were impressed. But then he turned to Adam, and this time his dark voice had the merest hint of urgency.

"Engine room. Go quickly."

Adam's own eyes widened and he backed away. Then he turned and ran on the leveled stairs.

Darian feigned unconsciousness, and as the younger Mantarian passed by he surged up and attempted to trip him. Adam dodged easily, and growled as he kicked Darian back down the stairs. He turned and grimaced at the human, but he didn't slow down.

Darian's heart sank - he tried to make his legs move, but the pain drove him back down to his knees. He heard another scream, this one so loud and so terrifying that his skin crawled and his teeth hurt from the shrill vibration in the air.

Linsey was attacking.

fORty thRee

As a child Linsey was constantly getting into fights, most usually with other girls. She had fought both men and women during training at the academy. And during her first commission she had brazenly taken on three Impalan deckhands, all of whom were twice as large as she was, all at the same time.

But every hand-to-hand battle the felid had fought, she had kept her senses about her. Every time, she was thinking through the battle. Restraining herself to higher thought – the proper aristocrat strategizing and taking down her opponent in the most efficient, effective way possible. Textbook.

Now the animal inside her took over.

She let it reign free.

Vek stood his ground with customary smirk on his face. But at her feral, shrieking battle cry all the other brigands began to stumble and fell backwards. Wide-eyed, they instinctively jerked away in shock.

Linsey was a blur as she tore over the deck boards straight at Vek, claws ripping up splinters with each step. Vek reeled back his right arm to meet her momentum with a simple punch – but at the very last moment she changed direction, a forty-five degree turn. Instead of slamming into Vek, her talon whipped through the air and tore across the throat of the armed brigand standing to the right of Drago. Balling up her body during the strike, her feet came up to follow the path of her slash and impacted her victim's chest. The man fell backwards as she rebounded off of him and twisted. Cartwheeling in the air, her right arm came around in a wide arc with the now-bloody talon extended.

The razored edge seared along Vek's left upper shoulder and neck, raking a path that normally would have nearly decapitated a foe. The fabric of his shirt was slit easily, but the edge had no purchase on his body. In the intensity of the wildfire that raged in her mind, Linsey only felt a hard jarring up the bone of her arm from scraping across the Drago's thick armoring scales. She landed on her feet behind him, coming down to a crouch to present as small a target as possible.

Vek was knocked sideways by the momentum in her blow, but he did not fall. He snarled and turned to face her again, his own natural arm blades flashing out. Linsey could see the red blazing in his eyes, and let out a lingering deep growl in response.

The man with the gun that Linsey had slashed stumbled backwards, clutching at his throat as blood spilled down his body. The heavy gun clattered onto the deck as he tried to gurgle a scream. From behind him where the ruined stairs to the main deck had been, three surviving Navy crew rushed forward. Linsey could see they had been spurred by the ferocity of her own attack, and the look on their faces told her they would give no quarter.

"She's mine," Vek growled to his charges. His torn shirt fell forwards awkwardly across his chest. In irritation he grabbed and tore it off, to reveal an upper body bristling with scaled muscles. "Kill the others."

The four remaining pirates that had come on the skiff rushed the Navy crew, brandishing long wicked knives. The gun that had been dropped seemed to be the only one, and all the men on both sides earnestly began a raging melee to acquire it, just to the right of where Linsey and Vek faced each other.

Linsey snarled once again, a lifting whine filling the air from her mouth as she pulled back her lips to show her teeth. Opening her mouth, she sucked in breath to buoy herself for her next attack.

But Vek attacked first, taking a long step toward her and planting a foot before curling his arm around in a jabbing punch. Instinctively responding to the forward movement of his leg, Linsey erupted and threw herself at him.

The sharp scales on the back of Vek's arm had been stuck out, but the blow was far short of Linsey's original position. Linsey realized too late that he had simply feinted – had made an aggressive move to get her to launch herself. Then he would let the natural blades on his arm provide both his defense and his attack.

The hard edges of the Drago's scales dug in and ripped across her flank, and the strength of his jab knocked her sideways. With no scales of her own to protect her, Linsey's left arm, side and chest were slashed. She screamed in pain and rolled as she fell, landing heavily on her shoulder on the deck boards.

Vek laughed as he stood defiantly. "Come on, kitty kitty. Is that all you've got? Ripped my shirt – good for you. I'll have you sew me a new one. Or I'll make one out of your skin. Which would you prefer?"

Linsey breathed out a long painful moan as she came to a crouch again, her injured left arm pulled in protectively around her bleeding chest. Her eyes were bleary and she huffed out staggered breaths to control herself.

"Tell you what," he smiled. He leaned comically sideways and dropped out an open arm in casual indifference to her rage. "Stop now and I'll let you liv-"

Linsey came at him again, his irrelevant words garbled noise in her ears. This time she came in low, taking a leap to land on her hands before springing with all claws on her hands and feet extended.

Vek had no time to prepare. Her hands pushed squarely against his shoulders and her feet scrabbled to dig in just below his waist, bowling him backwards. Linsey's teeth had closed around left side of his face before they hit the deck. She tasted his sweat and hard texture as her strong jaws locked down onto the scales of his face - but no blood.

The pair struck the ground intertwined, Vek snarling in pain himself as the claws on Linsey's feet bit into his only unprotected, sensitive areas. Her sharp claws and razor talon ripped at his upper body for only a moment before he was able to react with a heavy and hard punch to her midsection.

She had expected him to strike her, and her strong abdominal muscles took the brunt of the impact. She was searching for an opportunity – just a flicker of an opening that she could use. But as he pushed her back she found it impossible to hold onto him with her fangs – there was no purchase against his impervious armor covering.

She stabbed out her talon at his face, and felt the sickening feeling of his left eye being pierced before his arm came across to deflect the blow.

Vek screamed.

He had already started to bring up his feet when he had to deflect her thrust, and he kicked her with both heels hard against her body to throw her off of him. He snarled angrily and patted his hand urgently against his face, trying to find the limits of his injury.

Even having achieved a successful attack, Linsey knew it was not over. She kept her guard up, crouching again to try to regain her sense of equilibrium. Her chest ached with the deep cuts she'd received, and her left arm gave intense spasms of pain if she tried to move it.

Vek moaned and gritted his teeth, heel of his hand pressed to the socket of his ruined eye as it seeped dark black blood. Just beyond him Linsey could see two brigands still fighting with Ceres Hall, who appeared to be defending an injured comrade. The two seemed to be the last Navy crew alive - she could not see Darian, or the gun that had been on the deck.

How much longer? Her mind blurted out as she though of Max. *What if Adam caught him?* She didn't think she could take much more of the battle with Vek. She could see he was concentrating on controlling his anger. But his next words to her showed a tinge of pain, the edge of control wavering.

"I'm going to make you want to die." He came at her – this time with no pretense or strategy. His bull rush proved he was ready for a close-quarters fight he knew he would win. He'd always won.

Her talon retracted into her hand to favor brute strength punches as she rose to meet him, and she slammed first her left fist into his chest and then her right into his face, her body curling up to so she could try to use her feet again.

Seemingly impervious to the punches, his hand came around and wrapped her throat, gripping and pulling her towards him. His other arm struck out – led by a single pointed digit tipped with a hard sharp claw. Linsey tried to jerk her face away to dodge, but he was faster.

She squealed sharply as excruciating pain seared into her. Her legs spasmed and her head jerked away from him, making blood spit on the deck boards as she convulsed and rolled backwards. All she could see was bleary red. Then black. Her claws fully retracted, she thrust her hands at her face, exactly the way Vek had a moment ago when she'd taken his-

My eye!

Now Vek laughed again with a loud growling clacking of his tongue. "How you like that, sweetheart? I know exactly how much that hurts."

Linsey couldn't think. Her legs felt useless and weak, and her left arm fell to her side, suddenly unable to respond to the commands she gave it. The animal inside her that had pushed her forwards so hard and at such intensity was suddenly pulling her back. Telling her to curl up. To submit.

The Drago was over her, grabbing her by her hair and yanking her up.

"And I'm gonna take both of yours. I promise."

I can't, she said weakly in her mind as she slumped in his grip.

He kicked his leg over her back and leaned down, wrapping his other bulbous muscled forearm around her neck. Through the image from her bleary right eye, she was able to see him peer around at her face with his toothy grin. He seemed to be studying the wound he'd given her.

"Oh... oh, it's gone sweetie." He squeezed his arm muscle roughly around her throat, cutting off her air and compacting the dizziness she felt. Then the anger in his voice was gone, replaced with calm control as he whispered to her.

"Eye for an eye, I guess." He eased off the pressure for a moment, leaning an inch from her ear. "But you gave me a tough time. So I guess I'll give you a tough time, when we get back."

He started to squeeze again, and she choked, gripping at his arm that locked her head. She strained, but it was useless – her worn claws scrabbling uselessly against the scales on his face. Irritated, he tilted his head upwards to keep his remaining eye from her reach as he gradually forced consciousness from her. Her vision went dark, and she struggled to pull in one final breath as her muscles became loose.

Max. Please, Max. Make this end.

But then she felt it. His head was lifted, tilted back to avoid her claws. The scales on his neck, rather than being folded together down on one another, were flayed outwards. She stuck the fingers of her gnarled right hand up to them, the hard sharp edges one of the last things she could feel in her whole body. She made a fist, and with her withering strength pushed it softly against his throat. Through the murk she heard him chuckle at her feeble attempt. A shroud of black came down on her, floating like a heavy curtain onto her mind.

Her talon shot out. Piercing through the tiny gap she had felt in his scales. Through his throat. Right up to tear across his brain stem.

forty four

Darian crawled up the shattered stairs to the *Kristoff*'s bridge, all the while hearing the angry yells and cracks of fighting between the surviving Navy crew and the brigands that had come aboard in the skiff. He'd reached the top what felt like moments after Linsey's first battle cry, ready to try anything he could think of to distract their foes or put himself between Linsey and Vek.

As his sight crested the floorboards of the bridge deck, he immediately saw a the heavy lump of a Navy-issue spike gun lying within easy reach. He grabbed it and looked about to get his bearings, trying to find someone worth shooting. He was unaccustomed to its bulky size and heavy weight – it was not a weapon designed for the relatively weak and small hands of a human.

To his right were two brigands with knives attacking Ceres Hall, who stood defiantly protecting an unconscious colleague. Right in front of him was Vek – his muscular shirtless back exposed and head tilted far back. He was hunched over with his arms tightly around something.

I'm too late!

"Hoy!" Darian called angrily, pointing the muzzle of his heavy weapon at the Drago's back. But he didn't fire, afraid the spike from the gun would go right through into the only place that Linsey could be.

Vek quivered, the muscles on his back seeming to vibrate as his knees buckled under him. Darian heard a hissing gurgle, squinting to see the Drago's eyes bug out wide as bloody drool erupted from the sides of his mouth. Then the male pitched forwards, slumping over a large lump in front of his body Darian could not see.

A scream of pain came from his right and he whirled his face and the gun he held in its direction. One of the pirates had skewered Hall through the chest - the man stood with eyes blazing and face pulled taut. The pirate with the sword laughed as he held his enemy up on the blade.

Darian pulled the trigger of his gun, causing him to be momentarily blinded by a white flash erupting from its muzzle. The kickback from the launch of the weapon's heavy payload made it feel as if all the tendons in his wrist had suddenly been ripped free from their muscles. He yelled in pain and cursed, blinking his eyes to try to get them to recover from the intensity of the light from the spike's emission.

The brigand who had held the sword was simply gone. There were streaks of blood on the *Kristoff*'s far railing, but the man had been blown completely off the side of the ship by the impact of the transuranic round. Hall fell to his knees on the deck, holding the blade that penetrated him and fighting for breath. The other rough who had been attacking simply stood in shock, gaping at Darian.

The human's wrist burned, feeling like it was going to fall apart simply with the weight of the gun in his hand. He gripped it with the other, trying to hold steady while aligning the muzzle to point at the last rough standing. He winced and tried to fathom in his mind what his arm was going to feel like if he had to fire the heavy weapon again. He wasn't even sure his fingers would obey him.

"Jump," he hissed at the dirty pirate. He felt a tear run from his red eyes down his cheek as he struggled against the searing pain in his legs and in his wrist. "Over the side, or I swear I'll blow your head off."

The man swallowed hard and backed away to the edge of the boat. He stood at the edge for a moment, hesitating to move any further towards what would almost surely be a fatal drop to the ground far below.

"Take your chances with the fall, or your chances with a spike. Two seconds to decide."

Incredibly, Darian's thumb obeyed his mind's commands and came up over the back of his weapon to push the power emission control to its maximum setting. The gun hummed loudly, as if begging to release its deadly payload.

"One…"

The man hopped up on the railing, swinging his legs over and jumping. He disappeared from view, and Darian heard his terrified scream fade away. The human dropped the gun, letting out a cry of pain himself as he clutched his strained extremity. But he focused on himself only a moment before jerking his head around to look at where Vek and Linsey had fallen.

Vek was still in the same position, lifelessly folded over top of the felid.

"Linsey!" He called, the pain in his voice turning the end of her name into a high-pitched pleading squeak. There was no movement from the bodies.

"We've got to get... away."

Darian turned to the voice at his right. Hall was still on his knees, with bleary eyes distant and arms limp at his sides. He had managed to pull out the blade that had pierced his chest, but that seemed to be the limit of his remaining strength.

"On that skiff," he continued as his head turned slowly to let him gaze at the boat the pirates had come on. "The *Kristoff*... will explode... any minute now."

"Explode?" Darian almost yelped in surprise.

"Your friend..." Hall wheezed as his head swiveled slowly back in the human's direction. "That's what... That's his job. Blow us up. Take out both ships." He coughed a gob of bloody phlegm, baring his teeth against his pain. "I can't breathe. I can't..." The man fell sideways to the deck, but continued to wheeze and clutch his chest. When he spoke again Darian could barely hear him. "Help me. Please... help me."

Darian took a deep breath, then surged upwards onto his feet with a long growl of pain. He could feel the bits of wood splinter that had embedded themselves in his muscles shift and grate, each one of them a stabbing pain as he moved. But he did move – urgently, pushed forwards by his mind's screaming fear.

Max!

He grabbed Hall, half dragging him to the skiff and pushing him roughly into it. Then he stumbled quickly back for the unconscious body Hall had been protecting, using every ounce of strength in him to lift the man onto his back. His legs burned as he threw the second survivor over the side into the tiny boat. Hall was no help as he lay in the front of the craft, hand still clutched to his punctured chest.

One more, his mind blearily told him. *Then Max.*

Turning back again he shuffled and stumbled towards the Drago's arched form halfway across the boat.

From just beyond the bridge he heard voices yelling – more pirate roughs coming over and up into the skewered remains of the *Kristoff*. They were climbing around, coming to put the battle to an end.

He gripped Vek's scaled shoulder, shoving against the loose sweaty muscle to push him off of Linsey. The Drago's body fell limply to the side, eyes still bugged out and staring, surprised, off into infinity.

Linsey had fallen slightly to the side with the Drago, his arm around her in a macabre embrace. Then Darian saw her own arm bent upwards with her razor talon still embedded in his throat. The human swallowed as he gazed at them, then shook off his horrified fascination at the scene to pull the female commander's hand out of Vek's fatal wound.

In a daze Darian gripped her body and hoisted it to his shoulders. She was surprisingly light, but at the same time he found it almost impossible to keep steady as he trudged back to the skiff. When he got there he was not gentle – he simply tossed her over the side and turned away.

"Get around there! Get around that! That's the bridge up there!"

The calls from just past the broken back of the *Kristoff* were clear now – voices of roughs yelling at each other to rush to where they expected Vek would be waiting for them. Darian's heart fell down into his gut. It didn't seem possible to him to go all the way down into the bowels of the ship. To overcome Adam, to rescue Max-

"Mister Carver..."

Darian stood at the edge of the skiff and looked back into it. Linsey's face stared at him, eyes shut. Red tears streamed from her gored left eye, making Darian wince as he looked at her bruised face. She was bleeding badly from her side as well, her arm in an awkward position as she clutched it to her injured chest. Her voice had been barely a whisper.

"Ca- Captain! Max! I have to get M-"

"I won't blame you..." her voice wavered, almost unintelligible. ".. if you go. Your father... made the same choice. I understand it." Her right eye slit open for a moment, the green pool of its iris gently but steadily holding him. As she lost strength Darian had to strain to hear her whisper.

"It's all right. It's all right now."

Darian's mind froze. A pain shot over his back and up his neck as if a rod of iron had hit him, pulling the air from his lungs. His mouth gaped open as he looked at the three in the boat, then turned to look back at the fractured staircase. The calls of the roughs approaching came again.

What do I do?

Like a crushing pressure on his spine, he could feel his spirit crack.

forty five

Max had found the sail exactly where he'd thought it would be – in the auxiliary storage room as far away from the engine room as was possible. In his two years out in the rough, he'd been told one thing over and over again by his mentors. Never – ever - bring a sail near an engine core.

He had just gathered up the crystal-studded ream of fabric when the *Kristoff* had pitched up and stalled, falling backwards to slam into the *Blackavar*. Even though he knew the maneuver was coming, he was unable to keep his footing. The Mantarian had fallen heavily against the wall of the storage room, pelted by supply containers and cleaning equipment as the vessel lurched and snapped around him. The bowsprit of the *Blackavar* had penetrated the hull easily – shattering and ramming its way like a stake through the heart of the smaller ship.

For a moment in the shock after impact, Max wondered if the engines had been completely destroyed – whether his desperate plan even had a hope of succeeding. He started to get up.

Even if the engines are stopped, the residual power in a battery will have enough stored energy to flood this sail. A hundred times over. Wrapped up and over and onto itself around a battery, he knew the special fabric would exponentially concentrate and feed back power into a chain reaction.

From the fact that he could feel gravity's steady pull, he knew they were still safely in the air – the misshapen and cobbled engines of the *Blackavar* strong enough to hold both vessels aloft.

Dammit. He knew the brigands' craft could take on any ship in the Navy, and would most probably win. *I have to do this. I have to, no matter what. Vek won't stop until he's killed the Queen.*

Stumbling and bumping off the broken timbers of the walls and bulk-heads, he made his way down into the bowels of the destroyed ship. A quarter of the way to his destination he ran into the hull of the *Blackavar*. The huge craft's skin did not even appear damaged - its bulk having withstood the enormous impact and its reinforced structure proving far superior to the *Kristoff*'s standard Navy construction for a light escort. Max stared at the enormous hull plates for a moment, before he pushed aside his amazement to figure out a way to get to the engine room. Only by squeezing carefully past the tattered and cracked edges of the broken walls was he able to edge further downwards. As he came down the last set of tilted stairs to his destination, it occurred to him that it was his third trip back to the same spot in two days. But this time he did not think of Karthow, or of Vek for that matter – he did-n't have time to linger. Taking a deep breath he burst in through the broken engine room door, expecting to be overwhelmed by black smoke and carb dust.

Hot steam and a burning smell buffeted against his face, but the room was surprisingly clear of smoke. The engine appeared to have seized when they were hit by the larger ship, and the emergency vent that Max has slipped through to escape the previous day was still open. Almost all the black acrid carb dust had been pushed out by the hot air venting from the engine. Max ducked under the wafting stream, his skin already sweating from the stark temperature change as he headed straight for the battery pack terminals. He pulled out the positive lead, then its negative partner, and dropped them onto the floor before he yanked off the cover of the battery casing. Bringing up the sail he had stuffed under his arm, he started to wrap it tightly around the exposed surfaces on the inside of the power cell. With every loop he made sure that the largest number of crystals in the fabric pressed against the energy storage substrate. And every loop his mind screamed at him.

What do you never, ever do? What is the stupidest thing you can possibly think of doing on a ship?

He grunted as he finished, tugging the end of the sail tightly so that it draped out of the battery case. Grabbing the positive lead he had dropped on the floor, he wound the yellow channel fiber embedded in the sail around it. Sighing, he looked at his work for a moment,.

I'm done. That's it. Well.. He blew out his breath and reached reluctantly for the negative lead.

He was rocked sideways by a hard punch to his face. Falling to the deck with a sharp cry of pain, he rolled onto his back and looked up in surprise. Adam stood over him, grinning gleefully as his chest heaved with exaltation.

"You're done. I beat you."

Max started to get up, but Adam kicked him hard in the crotch with a powerful hind leg. The older brother clutched himself and growled out a seething moan, huffing from the pain.

"Survival of the fittest. Now you finally see that you're not the best."

"I never wanted to be the best." Max gritted. "That's what Vek wants. You think he cares about you? Hah - you're nothing. He's your master and you're only as good as what you can give him."

"He's not my master!" Adam shouted back at him. "And you're not my brother."

"No," Max agreed, his face hard and sure now. He slowly got up. "I know who my brothers are."

Adam's eyes blazed with hatred, and he jumped, kicking out at Max's face again. But this time Max grabbed Adam's foot with one quick hand and hammered a fist into it with the other. Adam yelped in pain and fell awkwardly forwards as he lost his balance. For a moment Max could see his brother's eyes – scared. Angry. And lost in terror. Lost forever.

Adam punched - Max kicked. With angry snarls they wrestled and tore at each other.

Next to them the negative lead from the battery pack lay on the floor, waiting patiently for its destiny.

forty six

The skiff sped away.

She was barely able to see, but Linsey managed to keep her remaining eye fixed on Darian as he piloted. His face was detached and empty, all its muscles drained. A single tear ran down his cheek and dripped off his chin.

White light filled her vision, and she hunched her eyes shut from the glare. Then the hot blast wave came – buffeting against the back of the skiff and shoving it forward with its force. She winced against the painful roar of the explosion that filled her ears.

Then the skiff safely straightened out.

Linsey could hear Darian's soft sobs as she drifted to unconsciousness.

forty seven

Linsey was floating, softly embraced by white. The smell of wood and spice came to her, and she smiled. A comfort she hadn't known in years held her as the sense of her body started to return.

The pain was dull - aching as if far away, but constant. She felt dizzy. If it were not for the stable caress of fabric on her body she would have sworn she was spinning – rotating in one spot while lying on her back.

She opened her eyes. Above her body she saw the blurry wooden plank boards of the ceiling. She blinked to clear her vision, but the image was still shifted somehow - not normal. She felt as if she could not tell how tall the room was.

She shut her eyes and concentrated, trying to get her memory to refresh and tell her where she was.

My eye, she thought. *My eye is gone.*

A tightness came to her throat, and she moved her arms instinctively to bring her hands to her mouth in response to the shock that gripped her. Her left arm did not move, and she felt the dull pain from it lance up her bones as she tried. She moaned, and a tear trickled out of her closed right eye as she covered her face with her right hand. There was a patch on her face.

"Welcome back."

Vrue.

Linsey's eye opened again, and she blinked away the water in it. She tilted her head to the side, and looked up at the huge Ursid.

He stared at her for a long moment, his face changing from worry to sadness as he reflected her own visage.

"I'm sorry, Linsey. I wasn't there for you."

She looked back at him, swallowing once as she realized how much she owed to him. How much of him had become what she wanted to be. "You were there," she whispered at him, never breaking her stare. "You were always there."

Vrue flushed, averting his eyes up to the ceiling for a moment as he coped with her words. She didn't want to punish him, and looked away to give him the space he needed away from her eyes.

"Where am I?"

"My bed," he responded in voice that still showed the strain of his feeling of responsibility for her. "On the *Archer*. Still two days to Station from here."

A flash of surprise leapt in her chest as she suddenly felt very out of place - she could feel she had no clothes on under the covers. Her eyes widened and she turned her head to look left, then glanced right. The bed was enormous. Soft. Layered with sheets that took away the tension in her skin, and with cushions that held her gently in place. She realized the pleasant smell surrounding her that she had been ruminating on was Vrue's own scent. Though surprised, she felt protected. "Y- Your bed, sir? I-"

"Heh. Your dignity's still solid." He cracked a smile. "Miss Kelch has been tending to you. I won't have you swinging in a hammock while you're healing. And this is the finest bed on the ship - probably in the whole fleet. Worthy of a hero, I think."

Linsey looked back at him sternly. "I'm not a hero. Mister Ford and Mister Carver-"

"Yes, I met him, your Mister Carver. Fixed up his legs - seems a strong lad. Been hit hard by what you been through, though. Not talking to anyone, except maybe me. He's been asking for you, but I wanted to keep him away until you woke up."

Linsey gulped down her fear of facing the human. "I would like to see him."

Vrue nodded. "I'd suggest some clothes, Miss." He smiled and turned to move to the large desk up against the side of the room. "Lest you be giving the boy distraction."

Linsey grabbed the covers in her hand, and tried to sit up. She winced and squeaked out a moan at the pain that ran up her left side, falling at once back to the pillows of the bed.

"I think a top half will be sufficient. You're not going to be moving much for a while with the nasty tears you took to your side and your bosom."

Linsey gritted her teeth against the pain, and slit her right eye open to look at Vrue as he returned to her bedside with one of his colossal shirts. She took a few breaths to get through the pain, then cocked a brow at him. He appeared embarrassed for a moment.

"Okay, well- fine. I peeked at you while they were taking care of your cuts and bruises, all right? Just making sure you were being taken care of properly."

She shut her eye but made a wry grin.

He put the shirt on the bed beside her and turned, putting his hands behind his back as he sauntered to the door. "Just proper, you being my responsibility," he quietly argued with himself as he left the room.

Linsey struggled through the process of edging herself up to sitting, motions that tested the limits of whatever painkillers she had been given. By the time she had pulled the shirt awkwardly over her head and stuck her single good arm out of the right sleeve, she was huffing breath and sweating from exertion. She sat still, breathing long slow breaths to let the drugs in her system take back their hold on her pain.

A knock at the door. She flushed in response, afraid she would not be able to deal with the confrontation. But she took another breath and forced herself to respond.

"Enter."

The door swung open, just far enough for Darian Carver to step through. He turned without really looking at her, and closed the door as quietly as he could. Then he just stood there, facing the door.

"I am decent, Mister Carver," she said quickly, staring at his back.

"I know," he whispered in response.

She stared at his back, feeling her face burn and the shaking well up in her lungs as she struggled to keep her composure. Her heart forced the hard words up and out of her mouth.

"Your father chose me. Over all the others he could have saved. He chose me even over himself. In an instant - he decided that was what he wanted."

The words felt like fire coming from her lungs, and her eyes watered from the heat of their release.

"I'm sorry Darian. I'm so sorry."

He turned, finally, looking over his shoulder at her for a moment before his body came around to face her. He nodded, blinking and taking a breath of his own.

"How come you never told me?"

Linsey shut her eye and thought about how to answer. It didn't seem real. All the time she'd been waiting to tell him - explain to him what had happened. And now, she couldn't fathom how to word it.

"I didn't-", she started, and stopped. Her head hurt as she searched for words. "I didn't know how to tell you, so that you would understand. I didn't think that it mattered."

"Was it... was it like what happened... to us?"

"Yes and no," she said softly, looking down at the covers of the bed in thought. "Your father cared for me, the same way you cared for Mister..."

"Max."

She looked up at him.

"Yes. The same way you cared for Max. And he cared for you." She was silent for only a moment as they gazed at each other. "If your positions were reversed, would you have... done... what he-"

"Yes," he answered stiffly, cutting off her question. "And somehow that makes it easier. And harder."

"I know," she slowly nodded. "But you understand it. That is the hardest part."

"I don't think I'll ever really understand. But... I keep thinking of something you said. That the parts of us that matter can't die." He swallowed and leaned back against the wall near the door, eyes looking to the ceiling. "Max changed me. Made me who I am, just like... just like you have." He paused and looked back down at her for a long moment.

"I'm not mad at you Linsey. I'm not mad at anyone any more."

"I am glad to hear that, although I would not blame you if you were. You've had a rough time. You've lost many things."

"I've gained some things too. You. Captain Vrue." He smiled finally. "Things that will change me still. Changes I look forward to."

Linsey felt herself smile in response, and the pressure on her shoulders receded. She knew she would always be connected to Darian, and felt a flush again as she realized her pride in him.

"I will be off my feet for a while, I believe. Not liable to change many people while my body heals itself."

"Heh. That's ok. I've got Captain Vrue. He's letting me stay on board. Something about being short a first and second officer."

"Oh, really?" Linsey cocked her brow again.

"I told him I was a Captain too," Darian smiled. "That you'd promoted me."

Linsey rolled her eye, feeling suddenly embarrassed as she reflected on the brash action she'd taken under the duress of their situation.

"He said anyone you thought was a Captain was someone he wanted to keep around."

Linsey chuckled at the audacity of it, and tilted her head forward so that her hair fell across her brow. She blew it upwards with a soft puff of breath, then looked out of the top of her eyes at him.

"You are where you should be now, Mister Carver. You are no longer alone. You never will be, again."

Darian smiled, and with his right hand reached out and opened the door. He didn't speak. He just looked at her for a long moment, before sliding through the portal and closing it behind him.